HUSKY LOVE

FRIENDS OF GAYNOR BEACH ANIMAL RESCUE

GABBI GREY

BLURB

DANNY

I may be young, but I've done a hell of a lot of growing up in the past year. I watched my big brother deal with the challenges of loving someone, went through some medical stuff myself, and changed my career plans and ultimately, my city. Gaynor Beach is smaller than where I was, but it has two attractions—my brother's big new house, where he's letting me live for now, and Rob Dunn. When I met Rob, just, damn. Like my brother, I wanted to help that sweet, stubborn guy and his cute kids get back on their feet. Maybe the rescue husky wasn't the right gesture, despite Rob's connection to him, but a dog is love on four paws, and I plan to be there to help all the way.

ROB

I fled my abusive husband with my two kids and the clothes on our backs. I'm grateful every day for the support the Gaynor Beach folks have given us…okay, I'm not sure I'm precisely grateful for the rambunctious young husky Danny Reynolds gave us, but Trouble makes my kids smile, and that's a big win in my eyes. I'm determined to get back on my feet. I hate relying on other people to help us, but somehow it doesn't bother me as much when it comes from Danny. It's nice to have a real friend after all those isolated years, but do I want to keep him in the friend zone?

This slow-burn small-town gay romance novel is about fresh starts, accepting help, two sweet kids, and an adorable husky named Trouble.

Edits by ELF

Cover by Leanne Clugston

Kaje
Renae
ELF
Wendy
Leanne
The Cullens

PROLOGUE

ROB

I clutched my children. How I could possibly have sunk so low? How had things gotten so bad? How had I allowed my husband to do the things he had?

The nice police officer offered a smile. Her blonde hair was pulled back into a ponytail, and her blue eyes seemed kind. My four-year-old daughter, Hallie, had the same coloring. Well, her hair was almost white, while Officer Greenaway's was on the darker side.

Will Hallie's hair darken as she ages? Or will it stay so light forever?

And why are you thinking about this when you have bigger issues to deal with?

"Are you going to take my children away from me?"

Hallie, who was curled into my side, wrapped her tiny arms around my waist. Or at least she tried to.

One-year-old Thomas slept in my arms. He'd been underweight when he'd been born, and I'd done everything I could to help him gain weight and be healthy. He'd recently made it into the normal range. Not that my kids had to ever be normal. They were perfect just the way they were. And I'd been damn lucky to be chosen to adopt them.

But everything changed after Thomas's arrival. I'd been so focused on getting him healthy that sometimes Gerard had come second to our son's needs. He'd accused me of neglecting him, which I'd never understood. The verbal tirades had tripped into abuse, and I hadn't even realized.

"Mr. Brewster—"

"Could you call me Rob? Mr. Brewster is Gerard's name…" And I didn't have the money or energy to change my name back to Dunn—even if I wanted to be connected to my parents again. Which I didn't. "Just…Rob."

She smiled. "Okay, Rob." She tapped her pen on her notebook. "These allegations of abuse—"

"Allegations?" I tried to calm myself. "He broke my nose. He…" I glanced down at Hallie, then back up at the police officer. I couldn't say the words aloud, but the bruises on her beautiful, pale skin should've been enough.

"He claims you walked into a door and that you were the one who grabbed your daughter by the arm."

Of course he did.

I girded my loins. "Check the nanny cam. It's in Hallie's bedroom. If *he* didn't find it, it should show everything that happened."

She cocked her head. "You thought this might happen? Or were you worried about a babysitter?"

"There's no babysitter. I haven't left the house since we adopted Hallie." I winced. "That came out wrong. I mean, I took her to the park. I wanted to enroll her in daycare so I could have a bit of a break, but Gerard said we couldn't afford it."

"Oh?"

I wanted to cry. "Gerard said that even though he lived

in a mansion there was never money for *luxuries*." I wouldn't talk about the thousands of dollars he spent on electronics for his gaming addiction. Maybe we really didn't have anything left over after that. But somehow, I doubted that. He drove an expensive car, and we lived in one of the most expensive suburbs of Los Angeles. I'd believed I'd found the jackpot when Gerard chose me.

We'd married and, at first, his little criticisms were because he *wanted the best* for me. Then Hallie came along, and everything seemed good. Then came the *constructive criticism*. I'd always been accused of being too sensitive, especially by my cruel family, so I thought this was normal. I'd accepted he loved me and Hallie and was showing us his love in his own way. I didn't think he could be cruel. Although, in hindsight, that was a lack of imagination on my part. This got worse after we brought Thomas home. I thought we were giving the kids a loving home.

I'd been so very, very wrong.

"Will you look into our finances?" I wanted to know the truth. Even if I didn't get a penny, I needed to know.

"Did your husband…" She tapped her pen.

"Hallie?"

She nodded.

"No. I can say that honestly. She's never out of my sight."

"But surely when you slept?"

I fought the bile rising in my gorge. "He has a temper and likes to be the boss." I hesitated, then added, "I think maybe he likes when I'm afraid of him, but he's…not that."

She didn't appear convinced.

"Honestly." I gestured to my nose. For my trouble, a wave of nausea rose. "Am I going to lose my children?"

"Do you think you deserve to lose them?"

I glanced down at Hallie's ringlet curls and then to Thomas, who slept deeply in my arms. "It'll kill me." I met the police officer's gaze. "But I didn't keep them safe."

I gazed at Thomas. "No." I needed her to understand. "Gerard didn't touch the baby. He'd yell, and sometimes it scared the children, but the bruises on Hallie were the first time…" I drew in a breath. "I ran before anything worse happened."

Another tap of the pen.

The smell of antiseptic wafted over me. I wanted out of this hospital so badly, but I was terrified my children wouldn't be allowed to come with me.

"There's a significant age difference between you and your husband." No derision in *husband*. Thank God she didn't appear to be homophobic.

But she was right about the age difference. Twenty-two years was significant.

"You were how old when you adopted Hallie?"

My daughter stirred at her name, then clutched me even tighter.

"I was twenty." She knew this. Undoubtedly, she could do the math.

"And you'd already been married…"

"Almost two years."

"So you were eighteen when you married? And he was forty?"

"Nineteen." As if that made a lick of difference. "Look, I'm sure Gerard will tell you how he rescued me. He's not lying. I was in a bad place with zero hope. I thought he was my savior. And for a while, things were great."

She held my gaze.

"We were so happy when we adopted Hallie. Her mom…" I hesitated. Marie had been in a bad place. I'd known her from when we'd been homeless together. We'd lost touch when I landed in a good place. Her turning up on my doorstep, eight months pregnant, had just…been one of those things. Like it'd been meant to be.

Gerard had been the one to suggest we adopt the baby.

I'd suspected Marie had been raped, and she also used drugs on and off. She wasn't in a position to raise a child, even if I'd been able to give her all the money she'd need. And I hadn't been able to—but I could give her baby a loving home.

"And Thomas?" The officer looked at the baby in my arms. His darker skin often raised questions.

"We put our names in with an adoption agency. In the end, though, a girl approached us privately. I think she'd heard from Marie how we helped her out, and…" I swallowed. "Cantrice wanted us to privately adopt Thomas." I cradled my infant son against my chest.

"Private adoption?"

I nodded.

"So it was finalized after six months?"

"Yeah." I gazed down at my son. "That was six months ago."

"Do you know where Cantrice is now?"

I shook my head. "She asked for money so she could go to New York. I don't know how sincere she was about leaving LA, but Gerard was happy to give her the money once the adoption was finalized." Panic at the thought of her returning and demanding to take Thomas back welled within me. Given how poorly I'd taken care of myself, she wouldn't be wrong in questioning my ability to care for him.

Except I would've laid my life on the line for him. Damn near had.

"Do you have a place to go?"

I shook my head. "No. I mean, can't I go home?"

The officer arched an eyebrow. "Sure. And you can get a restraining order in case he's released, but—"

"Released?" I squeaked that, and Hallie held on tighter.

"Yes. I mean, I'm certain the prosecutor will try to keep him in jail, but the judge might offer bail."

"Which he'd be able to post."

"Right." She smiled at Hallie. "Do you have money?"

I swallowed. "I have a twenty in my wallet."

"That's it?"

"Yeah."

"Let me make a call." She pocketed her notebook and stepped out of the room.

I tried to stave off the shakes. Four hours ago… I wanted to say I'd been happy, but that wouldn't have been true. I wanted to say I'd felt safe, but that wouldn't have been true. Finally, I wanted to say I'd known what my future held in store, but that wasn't true either.

Officer Greenaway returned about fifteen minutes later, her face set in a grim line. "We don't have any open shelter beds for men with children right now."

Of course they didn't. "I'm not giving up my children." If they went somewhere else, I might never see them again.

"I called a friend. He's a social worker down in Gaynor Beach. Have you ever heard of the town?"

I wracked my brain. I knew a few places around Los Angeles, but not many. I'd grown up in Missouri and hadn't looked back after being booted out at sixteen. I'd had enough cash to get to LA, and I'd thought…huh. I wasn't sure what I'd thought. Not that I'd be living on the streets for two years. I'd had dreams of finishing high school and maybe college. I'd believed after I married

Gerard that he'd support me to get my GED. That hadn't happened either. I blinked. "Gaynor Beach?"

"It's a couple of hours south of here. Between Huntington Beach and Oceanside. On the way to San Diego."

Slowly, I nodded. I knew San Diego. Had never been there, but I understood it was south of here.

"My friend can drive up here to take you back. He's got a place you can stay for the night and then he has a line on a house you might be able to stay in. It's a small house—"

"I don't care." I needed to show appropriate gratitude while not losing my ever-loving shit at the kindness of this woman. "We…" I winced. "We need car seats." We hadn't had them when we'd come to the hospital because everything had been so chaotic. I hadn't even thought about it as I'd clutched my children's hands in the ambulance.

"My friend is the father of several children. He's got car seats." She eyed me. "I can go back to the house and get a few things—"

"No. We need to leave. Now." I needed to get out of LA as soon as possible. As fast as we could move.

"He's safe in jail."

"You said he might get out." I might not have a high school diploma, but I'd watched enough television and news shows to know that many first-time offenders got bail if they could afford it. And that restraining orders were useless.

Officer Greenaway nodded. "Is there anyone you want to call? To let them know you're going away but that you're okay? You shouldn't tell them where you're going, of course…"

I didn't feel okay, and I definitely didn't have anyone to call. Gerard had made certain I had no one. "We're good."

A nurse entered the room carrying a cloth bag. "Diapers, formula, wipes, and a few snacks for the little one." She smiled at Hallie, who just burrowed into me more.

I could barely tell where I ended and she began.

Then the nurse put a pile of clothes on the exam table. "For you."

I gazed down and winced. Yeah, the shirt soaked in blood wasn't a good look. Even my track pants hadn't escaped the ordeal. But I'd keep them because they were all I had. I'd figure out how to get the blood out. "Thank you."

"Why don't I hold the little one while you change? It will be nice to be in fresh clothes." The woman held out her tanned arms.

Her kind, dark-brown eyes mesmerized me as I considered her offer. The gray streaks somehow assured me. Not just that she could hold Thomas properly, but that she'd seen shit like this before. I was quite certain I wasn't the only battered husband who'd graced the corridors of this hospital. I was lucky I was able to walk out. It could've been so much worse.

I handed my baby boy over to her and tried to untangle myself from Hallie.

Officer Greenaway held out her hands.

Reluctantly, I tried to encourage Hallie to go to the woman.

My girl was having none of that. She started howling.

The police officer backed up. "We'll leave you to change."

"Can't you just turn around?" I didn't want Thomas out of my sight.

"We'll be just outside the door, right there…" She pointed to the door.

I weighed the idea of privacy versus letting Thomas out of my sight for a moment. I didn't have any other marks on me, but I didn't need to be scrutinized. Finally, I nodded.

The two women stepped outside the room.

I toed off my running shoes, relieved to see they weren't speckled with blood. "Sweetheart, Papa needs to get his clothes changed. Will you sit in the chair while I do that?" As open and free as I tried to be with my kids about nudity, I always hesitated with Hallie. I'd grown up in a repressed household, and I didn't want my daughter to have the same hangups. On the other hand, I was always conscious of being perceived as being some kind of deviant because I was gay.

Apparently my own hangups remained.

Still, Hallie sat on the hard plastic chair while I quickly changed. I nabbed a plastic bag, dumped the bloodstained clothes in it, tied it, then rearranged the supplies in the cloth bag so my soiled things sat at the bottom and everything I needed to take care of my son was on top.

Tears pricked the backs of my eyes. All these people were strangers to me—and yet they were generously opening their hearts and helping me. I didn't feel worthy.

I never felt worthy.

As I gazed at my daughter, the dawning realization I had to do better struck me with the force of a two-by-four to the solar plexus. I was all she had. All Thomas had. No more Gerard to back me up. Not that he'd done much of it, anyway. But now, if something happened to me, my babies had no one. That thought saddened and terrified. What if…they let Gerard take them? Or, worse, they called my parents?

I vowed to see a lawyer as soon as I could. I had no idea who I might nominate as a guardian, but just about anyone else—except Gerard—would be better than my parents. At least I hoped I could do this. *God, you know nothing about the law, about children, or about your rights.* I'd understood adoption rules because we'd been deep in the weeds. The rest hadn't seemed important. *How's that working out for you?*

Hallie, having clearly run out of patience, held her arms open.

I scooped her into mine, holding her close. "We need to find Thomas." The nice people said they'd be just outside, but what if they'd been lying? What if they'd tricked me?

Panic seized my heart as I barged into the corridor.

To find the nice nurse holding a sleeping Thomas who was, apparently, oblivious to everything going on around him. I swore he'd sleep through an earthquake.

Hallie was the opposite. Even in sleep, she was hypervigilant—waking at every noise and often coming to see me. That irritated the shit out of Gerard, if she woke him by accident, but I liked that she felt she could come to me when she was scared. That I was her port in the storm.

The nice nurse indicated the room with her head.

I went back in and she followed. Instead of trying to hand back Thomas, she sat in a chair with armrests and settled him—and apparently herself—comfortably.

She eyed me. "Why don't you lie on the bed and try to get some rest? Officer Greenaway said it'll be a few hours."

Until what? I wanted to ask. But hadn't the kind woman said something about a social worker coming from Gaynor Beach? That we'd have somewhere safe to stay for the night? I clung to that hope, even as I positioned myself on the bed with Hallie tucked against me.

Against all odds, I managed a bit of sleep and was groggy when someone shook me awake. I blinked in the bright light, disoriented until I caught sight of Officer Greenaway.

Hallie didn't stir when I untangled myself and managed to sit up.

The officer stepped back to reveal a tall, slender man. His tanned skin glowed in the overhead light, his beard was neatly trimmed, and he had a cautious grin. What I mostly noticed, though, was the eyes. He had kind dark-brown eyes that offered a promise of solace in this dark moment I found myself in.

"My name is Anthony Rodrigues. I'm a social worker from Gaynor Beach. If you like, I can take you to a safe place for the night and help you start fresh. We'll take care of you."

I sobbed.

CHAPTER 1

DANNY

"Gracie," I whined to my annoying big sister.

"Danny," she whined back.

I smacked her arm.

She smacked me right back.

Harder.

A sign of affection in our family.

Then she met my gaze. "What?"

As I sat in her living room, I took a moment to admire her moxie. Moving away from home at eighteen so she could become an actor. Los Angeles wasn't too far from our family home in Huntington Beach, but that distance felt especially huge today.

I pointed to my books. "School is so hard."

She scratched my shorn hair as I sat at the table and she stood above me. I didn't like how it looked when it grew out, so I always kept it short—much to Mama's dismay. She preferred the natural look and despaired when any of her children did treatments and used products. My choice to be practically bald didn't appease her, even though I didn't use anything in my hair.

"Uh, Danny, you're premed." Her gaze softened as she smiled. "Did you honestly think you'd just sail through undergrad and right into the School of Medicine at UCLA?"

"Well, frankly, yes."

She rolled her eyes.

I smacked her arm again. Lighter, I thought. "Gracie, I aced all my classes in high school. Had a near-perfect SAT score. Am on scholarship for premed at UCLA. This should be easy for me." Because all my life, I'd wanted to be a doctor. Like, a cardiologist or oncologist or thoracic surgeon. Big names for big ambitions. Big dreams. I was going to make my parents proud. They sacrificed a lot for all of their seven children. As the youngest, there shouldn't have been anything left over for me, but they'd put as much heart into me as they had with my older twin sisters—Leticia and Felicia.

"Just because everything that came before was easy doesn't mean it'll be that way now." Gracie scowled. "Maybe it's good you're being tested now instead of when you're in a position to actually harm someone."

Again, with the scratching my scalp. She played with my hair to drive me nuts.

"Not everyone is cut out to be a doctor, little bro."

"You know I hate it when you call me that."

"And so, I will continue to do so." She rose from the kitchen table. "You want something to drink? You can't be hungry again—"

"I am." I patted my not-so-taut abdomen. I wasn't fat…but I wasn't slender either. I was heftier than my brother James, and that bothered me. Mama was always trying to show her love through food. Gracie, Leticia, and Felicia all inherited our grandmother's slender frame—willowy. I, along with my brother James and my sister

Whitney, had gotten our grandfather's and father's genes—hefty. Whitney's curves weren't too much. James managed to keep himself fit. Especially now he was helping take care of some dog down in Gaynor Beach that seemed to need constant walks, judging by his fake-bitching. I wasn't as lucky. Then again, a few pounds never hurt anyone. "I am hungry. Have you heard from James lately?"

Gracie tossed a piece of leftover pizza into the microwave and refilled my water glass.

I was grateful but annoyed. I could've done both those things myself. She liked to mother me, and today, arguing with her wasn't worth the effort.

"Not since Thanksgiving when Colin told us the Hep C was gone." Colin was James's boyfriend. And a super nice guy with an awesome dog.

"So…Colin needs a liver transplant next. Do you think James will consider donating?" Our brother was just a big teddy bear. So accommodating. So kind. So understanding. I was none of those things. Or at least I didn't see myself that way. I was too focused on academics to deal with anything else. This whole liver-transplant thing fascinated me, though.

"I don't know." Gracie pulled the piping-hot slice of pizza from the microwave, plated it, and tossed that my way.

"They say that donations are best done with the same race and gender. Or, at least, those yield the best results."

Gracie arched an eyebrow. "You've looked into this?"

I shrugged. "I'm premed, Gracie, and considering being a surgeon. Of course I looked into it." Not as a donor or anything…just to see what might be involved. Especially if James wanted to donate. At least he and Colin were both guys. But James was Black and Colin was white. I tried to tell myself that things like that didn't matter, but the odds of compatibility were a bit lower between them. No matter how much James might want to be a good match, if he had the wrong blood type, that wasn't something wishing could fix.

"You're thinking really hard, Daniel."

I glowered. She knew I hated when she used my full name.

She merely smiled and pointed to my pizza. "Eat it while it's hot. Then we can go for a walk. Let's see if we can grab Cindy's dogs and take them for a trek around Hancock Park. You need a break from studying."

Gracie lived in La Brea, which, as she liked to point out, was central to everything. She worked in a high-end dining establishment as a hostess when she wasn't out pounding the pavement for auditions. She hadn't had her breakthrough yet, but I had high hopes for her. My sister was damn talented. And sure, I was biased. I might be closer in age to Whitney, but Gracie had been the best big sister. "Sure, a break sounds good." I scrunched my nose. "Can you get the dogs without me?"

My sister laughed. "You don't want to see Cindy?"

"Uh…no. Why did you tell her I was pan?"

"Because you are." Gracie narrowed her eyes. "You're out, Danny. Or at least that's what you've always said—"

"I am."

"So why the fuss about Cindy?"

I considered. "I've dated men and women, but Cindy's…"

"Aggressive?"

"Assertive," I countered. "And that's usually okay, but…"

"She's not your type?"

That was a hard question to answer because I'd never considered myself as having a *type*. Knowing myself, though, meant certain things turned me on and certain things were off-putting. "I know she's smart."

Which was a turn-on.

"But she's also…really set on dating me. And that's just not in the cards right now, you know what I mean?"

Gracie nodded. "Okay, I'll go get the dogs and you hang tight." She put on her lightweight jacket and headed out. Early December in Los Angeles could be hit-or-miss temperature-wise. We'd gone through a spell of cool weather earlier in the fall, but we were in the mid-sixties with sunny days this week.

My phone pinged with a text from James.

—*We need some assistance to do some physical labor. You up to helping? I don't want Colin to overdo it.* —

I replied. —*Sure. What does this involve?* —

—*Tomorrow we're moving my stuff to Colin's and I'm renting my place out to*—

I waited for a full minute, about to prompt, but then he finished.

—*A family in need. I'll explain when you come down.* —

—*Sure, be there at eight.* —

He gave me the thumbs-up emoji, then a string of hearts. That was James…showing affection in any way possible. I eyed my chemistry textbook. Tomorrow was study day with a major test on Monday. Except James rarely asked things of me, despite me being single and most able to help. Martin had his little daughter, with another one on the way. Whitney was busy with grad school, and Gracie's schedule was unpredictable. Thanks to my scholarship and a bit of help from Mama and Daddy, I didn't need to work. Which meant I had all the time in the world to lend a hand and still focus and study…

And yet I didn't. My mind was always elsewhere. Restlessness had set in, even as med school neared.

Gracie poked her head in the door. "Two Dalmatians at the ready. You know I can walk them both alone…"

She could, of course. My sister was wicked-strong. Still, I grabbed my keys. I had one for her place so I could come over when I needed reassurance. I locked the door, then took one of the leashes. Honestly, I'd tried to figure out how to tell Lucy and Linus apart, but I was clueless. Well, except for Linus's big dick. It wasn't his fault that his penis hung out. If they'd been better behaved, they might actually respond to their names. Cindy hadn't quite got the training down, so both dogs sort of did what they wanted —which was why Gracie appreciated when I walked one with her.

We did about six miles before heading back to her fourth-floor studio apartment. She was in the heart of La Brea, close to the restaurant and within spitting distance of all the major studios.

Or at least that was my perspective.

I, on the other hand, felt the hands of time creeping up on me. Becoming a doctor was going to take me eleven or twelve years through residency. Gracie could hit it big in the next month, or even the next year, but becoming an MD had no shortcuts.

While Gracie returned the dogs to a grateful Cindy, I closed up my textbooks and put them back into my knapsack. I promised myself that I'd look at them after I helped James tomorrow, even as I knew that to be a lie. After whatever physical activity was too much for just James? I'd likely be too tired. I'd drive from LA to Gaynor Beach in the morning—which meant being on the road by six. At least, early on a Saturday morning, the trip would fly by. But I'd have to drive back up afterward. I texted Mama and asked if I could stay tomorrow night at the family home in Huntington Beach. That was partway between Gaynor Beach and LA. Would get me closer to my dorm without actually landing me there. Maybe I'd study at Mama's.

Ha.

No, I wouldn't. I'd flop on her couch and watch reruns with Daddy. Or a game, if there was one. I wasn't big on sports, but Daddy kept up with all the California teams.

Mama texted back that she'd make Mission-style burritos.

I countered with a request for a cobb salad.

She said she'd make both.

Which should've made me feel guilty. Mama's heart wasn't so good, and she needed to take it easy. And I patted my stomach, which didn't need more high-calorie foods. *Oh crap.* I texted back that I might be eating dinner with Colin and James.

She said she'd put something aside for me *just in case.*

Knowing me, I'd be tempted to eat it, even if I'd consumed plenty at my brother's place.

"Cindy says *hi.*" Gracie bounded into the room, still full of energy.

"You want a dog."

She shook her head. "I get to watch Widget when Colin and James are at the hospital. Cindy lets me borrow hers. Germaine fosters, so he's usually got one or two as well…"

I cocked an eyebrow.

"Okay, yeah, I wouldn't mind a furry companion of my own. But you know I can't, Danny."

"If you met someone…"

She tossed a throw pillow at my head, which I caught with ease. "It could happen. You're not the only lesbian in LA."

"I might've…"

"Oh…?"

"There's an app for that."

"And?"

"I can't find anyone who's my type."

"And what type is that?"

She tapped her lips. "Attractive—although that's not the most important."

"Yet you listed it first."

She held up another throw pillow as a threat.

"There's more?" I loved needling her.

"Smart."

"That's a given." I didn't say the *duh*—it was understood.

Grace slashed her hand through the air. "I want someone who gets me. Who doesn't question the insanity of what I'm doing. Who will understand when I'm upset that I didn't get a job. Who won't mind the crazy hours I work."

"Those all sound like reasonable things."

She rolled her eyes. "I haven't met a single woman who matches any of those criteria. It's like I'm asking too much."

I grabbed her and pulled her into a bear hug. I wasn't as tall as James's six four, but I held my own. Taller than Gracie's five ten, that was for certain. Well, by an inch or two. "You'll find the right woman, I promise."

A snicker escaped, even as she held me tight. "I might just hold you to that promise. You can interview the local lesbians and bi women for me."

This time, I whacked her with a pillow.

Five minutes later, I was on my way back to my dorm for a good night's sleep. I was excited to see Colin and James again, but barely gave a thought to the reason they needed me. James asked, I responded. Easy as that.

CHAPTER 2

ROB

I HADN'T THOUGHT I'D SLEEP, BUT ONCE WE ARRIVED AT the shelter in Gaynor Beach and Anthony gave us a secure room, fatigue overtook me. The adrenaline that had sustained me from the moment Gerard had broken my nose evaporated.

With Anthony's help, I got Thomas changed, fed, and down for the count in the small crib.

Hallie wouldn't let go of me, and I made the executive decision she was fine in the pajamas she still wore. I also decided I'd crash in the clothes I had on. Again, with Anthony's help, Hallie and I got into the single bed.

Gerard never allowed co-sleeping. I understood the practice could be dangerous, but I also always wanted to be as close to the kids as I could. Possibly because I'd unconsciously worried Gerard might get angry with them when I wasn't around.

Well, probably.

Anthony shut the door, and in just a moment Hallie was out. I turned the lock, checking twice that the door was secure. Told myself Gerard had no way to find us. The folks at safe house were used to abusive spouses and wouldn't let him in if he did. We were fine. We were safe. *For now.* Sleep took a lot longer in claiming me, but exhaustion muffled my thoughts, and eventually it did.

I hadn't bothered to set an alarm because my adorable son, no matter the circumstances, woke up at six-thirty. Didn't matter what time he went to bed or how many times he woke up in the night—come six-thirty, he was awake and ready to go.

We'd gotten about six hours of sleep, so I was actually okay when I slipped out of bed to take care of him. I wanted a shower, but I couldn't leave the kids. I'd met a caretaker last night, and Anthony had mentioned someone being around in the morning, but I'd only focused on the bed.

"Hey, little man." I whispered the words since Hallie still lay curled under the blankets. *At least she didn't have a nightmare.* My daughter had them fairly often, and I'd need to soothe her back to sleep.

Much to Gerard's consternation.

Why did he even want kids? Come to that, why did he even want me?

I could ask the question, but I could also now recognize the answer. I'd thought he wanted a legacy, to have kids carry on his name. The last six months had opened my eyes to the truth. The man loved to control people. To play God with people's lives. From the little he said about his job, he got to boss people around a lot. He also said everyone who worked for him was a moron. I'd once tried to talk to him about his job. His rebuke, along with the name he'd called me, ensured I shelved that curiosity.

Which made me wonder just how much power he really had. Why not fire the ones who weren't doing the job and hire smarter people? Although maybe he liked being around people he felt superior to. Much of me doubted these people he derided were as stupid as he implied. And I now suspected what he said about being the big boss was also horseshit.

Thomas giggled as I blew a raspberry on his tummy. He was such a happy kid—completely oblivious to the surrounding turmoil. His luminous dark-brown eyes gazed up at me as I finished changing his diaper, then I slipped him into an outfit the nice people at the hospital had provided. We'd need more stuff soon. Maybe I should've run home for a quick retrieval. Gerard was in jail. He couldn't have hurt me.

Yet I wouldn't have had the strength to walk in that door. Although the broken nose had been a shock to my system, it shouldn't have been. This was, truly, the conclusion of a toxic relationship. Only, until the moment his fist had connected with my face, I'd still believed I could somehow make us work. That if we just bonded as a family that everything would be okay.

Fucking idiot.

I didn't like putting myself down, but the cruel words of my parents, and now Gerard, were hard to deny. I wasn't smart. I didn't know how things worked. I'd managed to figure out how to cook, clean, raise children, and not be a complete disaster in the process. Except Gerard was always explaining how my mistakes were my own fault. Telling me I wasn't—

"Papa?" Hallie's small voice rang out in the small room which held only the bed, the crib, and a dresser.

"Yes, baby."

"I have to pee."

"Of course." I did as well, but I'd just have to wait until the kids were comfortable. "There's a bathroom in here." I guided her to the bathroom with Thomas on my hip. To my relief, there was a potty-training seat, and she was able to pee easily. A little stepstool helped her reach the sink so she could wash her hands.

When she was done, we went back into the room. "Honey, can you watch Thomas?"

"Yep." She'd never said no. She probably didn't even know that was an option. Without being asked, she sat on the little mat on the floor and held open her arms.

I gently placed Thomas in them. Immediately, he pushed up, stood, and toddled over to a little plastic chest. I hadn't even noticed it.

I murmured to Hallie, "Do you think there are toys in there?"

"Oh yes." Hallie scrambled over as well.

After raising the lid, I found the safety latch and made sure it wouldn't close on little fingers.

Thomas already had pulled out some colorful rings and had one in his mouth.

Working off the assumption everything had been properly sanitized, I scooped him up safely into the crib with his new treasures, pressed a kiss to the top of Hallie's head, then made a beeline to the bathroom. Knowing my daughter would be okay for a few minutes, I decided to take a thirty-second shower. My face still ached, and I'd need to keep the bandage clean, but I needed a moment to rinse off some of the gross stinky sweat from last night. I regretted sleeping in my clothes, but I hadn't really had a choice. Hopefully today I'd have the opportunity to grab something fresh.

Doesn't matter. The kids are the priority.

Right. I needed to focus. In the shower, I lathered up and then rinsed off as quickly as I could, ever mindful that something bad might happen. The vigilance never let up. As soon as I was clean, I rinsed off, shut off the water, and hopped out. I did a quick rubdown, then tied a towel around my waist and opened the bathroom door.

Hallie sat beside the crib as she read Thomas a story. I didn't recognize the book, and Hallie couldn't read, so she was likely making up a story to fit the pictures. Her creativity knew no bounds. That was one of the reasons I could leave her to her own devices and she'd be perfectly happy to just sit in her room with a pile of toys and books. She didn't need me to guide her—she could figure it out by herself.

Thomas, on the other hand, required guidance. Appropriate for a one-year-old. I got the feeling, though, that he wouldn't have Hallie's quietness. From the beginning, she'd been undemanding. Thomas very much wanted to have everyone's attention. Although he was adorable, that much energy was also exhausting.

"Papa?" Hallie blinked up at me.

"Everything's okay, sweetheart."

"You have an owie." She pointed to my face.

"I banged my nose. I'll be fine, just like when you skinned your knee."

Her solemn blue eyes held my gaze. If any four-year-old was capable of calling bullshit, it would be her. Still, she offered a small smile. "I'll keep reading."

Thomas put an arm through the bars and seized the book in his tiny fist, but the solid cardboard didn't crumple. Thank God. I didn't know what I'd do if he destroyed something and I'd have to repair it.

I scooted back into the bathroom, and after a quick search, found a new deodorant as well as a toothbrush and toothpaste. There were tiny brushes as well. Which reminded me that my kids hadn't brushed their teeth last night. Small everyday things were starting to pile up and, if I didn't miss my mark, we were headed toward a Hallie

meltdown. She thrived on routine, and with everything
that had happened, I was surprised she hadn't lost it yet.
Or, perhaps, she sensed I wouldn't be able to cope, and
she'd somehow hold on.

Wishful thinking.

My child was empathetic, but I didn't think she was
capable of understanding how her meltdowns affected me.
I was always careful to never show how I felt about things.
I didn't want my negative emotions to affect her.

She probably knows.

Yeah, probably.

I put the borrowed clothes back on.

No, not borrowed. Gifted. And they fit pretty well.

I padded out of the bathroom with my socks in one
hand and a toothbrush in the other. "Hallie?"

She glanced up. "Thomas first."

"Of course. Come on, little man."

My boy held his arms out, and I easily scooped him
into my arms. Despite being born underweight, he was
now in the ninety-seventh percentile for height and weight.
I was super proud of how far he'd come. He was a healthy
chunk of happy baby. Toddler, I corrected. In just a couple
of days, he'd have his first birthday.

What kind of celebration will that be now? No gifts, no party?
He wouldn't care, of course. Wouldn't understand. But I
would. I'd carefully documented everything from my
children's lives and had beautiful scrapbooks. All
abandoned. I still had some of the photos on my phone,
but Gerard paid the phone bill, so God only knew when it
would be cut off. Even if I knew how to change it to my
name, I didn't have the money to pay for the plan.

Thomas bopped me on the side of the head. Not hard.
But not gentle either. "Ba!"

I chuckled. "Okay, let's get this done."

Ten minutes later, both kids had brushed teeth, and I'd tamed Hallie's hair. Her fine blonde locks curled naturally. They also tangled continuously, so keeping up with the brushing was critical.

"Maybe we should put on our shoes?"

"Papa, I'm hungry."

I wasn't, but relief washed over me that she wanted food. I worried constantly about her waifishness. She ate plenty, but always seemed so fragile. Unlike Thomas, who was finally as solid as a toddler could get. "I suppose we could go and see if we can find food. Uh…" I glanced around. "Let's put on our shoes first." I could barely remember the walk from the front door to our second-story room. This place felt less industrial than I'd expected and more like a house. But I hadn't been given a tour, and I didn't want to wander into something I shouldn't.

Just as I finished tying Hallie's laces, a soft knock sounded at the door. When I picked up Thomas and rose to answer it, she cowered behind me.

I paused with my hand on the lock. "Who's there?"

"Anthony? We met last night."

"Oh, sure." Thomas grabbed my hair as I opened the door, and I gasped.

Anthony smiled, stepped forward, and gently extricated my hair from my son's grasp. "That's a strong grip."

In response, Thomas twisted and threw himself into Anthony's arms.

Fortunately, the social worker caught him easily, hefted him in the air, then settled him on his hip. A flush of exertion overtook the man's tanned skin, and his eyes sparkled in amusement. "I thought he was easygoing last night. Clearly my recollection was correct."

Hallie gripped my jeans tighter.

"Did you want to come in?" I slowly loosened her grip,

then gently pulled her up into my arms. I wasn't a big guy —certainly not tall like Anthony—but I could still lift Hallie. If Thomas kept growing like he was, he'd be a much bigger armful at four.

"I could, but I was thinking you might like to come down to the kitchen and have some breakfast."

"Will there be other people?" I was painfully aware of my bruised face and bandaged nose. I didn't want pity or questions, and Hallie was shy even before last night.

"We have two other women here, and both have already eaten. We'll have the kitchen to ourselves." He cocked his head. "Do you like avocado?"

Thomas clapped his hands.

Anthony laughed.

Hallie buried her face in my shirt. One step forward…

We followed Anthony downstairs, and I sat with the kids at the table while he set about making a breakfast of avocado toast, eggs, and sausages. I wanted to help, but Hallie clung to me like a limpet, huddled in my lap. Anthony had slipped Thomas into the chair with practiced ease, getting my son's flailing legs in the right holes and the belt buckled even faster than I could. The social worker quickly sliced an avocado and passed Thomas a bit, smiling as my kid mashed it on the tray.

"You're good with kids," I said.

Anthony grinned as he sliced the rest of the avocado. "My husband and I have four-year-old twins. Zayden and Alicia."

"Oh my God."

He grinned. "Yeah, we pretty much say that every day. We also have a foster daughter." He blinked a couple of times and sobered, a shine coming to his eyes. "But it looks like we're going to be able to adopt her soon."

The palpability of his emotion hit me. Joy? Sadness? I couldn't be certain. "That's good?"

"That's great." He shook his head a little. "I love kids so much, and Laura...well, all kids need love, right? Some are just luckier than others."

"I'd say she's lucky to have you and your husband."

He appeared to consider. "Yeah, you could say that. I wasn't sure how things were going to pan out. We were an emergency foster for her. But she just...settled right in. Like she was always meant to be with us. The twins adore her. And she them," he quickly added. "She's even won Crumpy's heart."

"Crumpy?"

"Our seal-point Himalayan cat. Scott had him before the twins showed up, and at first, grumpy-cat wasn't quite certain what to make of those two characters."

I wanted to ask if one of the men was the biological father, but that was so none of my business. It never mattered how a family was made—just that it was full of love.

"Papa?" Hallie tugged on my shirt.

"Yes, sweetheart?"

She wrapped her tiny arms around my neck.

I breathed in her scent.

"We'll take care of you three." Anthony spoke quietly. "I'm taking you to a different house today—a donated space. It'll be all yours. It's small—just one bedroom and a den—"

"I don't care—"

"I imagine you don't." He brought a plate of avocado toast cut into four with a little bowl of sliced fruit as well. He placed the bowl before Thomas, who dug in with both hands. Then he put the plate on the table. "If you're up for it," he said to Hallie.

She ducked her head against my shoulder again.

"How is there a house available?" This felt way too easy.

Anthony grinned again. "The guy who owns it is moving in with his boyfriend. He didn't want to sell just yet…you know…"

I did know. Lack of having a place to escape to when things went sideways was what had led to my predicament.

"…so he wants to keep his place, but doesn't want it to sit empty. I called him when I realized you'd need a longer placement than we have space for here. The room you're in is promised to another family tomorrow."

"I can't afford rent."

He held my gaze. "Don't worry about that right now. Let's get you and the kids settled, and then we can figure things out."

"I need to get a job." I gripped Hallie even tighter. "But I've never had one. I know my social security number, though. But if I give that, will Gerard be able to find me?"

"Let's not worry about that right now," Anthony repeated. "You've got a lot to deal with. Let's get you safe first, and then we can figure out the rest."

Damn. "Look, Anthony, I really appreciate this."

He stirred the scrambled eggs. "I know you do."

"But I don't want to be beholden to another person. That's the correct word, right? That I don't want to owe anyone else?"

"That's the right word." He continued to stir the eggs. "You won't be beholden, Rob. Sometimes…" He added a sprinkle of salt and pepper. "Sometimes there are people in the world who just want to help. They've had a run of good luck, and they want to share. Or something bad happened to them once, and they got help and now they want to do the same thing. Pay it forward."

My mind spun.

"And you're eligible for some emergency funds. So we're going to go shopping for stuff for you and the kids. This afternoon, you'll move into your new house. We're going to set up counselling, and you'll see a pro bono lawyer about sorting out your situation." He plated the eggs. "It's up to you, but I got the impression you don't want to go back either to your house or your marriage."

"No fucking way."

Hallie clutched me tighter at my vehement words.

Anthony's gaze shot to mine.

"Sorry. Sorry, Hallie, Daddy said a bad word." I was such a screwup. My fault if Hallie said that at school one day.

Anthony shrugged. "Don't be. Just...sometimes the other person says they're sorry, makes a big, splashy apology, and the spouse forgives them. I'm actually relieved to hear you so certain you won't go back."

"I was worried who else my spouse might...impact." I dropped my eyes to Hallie, hoping my message was clear to Anthony and not her. The bruises on her arms were bad enough, but if he'd... No, I couldn't go there.

The social worker's eyes widened.

"Yeah, I didn't say that to the cops last night. But I lay awake in bed and replayed everything in my mind. He was going to do it. I think I knew that. That was why I put myself in the position to, um, get between." I gingerly pressed my nose. "I don't want Gerard near me or my children again. You can do that, right? Make certain he never gets to see them?"

He met my gaze. "Under certain circumstances, the other parent might be awarded supervised visitation."

My chest seized and my head swam. "You heard what

you just said, right?" I hugged Hallie tighter. Gerard would only touch her over my dead body.

Slowly, Anthony nodded. "But that's a long way off. The lawyer, Wynn Cavanah, will help you with a restraining order. We'll figure out when you might need to go back to LA to testify."

Hallie reached out to grab a slice of toast.

I loosened my grip a bit. "That sounds deceptively easy."

"It's not. The law is complicated. I won't go into specifics, but I've dealt with custody issues firsthand. Even when everyone's on the same page, the law might not agree. You'll have a good lawyer—"

"Who I can't pay—"

"—who will take good care of you." Anthony moved to the table with two plates. He placed one before me—with more toast and some eggs. Then he tapped a bit of cooled egg onto Thomas's tray.

He'd asked about allergies last night.

Thomas, who adored eggs, grabbed a handful and shoved it in his mouth.

Anthony put the plate before Hallie. "In case you like them too."

"I do." She blinked. "Eggs are good."

"Yes, eggs are very good." He moved back to the counter, snagged another plate, then joined me at the table. He grinned sheepishly. "Slow start this morning."

He'd been at my door at seven after having dropped me off near midnight. That felt Herculean to me. I was still an inch away from panic, my daughter was eating one-handed with the other clenched on my shirt, and Gerard might not be easy to ban from our lives. But as I took a bite of egg and the homey taste soothed me, Anthony's steady presence kept my fears under control. "Thank you. For all of it."

His eyes sparkled. "My pleasure."

CHAPTER 3

DANNY

I RUBBED MY FACE, TRYING TO INVIGORATE MYSELF. DESPITE my best intentions, I hadn't slept well. My roommate had stumbled in at three—drunk, high, and shocked at just having been dumped by the third girl in a row.

Now, Dwight tried hard…but the guy just didn't have a way with women. Oh, they'd agree to go out with him. Who wouldn't? Blond hair, blue eyes, California tan, tall… a damn attractive package. Unfortunately, he'd open his mouth, and that turned off just about everyone. He spouted right-wing conspiracy theories and drivel that made no sense.

I sort of shrugged and ignored him after having figured out early on that he couldn't be reasoned with. Why he insisted on attending a university in California while there were plenty in red states who would welcome him, I wasn't entirely clear. We had other right-wing students, for certain. And I respected some of them, for certain. Dwight, though? Not so much. And I struggled to reconcile the straightlaced dude, who believed in taking away rights of others, with the guy who regularly liked to get high.

He'd cried.

I'd gently suggested selecting women with similar interests. Surely he could find a woman with the same conspiracy views as him, right?

He'd vomited into his trash can.

I'd cleaned up that mess and him and tucked him into bed.

Out of an abundance of caution, though, I hadn't fallen back asleep. They'd told us a couple of harrowing stories in our freshman year, I supposed, to keep us on the straight and narrow. The girl who asphyxiated on her vomit and died was a scary one. I couldn't remember the others in as much detail. As much as Dwight annoyed me, I didn't want him dead. My hope was that, once I got into medical school, my caliber of roommate would improve. In fact, I could wish I'd have a single room. Probably couldn't afford it, though.

A strong extra-large coffee and a breakfast sandwich got me to Gaynor Beach. I stopped at Nice Buns to grab a second coffee and some sticky buns. The online reviews of the place were fantastic and, after I'd consumed one of said buns, I had to agree. I held out the box to James and Colin as we stood in front of James's house.

His soon-to-be former house.

"It's a nice place." I examined the bungalow. Barely more than a tiny house but cute. "A bit small."

He laughed. "Well, none of you ever descended en masse, did you?"

I cocked an eyebrow. "What's that supposed to mean?"

"Just…" He cleared his throat. "Right."

"What he's trying to say is that he wanted his

independence and was afraid if he bought a big house that you'd all visit. All the time." Colin grinned.

"Well…" James cleared his throat again. "Okay, you're not wrong. Although cost was a factor as well. I couldn't afford a bigger place."

"Good thing he can." I indicated Colin. "Because you know, now you're shacked up, Mama and Daddy are definitely going to come and visit. Often."

James groaned.

Colin laughed.

I grinned. Yeah, my brother was so easy to tease. "Okay, so what are we doing?"

"I've done several runs between here and Colin's house." James pointed to the SUV.

"Our house," Colin quickly interjected.

"Right." James let out a long breath. "Most of the computer equipment and electronics have gone. Everything else is boxed up. I figure you and I should be able to do it in a few trips."

I cocked my head. "You're not taking the furniture?"

"Nah." Colin leaned back against James's SUV. "My place has everything we need. We've found a not-for-profit that was looking for a solid desk, so they're picking that up shortly. The guy who's moving in has two young kids. So we've arranged for a kid's bed and a crib to be delivered."

James snickered. "We."

I gazed between the two men.

"Colin organized it," James asserted. "We found out late last night, and Colin arranged everything. Well, the desk we'd already found a home for. But the bed, crib, change table, and dresser have all been paid for by him. A delivery company is bringing them up from San Diego shortly."

I whistled. "I'm not going to ask what that cost you."

James cut me a look. When Colin wasn't looking, he indicated Colin with his chin.

Was James saying a lot or none of my business? Fair enough. Skinny white dude's skin was still pasty, despite having been in SoCal for more than a month. His pretty green eyes sparkled when he talked about James, but sometimes I caught a worried expression from each of them, when they thought the other wasn't looking. If he didn't get a liver transplant, then he was going to die, so that made sense.

This morning, in the bright sun, his coppery red hair shone. He looked better than he had in a while. Possibly because the meds had finally cleared up the Hep C. Or maybe because he was just that much in love with my brother.

Maybe both.

I peered into a window where a stack of boxes was visible. "So we run the rest of your stuff over to the house and then we clean for the new family?"

Colin snickered. "You don't think that house is white-glove clean already? James might not have been living there much, but he keeps it shining. In case Mama ever did show up."

James groaned.

I guffawed. Then considered. "Hey, where's Widget?" I *never* saw Colin without his French bulldog puppy.

"At home." James scratched his shorn hair. He kept his scalp nearly shaved while he had a nice beard.

I was always clean-shaven while my hair was…also short. "You left the baby home?"

"We needed the back seat empty to do this in as few loads as possible. She'll come back with us the final time. She and Colin are going to supervise as we put up

Christmas decorations for the new family, and then our place."

"I can help—" Colin started.

"No." James and I grinned. In unison, no less.

"Did you bring decorations?" I sipped my coffee.

"Yes." Colin shifted a little, then resettled. "I've bought outdoor decorations for both houses. As well as a few things for inside."

"A few?" James chuckled. "Bought out the store, just about. Mostly for here, though. We're going sparse this year until we figure out how we're going to organize *our* place." He gave a pointed look in Colin's direction. "See? I got it right."

Colin leaned over and kissed his cheek. "Thank you."

"Did you buy a real tree for in here?"

"Nah." James scratched his beard again. "We didn't want to make things too complicated, and some people are allergic. There's a nice artificial tree and several boxes of decorations. Anthony said he thought the guy might want to decorate with his kids, so we're leaving the indoor stuff alone for now. If he read the situation wrong, we can always help them. I'm more worried about doing the outside lights."

"Huh?"

He winced. "The guy's leaving a bad situation, and no one's supposed to know where he is. I just figured…"

"If this house is decorated like every other house, then it won't stand out." Colin grasped James's hand. "He's so smart."

"Actually, I think you decided that." James rubbed his eyes under his glasses. "We didn't get much sleep last night."

I almost piped up that I was also underslept, but I didn't want to compare a drunk roommate with helping a guy leaving a bad situation with two little kids. I clapped my hands together. "Okay, let's get this done."

Two hours and three runs later, all of James's personal belongings were at the house he now shared with Colin in West Beach. He'd have time to unpack later. The little house wasn't decorated yet, but the social worker, Anthony, had called with a heads-up to clear out for a bit.

We hunkered down at Boardwalk Book and Bites while Anthony helped the guy and his two kids arrive at the house. We didn't want to overwhelm them.

We sat outdoors with Widget at our feet, eying our food.

I tried to figure out if I could slip her something.

"Allergic to everything." James gave me the imperious older-brother glare. "She's not hard done by, no matter what she wants you to believe."

Widget blinked several times.

I gave her a sympathetic smile.

She huffed, then hunkered down.

"I admit when Anthony said a victim of domestic violence, I assumed he meant a woman." I eyed my lunch.

"Yeah." Colin sipped his drink. "We're all programmed to think that way."

"You said he's got kids?"

James nodded. "The guy's name is Rob. His daughter Hallie is four, and his son Thomas is a year." He bobbed his head. "I'm just glad we can help out."

"How much of a discount on the rent are you giving?" Not that it was any of my business, but I was super curious.

"I'm only charging him enough to cover utilities." James nudged Colin. "This guy won't let me contribute to his mortgage, so I can easily afford to keep paying mine."

"So basically, you're giving the place to the guy for nothing?"

James glanced back and forth between Colin and me. "We're lucky folks. Anthony heard I was looking to rent my place out and everything just sort of…came together. Anthony vouched for him, which is more than I'd get with a random renter. I'm sure the guy's not going to trash it, well, beyond normal kid stuff."

"Yeah, probably not."

"Plus, I don't want the house empty. So he's, like, doing me a favor."

I didn't call bullshit. I could've…but I didn't. I'd always known James had a generous nature. Colin's giving side had been a bit more of a surprise. He'd come from back east. An investment banker. I'd figured someone like that would be…snooty or entitled. And maybe he had been—I had no idea. I just knew the guy my brother loved was kind, compassionate, and a little shy around the massive Reynolds family.

James's phone pinged with an incoming text. "Anthony says we can go around. That Rob's expecting us."

We rose as a group, with Colin a little slower. James looked like he was going to offer to help, but Colin scowled. He was an independent guy, and obviously being dependent on others grated on him. We were always careful, when he came to the family home, not to baby him. But not to give him overly taxing chores either. He probably noticed—we weren't exactly known for being subtle.

En masse, we piled back into James's SUV for the brief drive back to Riverside. James's former residence was one of the smallest houses on the street, but it wasn't out of place. In relatively good shape, it now needed some festive stuff to make it look like all the other houses on the street.

James parked us out front, and I didn't spot another car. While we all got out, Colin, Widget, and I hung back a bit, letting James knock on the door. Then he backed up as well. I couldn't imagine what image we portrayed—two tall Black dudes and a scrawny white guy with cute copper-colored hair, and a snorting dog.

A guy, presumably Rob, stepped out of the house. Really, though, I noticed his daughter in his arms first—curly, blonde hair, a pair of jeans, and a purple sparkly sweatshirt that reminded me of Widget's harness. And she clung to her dad with a vise-like grip around his neck.

Next, my gaze followed his arm to the hand gripping a car seat. A small Black boy lay nestled there, fast asleep. He had a shock of natural curls and looked so restful in repose that a pang of envy ricocheted through me. Oh, what I wouldn't give for some sleep right now.

Finally, I noticed Rob. Damn, I should've paid attention to him first. Because the guy was…adorable. Half a foot shorter than me and on the thin side. Light-brown hair—shaggier at the top and cut short on the sides. Soulful gray eyes. The circles under his eyes spoke of exhaustion and, in fact, he yawned even as he eyed us cautiously.

Oh, and the bandage on his nose. He was lucky he didn't have matching black eyes. *That looks painful.*

"Hey, I'm Rob." He winced. "We fell asleep on the couch." He glanced at his daughter, then back at us. "Rough night."

James grinned. "Hi, Rob. I'm James." He gestured. "This is my house, and this is my boyfriend, Colin." He rubbed Colin's back. "And this is my brother, Danny."

"Daniel." I stood a little taller and tried to suck in my stomach.

James turned and full-on gaped at me.

Inwardly, I stood my ground. Yeah, okay, I normally hated my full name. I'd been named after the actor, Danny

Glover. Whom I loved. But in this moment, I wanted…to be an adult in a way I hadn't ever been before now, and that meant using the proper name my parents put on my birth certificate.

Rob blinked. "Oh. I like Danny. Sort of…softer."

"Well then, Danny's fine." I gazed down, then kicked the soft green grass with my toe. Finally, I looked back up. "I'm trying to be more grown up."

"You look pretty grown-up to me."

I startled for a moment at Rob's words. *Is he coming on to me?* I didn't think so, but I couldn't be certain. Even as I had the thought, his cheeks reddened slightly.

"Papa?"

He pulled Hallie closer. "Yes?"

"Who are they?"

He gazed over the three of us again. "They are the wonderful men who are here to set up your bed. You remember I told you that you were getting a big-girl bed?"

She nodded.

"And Thomas is getting a crib." He turned to us. "Would it be okay if we put the crib in my room? Then, when he cries, he won't wake Hallie. Not that he cries," he was quick to add. "I promise he's quiet. We won't disturb the neighbors."

Why would anyone care if the baby cried? Babies cried. That's what they did. Each of Felicia and Leticia's darlings had, at various times, howled the house down. Martin's daughter, Etta, was a little less like a siren.

A touch, anyway.

"We know it'll be fine." Colin gave Rob a sympathetic look.

Oh. Maybe it had been an issue in the last place for Rob. Maybe crying babies had annoyed the spouse who had broken Rob's nose. The white of the bandages matched the paleness of his skin, and I shoved down the anger that threatened to break through the surface every time I looked at him.

Before any of us could speak, a delivery van pulled up. I recalled Colin saying he'd hired a company from San Diego to come up and deliver everything.

A woman and a man stepped out. The woman held up the clipboard. "James Reynolds?"

My brother stepped forward. "Yes, that's me."

"Great, my name's Nikki. This is Fred. One bed, one changing table, one dresser, and one crib, right?"

"Right."

Rob gasped. "I can't afford that." He nearly toppled over, catching himself with a shoulder against the doorframe.

I strode over to his side, and pointed to the car seat. "Can I give you a hand? Just to take him inside where it's warmer? I'm sure Hallie has some toys she'd like to show me."

"But…"

I met his gaze.

Trust me on this. We've got this. We'll take care of you. Let someone help you.

Finally, he nodded, and held out the handle of the carrier.

I took it and balanced the precious weight of the sleeping infant.

Rob pushed off the doorframe, settled Hallie into a better position in his arms, and we went inside.

CHAPTER 4

ROB

As I ushered Danny into the house, with him carrying Thomas, it struck me that this was the first time someone else had hauled the carrier for me. Gerard certainly had never done it. And we'd been within walking distance of the medical clinic and stores, so I'd just pushed the double stroller.

In other words, no one had ever helped before.

I blinked rapidly. *He's just carrying your son. Don't make a big deal out of it.* And I wouldn't, I promised myself. I glanced over my shoulder at the other two men, but they just waved us on and turned to peer at something on the porch. I left them to do whatever, and followed Danny.

He moved to the couch, gently placed the carrier on the floor, straightened to his full height, and looked around. "You know, this is my brother's house and I've never seen the inside."

He spoke in a hushed tone around Thomas, which I appreciated. He needn't have bothered. Thomas could sleep through anything.

Danny stretched a little, rolling his shoulders back. He

was tall, although not as tall as his brother. He was also... I sought the right word. Not fat or chubby or anything like that. Just...solid. Both he and his brother had some heft to them. As opposed to myself who was short and... short and scrawny. No! Slender. Slim. Something that wasn't a word Gerard had used to make me feel bad about myself. Only now was I realizing just how often I repeated Gerard's cold criticism in my own head. I was determined to learn not to put myself down.

Gerard did enough of that for the both of us.

Danny smiled broadly. "My brother's lived here for a couple of months, and I've never even seen the place."

"It's a great place." I tried not to think of how small it was in comparison to my LA house because that didn't matter. We had a roof over our heads. For the moment, we were safe. "I love that Hallie's going to get her own room." I didn't mind sharing a room with Thomas. Having the crib next to the large bed would be a tight fit, but—having met James—I saw why the bed had to be so big. The guy was massive. And Colin wasn't a slouch either.

As Danny craned his neck, I offered up a smile. "Why don't you take a look around? Then you can say you've seen the place."

"Oh, I don't want to—"

"Really, it's okay." And Hallie was growing heavier in my arms.

As if sensing the issue, Danny nodded and headed down the hallway to the bathroom, bedroom, and den.

I lowered Hallie to the couch. "Do you want to read a book?"

She nodded silently, her gaze on where Danny had vanished.

Anthony had wanted to run us to the local bookstore to pick up a couple of things for Hallie.

I'd countered with a request to get to the library. Then, belatedly, realized I probably couldn't get a card…seeing as I didn't have ID.

Conveniently, Anthony's husband, Scott, was the head librarian. He was only too happy to issue me a card and help me select a bag full of books for Hallie. He'd also cooed over Thomas and talked about his own twins, insisting on showing me a photo. Which satisfied my curiosity as to whether one of them might be the father. Both Alicia and Zayden had Scott's red hair.

As Danny returned from the bedroom where Nikki and Fred were setting up the crib, James poked his head in the front door.

The brothers gave each other a long look I didn't have a clue of understanding.

James glanced toward me. "Would you mind if Colin and Widget come inside too?" He glanced behind him, then back at me. "My boyfriend is…not well. And he's also…"

"Stubborn?" Danny grinned. "Don't you let him hear you saying that." He turned to me. "He's not contagious or anything. Not that kind of illness."

"Of course he can come in." I glanced around, relieved there was a recliner as well as the couch. "Does he mind children?"

This time, Danny laughed. "He's survived our nieces and nephews. So has Widget—she's great with kids."

I blinked. "Widget?" I replayed the scene outside when I'd been so worried about making a good impression. Oh, who was I kidding? I was still worried about making a good impression. There'd been a dog on a leash…a small dog, I thought.

"Colin's French bulldog," James supplied.

Danny poked him in the ribs. "Your dog too, silly. She's the reason you two got together in the first place."

Which I'd sort of wondered about. None of my business, of course, but I always wondered how any gay couple wound up together. Oh, and straight ones as well. Pairing up confused me. Maybe if I'd better understood the process, I wouldn't have wound up with Gerard...

"Dogs are fine." I glanced at Thomas who still slept in his car seat. He loved dogs. So did Hallie, but she was far shyer when she didn't know them. The few we met in our local park were great with her, but she'd taken forever to warm up to them. I'd been eternally grateful to the generous owners who'd been so patient with her.

Right now, she sat on the couch with a new stuffed lion Anthony had so kindly gifted her. I'd quietly said we'd left her stuffed rabbit behind and I worried whether we should buy her another one. Anthony suggested something new—an animal who was brave. That left her the option to decide if the lion was brave and would protect her, or if she was brave like the lion. He said to leave that decision up to her. So far, she hadn't said anything—just gripped the animal tightly.

"Great, thanks." James disappeared back outside.

Danny eyed me. "This really okay? We can—"

"It's really okay." I offered up a genuine smile. "Danny, you all are doing so much for me. And..." I blinked. "I don't have anyone." God, I sounded so pathetic.

He moved swiftly to my side, then stopped at the last second.

Our gazes held—me staring up at him.

"You have us." He cleared his throat. "I mean, I'm in LA, but I'm just a phone call away." He dug in his pocket for his phone. "It's up to you, but I'd like your number. If that's too forward..."

I pulled my phone from my back pocket. "I just…it might get cut off."

"Well, you'll have me in your contacts, and you can call me if you get a new one. What's your number?"

Without hesitation, I gave it to him. I trusted him. I didn't really have a reason to…and yet I did.

He texted me and my phone pinged.

Carefully, I created a contact for him.

He grinned. "See? Now we're friends."

I blinked. Was it really that simple? And *just friends* felt like a safe space. I hadn't had a real friend since Marie and I had been on the streets together. That thought brought a pang of sadness that she'd probably never see Hallie grow up. But I would. I'd survived Gerard and, no matter what, I'd see my daughter become the woman she deserved to be.

"Hey."

Danny and I pivoted to see Colin entering the house. He started to remove his shoes.

"No worries about that," I said. "Keep them on." Everyone had worn theirs in so far. Well, except Fred and Nikki who wore cute plastic shoe covers. "I spotted a vacuum cleaner."

Danny snickered. "That would be James's doing. The man is super clean obsessed."

I smiled. "Well, that means the house is perfect for a crawling baby. And I'm grateful." Just as Danny started to move away, I took a risk and almost put my hand on his arm. In the end, it just hovered until I lowered it.

He stilled and gazed back at me.

"Thank you." I indicated my phone.

"Anytime," he replied.

"Yo, bro." James stuck his head in the doorway. "These lights aren't going to hang themselves."

Danny laughed. "No, they're not." He cast me one last look before heading out the door.

I pivoted to Colin. "Please, sit down. Does Widget need water? I don't have dog food, but Anthony stocked the fridge—"

Colin waved me off. "She's well-fed. And allergic to just about everything. A little bit of water would be great." He eyed Hallie. "But I can get it. I'll need to use one of the bowls, though. I didn't think to bring her water dish."

"Whatever you need." From the looks exchanged by the three men, Colin was as much to thank for all this as everyone else.

As he headed the few steps to the kitchen, I took a closer look at the cutest dog I'd ever seen.

She was mostly white with one black ear and the most adorable squished black nose, and her butt as she trotted after him sported a tightly curled little tail.

I'd never seen a dog built that way before. I assumed she was a puppy. *How big will she get? Will we be around to see her grow?* I glanced over at Hallie who still clung to her stuffie. Kids grew so fast. I assumed dogs were the same.

Sounds of slurping came from the kitchen, and I smiled. I knelt beside Thomas and gently traced his cheek.

He tried to bat my hand away.

"You need to wake up, little man." I hated to do it, but he needed a diaper change and, more importantly, not to sleep all day and be awake all night.

He'd been out for close to four hours. Despite everything we'd experienced, he'd napped.

I worried sometimes about how deeply he slept, but the doctor assured me his hearing was normal. That he was, despite his beginnings, a healthy baby.

"Hey." A soft whisper carried from the doorway.

I glanced over to find the delivery woman waving.

"We've finished the crib. I'm thinking changing table next?"

"Yes." I rose. "That would be amazing."

"Cool. Then we can do the dresser and, finally, the bed."

I pressed my hand over my heart. "Thank you."

Fred waved me off as he ducked behind Nikki to head outside.

She eyed her partner, grinned, and followed him.

"They seem like good folks." Colin reentered the room with Widget on her leash. "I've put the bowl in the dishwasher. James...well, there's plenty of crockery. For a guy who didn't want company, he's got enough to feed an army."

I eyed my two. "We use a lot of dishes."

"Well, the dishwasher will help with that. Do you mind if I...?" He pointed to the recliner.

"Please."

He sat.

Widget tried to jump onto his lap.

At the last moment, he put out his hand.

His grab missed as her shoulder collided with his fingers.

She landed hard on the floor.

I rushed over. "Oh, dear, is she okay? Were you worried about her being on the furniture? It's totally okay. I mean, I'm hoping my kids don't make a mess—"

"But they're kids," Colin supplied.

"Yeah." Heat crept into my cheeks. "They are."

Colin eyed me. "She's not able to jump this far yet, but she tries."

Feeling the unspoken request, I boldly scooped up the dog and gently laid her on the man's lap.

He smiled and petted the dog.

Who promptly licked him.

A win. I think. I hope.

"Papa?"

I moved to Hallie's side. "What, sweetheart?"

"Thirsty."

"Of course. Milk? Juice? Water?"

Her brow furrowed in concentration. Normally, she could make a decision quickly. Today, however, she seemed to struggle with everything. Finally, she whispered, "Juice."

"Okay. Can you watch Thomas while I get the juice?"

Slowly, she glanced over to Colin. Just as slowly, her gaze settled back on me. "Yes," she whispered.

"I can get the juice." Colin started to rise.

"No, it's fine." I waved him back down. I met Hallie's gaze. "Or would you prefer to come to the kitchen with me?" We were talking about half a dozen steps, but I would be out of her line of sight. That almost never happened.

"I'll watch Thomas." She slid off the couch and hunkered next to her brother in his car seat, never letting go of her stuffie.

"I'll be right back, sweetheart." I cast Colin a pleading look as I booted to the kitchen. I hoped he understood. Hell, I hoped I understood. I mouthed, *watch them?*

He nodded in reply.

Fortunately, Anthony had picked out kid-friendly kitchen things and, within a few moments, I was back with a small amount of juice in a plastic cup.

Hallie set her stuffie aside and took it with both hands.

I almost reminded her to be careful, but she didn't need the warning. She would do her very best. She always did. And that kind of broke my heart.

Fred and Nikki returned, carrying various boxes with what I assumed were the pieces to make up the changing table. They disappeared into the den, and I let out a breath.

"It'll be okay." Colin spoke quietly. "Within just a short period of time, everything will be set up, and we'll get out of your hair."

I ran my hand through my hair for what felt like the millionth time. "Is that a good thing?"

Colin cocked his head.

"I've just…everyone has been so helpful today. I couldn't have done it without you all."

"And you don't have to worry about that. We're a phone call away. I believe Anthony is as well." He held my gaze. "I'm new to Gaynor Beach. So is James. But we've been embraced by the community. Met plenty of great people. You will as well, just wait."

"Yeah…maybe…" Except strangers scared me. Sometimes I felt like I was a really bad judge of character. Like I couldn't tell if someone had good or bad intentions. Like I could wind up making another mistake. "Uh…cute puppy…how old is she?"

"Five months." Colin stroked her fur. "My family… chose to give her to me. And so we moved from back east to start a new life. No regrets."

"No regrets," I echoed.

If only it was that simple. "Oh, crap…would you like something to drink? I didn't even think—"

Colin started to wave me off, then stopped. "Actually, a water would be amazing. I have to stay hydrated."

That sounded super important to me. "Would you like ice? I remembered to fill the trays."

He grinned. "Ice water would be perfect." He gazed over to Hallie. "Do you think, when you come back, that she might want to meet Widget? No pressure." He eyed me. "Only if you think so."

Slowly, I nodded, although I wasn't sure Hallie would be up for it. Strange dog, strange people, I wasn't sure I was up for it. "Let me get you that ice water."

"Great." He grinned. Then indicated a pile of boxes next to an artificial Christmas tree. "Then perhaps you'll want to see what's in the boxes."

My heart sank. More gifts. More generosity. *Too much. It's just…too much.*

Colin's smile faltered. "Or you can do it as a family later on…when all the chaos is over."

Even as he said the words, Fred and Nikki tromped back in. "Changing table's done," she announced. Then they headed back outside.

This time, when she shut the door—unlike the thirty times before—Thomas awoke.

And let us know what he thought about his nap being rudely ended. Loudly.

Oh well, the peace was nice while it lasted.

I had no idea when quiet would return, but I hoped we'd survive until then.

Colin gently laid Widget on the floor. "Why don't I check on the status of everything?" He eyed my wailing child. "You've got your hands full."

"But—"

He waved me off. "Just…don't tell Danny and James. They're way too protective. I'm fine. Too much fussing."

Before I could argue, he headed down the hall to the bedroom and den.

Am I supposed to restrain him? Order him back into the chair?

Widget followed him, glancing around as she went.

I hustled over to Thomas, undid the straps, and scooped him out of the car seat. "Oh dear, buddy, you really need a change."

As always, he stopped crying once I held him. He was

quick to cry, quick to stop and, right on cue, quick to grin. He grabbed my face and planted a big, wet kiss on it. I thought this was adorable. I worried other adults would not.

"Hallie, sweetie, can you grab the plastic sheet out of the diaper bag?" Anthony insisted every parent needed a diaper knapsack and had not only purchased one, but had completely kitted it out for me. I had everything I could possibly need.

Within moments, Hallie had the plastic sheet laid on the floor. Then she had the fresh diaper, cream, and wipes organized as well.

I blinked back tears. "You're the best."

She merely grabbed her stuffie and positioned herself at Thomas's head as I laid him gently down. She ran her hands through his short hair and he gazed up at her with true adoration in his eyes. Despite everything, hope surged in me. At least they still had each other. And I had them. We all had each other. That had to count for something— had to mean something.

"They're doing a great job in there." Colin reappeared. "They've got the pieces of the bed and are putting it together. Apparently someone at the warehouse did the dresser so they just need to carry that in and secure it to the wall."

Relief flooded me. I didn't know how to secure furniture to the wall. Wouldn't even know what to buy in order to do it.

I put the clean diaper over Thomas so, if he peed, he wouldn't pee on me. Only had to make that mistake once to learn from the error. I wanted to ask Colin if he had kids, as I organized the dirty diaper and then used the wipe to clean up the mess. Nothing could be done about the smell, unfortunately. My son was…very healthy.

"That's almost as bad as dog, uh, stuff." Colin plopped back down on his chair and, before I could move, scooped Widget onto his lap.

I caught Hallie's eye. "Did you want to say *hi* to the puppy in a minute?"

She shook her head.

"Okay. That's fine. Thomas and I might, though. If that's okay?" I continued to hold Hallie's gaze, but the question was really directed at Colin.

"I think Widget would love that."

I finished securing Thomas's diaper, put his pants back on, and blew a raspberry on his belly. "Are you kidding? He adores dogs."

"That's great."

I scooped Thomas into my arms and pivoted toward Colin and Widget. Thomas's tendency to sometimes poke had me keeping him a bit of a distance away, but close enough for him to see. "Puppy?"

Thomas clapped.

Widget woofed.

In that moment, everything felt okay.

CHAPTER 5

DANNY

As I drove towards my parents' house in Huntington Beach, I reflected on my afternoon and early evening.

James and I got all the lights hung outside Rob's house, as well as some decorations that fit with the neighborhood.

Colin oversaw the installation of all the furniture for Rob's kids, and not just from his seat lounging on the recliner.

Much to James's consternation.

We'd made the beds with the sheets, blankets, and pillows. I suggested to James that we should come back to paint Hallie's bedroom something prettier, and he'd pointed out he had no idea how long the family would be staying or, just as important, who might come next. Not everyone would want a bedroom designed for a four-year-old girl. And, because the room didn't have a closet, the next renter might switch it back to a den.

I'd helped put away the few things Rob had acquired with the social worker's help. Rob's cheeks had turned an odd shade of pink when he admitted he hadn't brought anything with him to Gaynor Beach.

Which, in turn, made me want to track down his asshole ex and exact some revenge.

I wouldn't, of course.

Partly because I was a pacifist, partly because I was a chickenshit, but mostly because I didn't want any chance that Rob's ex might track him to Gaynor Beach via my relationship with James and the house. Nope. I also wouldn't do internet searches to satisfy my curiosity.

Much as that would kill me.

I'd keep my nose out of Rob's business.

Unless he asked me to get in it, of course.

Except…why would he? I was no one to him. Just the guy who helped him get settled. Just the guy who tried to keep the pity from spilling over. Mama and Daddy taught me about being empathetic of people's circumstances. Pointing out that people often didn't know everything that went on in another person's private life. Well, Rob's personal life was all over his face—with that broken nose. As well as written all over his daughter's face when she gazed up at us with wide eyes. Maybe all men scared her. Maybe dogs as well. If so, that was sad.

Colin said that although Hallie had been wary of Widget, Rob had actually sat on the ground for quite some time, just petting the puppy. Apparently, Thomas, when not toddling off and getting into *everything*, also really liked the puppy. Just Hallie hadn't warmed up to my brother's boyfriend's faithful companion. And, as I'd teased James, his little shadow as well. Clearly Widget loved James almost as much as Colin.

I took the exit from the 5 toward Huntington Beach.

And why wouldn't Widget adore James? My brother was truly the best man I knew. My other brother, Martin, was cool. And Daddy was awesome. But James had a generosity of spirit I could only envy. At times, in comparison, I felt petty.

Colin, James, and I had talked about what all Rob would need. I patted the steering wheel. I saw that sweet little girl acting afraid, and how Rob looked gutted every time she flinched. I saw the bruises on his face and the fear he tried to hide. And I wanted to help. I'd known people with abusive spouses, and it took a shitload of courage to get free of them. Rob was awesome, and I was pretty sure he had no idea that was true.

James had given them shelter. Colin had given them furniture. What had I done? Strung a few Christmas lights? But what could I offer that Rob would take? Descending on him with unwanted help would be worse than nothing. I could offer to babysit. From what my siblings said, no parent ever turned that down, and as a single dad, Rob would be starved for alone time. Except he didn't know me from Adam, and Hallie was scared of strangers. Odds were, it would be a while before either of them trusted me that much. I really wanted Rob to trust me.

Could I really give him my car? I'd suggested it to Colin and James, who'd seen my potential kind gesture as… interesting. I'd gotten the feeling, although I might've been wrong, that Colin thought the gift was over the top. Rich, coming from him. But…what about loaning it to Rob for a while? He'd need a way to get around town with two kids. I wanted to give money, but I just didn't have any to spare. Colin kept saying not to worry, but I didn't know what his finances looked like either.

Plus, everything I needed in LA was either on campus or a short bus ride away.

Yeah, over the top.

Was that really over the top? Okay, it probably was. But

for some strange reason I wanted to put a smile on Rob's face more than I'd wanted anything for a long time.

Night had fallen by the time I pulled into the driveway. I cut the engine and just sat for a moment as weariness overwhelmed me. Thank God I wasn't driving all the way back to LA tonight. I'd have to get an early start, though, if I wanted to get in a full day of studying biochem.

I didn't *want* to spend an entire day studying, but I needed to. My midterm grade sucked. My prof let me do work for extra credit, but she warned me if I didn't get a near-perfect grade on the exam, then I'd be repeating the course.

If I wanted to get into med school.

She'd tactfully pointed out that med school wasn't for everyone. That there were some really good alternate careers that weren't nearly as stressful but were equally as rewarding.

I sighed. She was right, of course. I *knew* she was right. But my heart wouldn't accept what my mind saw clearly—if I didn't get my shit together right fucking now, med school would forever be out of reach.

A knock on the window pulled me from my reverie.

Whitney stood at the door, pointing to her wrist.

Funny because she didn't wear a watch.

I grabbed my bag, opened my door, and hauled myself out. "What?" I might've snapped that.

She glared. "Mama needs to go to bed soon, and you're sitting out here mooning."

"I'm not mooning." I glared.

"Oh, so you didn't notice James's new tenant?"

My eyebrows shot up in surprise. I shut the car door, armed the alarm, and headed inside. "I don't have any idea what you're talking about."

"Well…" She did a little twirl. She wasn't as light on her feet as Gracie was, but she still did a good job. Years of jazz dancing hadn't gone to waste—even if she'd been really too short to have a shot at anything professional. Whitney was as petite as our mother while Gracie had the height.

"Well, what?"

"Gracie called James to ask how the day went and he said something about a guy and how you thought he was cute—"

"I did not." I opened the front door with more force than was strictly necessary.

"Did not think he was cute or did not realize James saw you thought he was cute…?"

I blinked. Twice. "Whit, I'm too tired for this shit—"

"Language." Mama's voice rang from the kitchen.

I winced. I *knew* better. No one swore in Mama's house.

Whit leaned in. "James said something about lean, handsome, and—"

"Whit." I hissed her name. "This time last night, he was getting beaten up by his husband. This conversation is so, so, so beyond inappropriate. He might be all those things. I didn't notice." *Liar.* "What he is, though, is a young father with two great kids who's hurting so hard that it comes off him in waves. He's trying to hold things together—for them as much as for himself—but he's barely holding on. He's totally overwhelmed and needs support… not someone panting after him because of how he does or does not look."

Whitney's dark eyes narrowed, and I could tell she was embarrassed.

"I would've said all those things." She poked her finger into my chest. "You didn't give me a chance."

"How are you, sweetheart?" Mama swept into the room. "My dear boy, you look so tired."

I managed a smile. "I am, Mama. Can I…just go to bed?"

Of course, she pressed the back of her hand to my forehead.

"I'm not sick, Mama, I promise. I just…didn't get much sleep last night. And today's been a long day. But we can talk over breakfast, I promise."

She held my gaze for a long time. "Okay."

Whitney looped her arm in mine. "I'll see him to bed."

Oh God, seriously? Can't I catch a break? Still, I'd never argue with Whit in front of Mama if it wasn't necessary. I loved my mom too much. And with her health these days… "Did you take your pills?"

She rolled her eyes and smacked my arm. "You think your father would let me get away with not taking them?"

"Uh…no."

"Right. Go to bed, and I'll see you in the morning." She gave Whitney a long look. "Behave."

Whitney pressed a hand to her forehead and swooned dramatically—giving Gracie a run for her money in the over-the-top department. "I'm always good."

Mama snickered as she headed back into the kitchen.

"Look, Whit—"

"Not here. Come with me." She whispered the words even as she propelled me to the back of the house where my small bedroom was tucked. When James moved out, earlier this year, he'd suggested I move into the much-bigger room our father had created for him in the basement.

I'd declined. Despite the minuteness of size, I liked my room. I had everything set up just the way I wanted. Plus, I was in LA most of the time for school. These days, I came home about as often as James did, so why force him into this smaller room? Now he had Colin, I was even more grateful I'd had the foresight not to move. Well, maybe not foresight. Just…the desire to keep things as they were.

Whit propelled me into my room and shut the door. "We need to talk."

I dropped my bag onto the floor, sat on my bed, and flopped back. I put my arm over my eyes. "Talk, Whit. Seriously, I'm exhausted." If I thought I could tell her about my redneck asshole drunk roommate and it *wouldn't* get back to Mama, then I would. But while Gracie could keep a secret, Whit was genetically incapable. Same with Leticia.

She thrust a business card into my hand.

I moved my arm so I could hold the card in front of me, but the writing blurred because of the overhead light. "Whit—"

She flipped off the overhead light and then flipped on my bedside lamp.

That *did not* make things better. "Whit." This time, I let all my exasperation sneak into my voice.

She sighed. "Dr. Marcia Patton."

"Who?" I squinted.

"She's a transplant hepatologist at Cedar Sinai. And, the most important part, is she's not Colin's liver doctor."

I closed my eyes and took a deep breath, fighting the impending headache. "I know what a hepatologist is. Why do *you* have her business card?" My mind swam.

"Because I went to see her to see if I was a candidate to donate."

I sat up so abruptly that the world spun for one very long moment. "Can you repeat that?"

Whit straightened. "Well, first Martin went. Wait, I

should go back a step. Leticia went through the family's medical records."

"Of course she did." Our eldest sister—older than her twin Felicia by mere moments, but one would never guess by the authoritative way she ruled us all—ran the show. Oh, Mama and Daddy thought they did, but our sister, from the moment she was born, was meant to keep everyone in line.

"So she checked blood types. Martin, you, and I are matches. Well, she and Felicia are as well, but since they're both pregnant—"

I waved her off. "And, in an obnoxiously short period of time will both have *five* kids each—"

"Right. Which is why she ruled out their husbands as well."

"Martin has a daughter and another one on the way."

"Yeah, but he…was more amenable."

"Leticia leaned on him harder."

Whit tapped her lips. "No. He was, like, genuinely willing to donate to Colin. I mean, the risks are minimal—"

"They include *death*, Whit."

She rolled her eyes. "Well, duh. So, like, he went and got tested first."

"No match?" I assumed by her windup that she'd been involved.

Another eye roll. "Martin's tissue didn't match" She held up her hand to cut me off at the pass. "But they thought they might be able to do a three-way…" She paused. "That sounds bad—"

"Whit." No question, I had zero shits left to give. My patience was beyond depleted.

"But I have a liver enzyme problem."

My gaze shot to hers as panic engulfed me.

She waved me off. "Minor problem. Like, not even a blip. They said they wouldn't have even found it if they hadn't been looking. They've given me a small list of foods and supplements to avoid and suggested I get retested next month and then every year for a while, till they're sure it's stable. But I'm out as a donor."

I winced…but that didn't sound too bad. If the doctors had been truly concerned, they would have done way more than that. Liver issues could be incredibly serious.

As Colin was finding out.

I waved my hand. "Okay, so Martin wasn't a match and you're out."

She shook her head. "But Martin insisted they do extra tests, and he's now in the bone marrow donor program. Given the scarcity of donors, if he's ever a match, they'll be all over that."

"He didn't have to do that."

"Of course he didn't." Whit examined one of her fingernails. "But, like, once he got it in his head that he could donate, he went looking to see what else he could do." She met my gaze. "Who knew? He's some kind of philanthropist."

I wasn't certain that was the right term, but I understood what she meant. "Okay…so we're down to me?"

"Yep." She popped the *p*. "Doctor Patton said to call as soon as you can. There's a two-day process. Well, if the initial blood tests are a match. They do more lab work, scans, x-rays, testing, and screening. If you pass all that, then you talk to a nurse about donating. If you survive all that, the next day you're back for consultations with… everyone. A psychologist, a social worker, a surgeon, and…" She tapped her lips. "Like, I can't remember."

I let out a long breath. "Whit, I've got finals. And, like,

school again just after New Year's. This is a big year for me."

She stepped forward and took my cheeks in her hands. "Danny, you know I love you, right?"

"Of course." Because for all of our battles—and there were many—we all loved each other.

"How will you feel if Colin dies waiting for a transplant and you might've been a match?"

I glared. Because she was right, of course. She often was.

Often.

Not always.

But more often than not.

"Whit."

"Danny." She feathered her hand through my hair. "Surely school would understand if you take a semester off. And…who knows…"

I waited. Dreaded what was coming next.

"You…" She winced. "You need a reset, Danny."

"How—"

"Your roommate might've let slip—"

"Whit."

She waved me off. "I went to visit you one day and douchebag got to talking all about you. Oh my God, Danny, that man has zero respect for you, women, Black people, the Constitution, democracy, or true Christians."

I cocked my head. "How much time did you spend with him?"

"Twelve minutes. Longest twelve minutes of my life."

Sounds about right.

"Look, he can be indiscreet—"

She snickered.

"But I never told him about my grades."

She eyed me. "You keep papers around? Your laptop

open? He totally seems like the kind of guy who would snoop."

Apparently she knew more than I did. "How…?"

"I dunno. I was waiting for you when he started in on how you were the perfect evidence of how stupid Black men are. Because you're flunking out of premed." She blew out a breath. "I coulda told him to shut up, but I wanted to see how far he'd sink. It's kind of fun to watch them tangle themselves up."

"And he didn't think you might…I don't know…tell me?" *Should have let him aspirate his vomit and die.*

That's mean.

So, apparently, is the fucking racist I've been rooming with. I'd have to see about swapping out after Christmas for someone else. Interesting that he'd never been openly hostile or racist to me. Of course I had seventy pounds and seven inches over the scrawny shit. Good-looking…but still a shit.

"I just sat there and gave him that smile. Basically, I played the bimbo." She pointed to her breasts. "Some men are truly that shallow."

"Ew. Gross." As a pansexual, I had an appreciation for breasts, flat chests, and everything in between. What I did *not* want to think about, however, was my sister's tits. I waved my hand. "We're getting off topic."

"The topic is you calling Dr. Patton's office first thing Monday morning, making an appointment, and going in."

I squinted. "Why isn't Colin asking me? Or James?"

"Because…" She did another twirl. "They don't know."

"Right."

"Because if they knew, they'd say not to do it."

"Right."

Whit leaned closer. "James wants to, but he's prediabetic. Had no idea."

"And you know this how?"

"He told Mama."

I arched an eyebrow.

She waved me off. "You don't want to know."

No, she was probably right—I was better off not knowing. "Won't Colin be upset? Or James?"

She wrinkled her nose. "Like, if Colin gets a new liver, I can't see how they would complain. And, besides, it's anonymous donation—they won't know who's giving to them, and you won't know who you're giving to."

"But you just said—"

"Make it anonymously. Colin will be told some good Samaritan wanted to donate part of their liver."

"*If* I'm a match."

"Yeah, there is that." She met and held my gaze. "I have a really good feeling, Danny. Like this is meant to be."

"Whit—"

"Didn't you ever feel like you were meant to be something greater than you are?"

"I'm planning on being a doctor. Maybe even a surgeon. Saving lives seems pretty noble."

"How's biochem going?"

I winced. "Maybe there's an out-of-state school who will accept a keen learner with bad science grades?"

She bopped me on the head. None too gently. "Find out if you're a match. If you are, take the semester off school and figure out what you really want to do with your life. If it's medical school, then take the class again, ace it, and you're good to go."

"Do Mama and Daddy know?"

"Hell fucking no." She snickered. "You think they'd let

you get away with this? Oh, when they ask who will take care of you after the surgery, just say me."

"You?" I arched an eyebrow.

"O ye of little faith." She placed a hand to her heart. "I will be the best nursemaid ever."

I didn't believe her.

But that didn't stop me from calling the doctor Monday morning.

CHAPTER 6

ROB

OUR FIRST NIGHT IN THE HOUSE, HALLIE WOUND UP IN MY bed. I couldn't blame her. Everything felt so still in this small town. We might've lived in a gated community in LA, but there'd still been noise. The city was bright, hectic, and never quiet.

Gaynor Beach was positively sedate in comparison. Like everyone had taken a tranquilizer and a nap.

Anthony had shown me a map of Gaynor Beach. The Riverside region, where we now lived, was close to downtown. Within walking distance, in fact. So I'd be able to take the kids everywhere—including down to the beach. The Pacific Ocean. Which, stunningly, I'd never seen. Two years in LA and I'd never made it that far west.

I could have, of course. Santa Monica wasn't far from where I'd lived when I was on the streets. Gerard's mansion in Brentwood had been within spitting distance, relatively speaking. But I'd never left our neighborhood.

Weirdly, I held the ocean as…sacred. Something to be enjoyed at the right time. That time, for me, hadn't come yet. Maybe now, with the kids, I could enjoy it.

Thomas stirred, and I hustled to scoop him out of his crib and over to the changing table quickly—before he got going with the noise. Sometimes he would wake up slowly, easing into wakefulness. He'd talk to himself and roll over, perhaps pull himself up, and have a big grin on his face when I came in.

Other times, he'd come fully awake, be mad at being alone, and howl to the heavens until I appeared.

Gerard had no patience for those times.

And you don't have to worry about that anymore.

A mantra I kept repeating to myself, but not actually believing.

As I changed Thomas's diaper and then put him in a new pair of red pants and a bright-blue shirt, I kept glancing over at Hallie. She'd had a rough night, so I was relieved to see her sleeping peacefully. Perhaps this afternoon, when Thomas went down for his nap, Hallie and I might be able to sleep as well. We needed to get into some kind of routine.

After putting socks on my son, I hefted him into my arms. I headed into the living room where I glanced at all the things that weren't mine but also sort of were.

Anthony assured me we could keep everything. That even if, by some miracle, we got all our stuff from the mansion in LA, we could still keep these wonderful gifts.

I eyed the bare Christmas tree.

Danny had offered to decorate it, but I'd seen Colin was fatigued and, unfortunately, Hallie hadn't warmed up to any of the men or even the precious dog. Much as I hadn't wanted to say goodbye—to any of them—I also hadn't wanted to put more strain on either Colin or Hallie.

So they'd left.

And my phone felt heavy in my pocket. James and Colin had insisted on giving me their numbers, in case anything happened and I needed help. That was sweet. But Danny's number daunted less than the others. We'd talked, only for a few minutes, but he felt like someone I could be friends with. And he'd been so good with Thomas. About ten times last night, I considered texting him. To thank him again, of course. Except then I would've had to text either James or Colin or both—to thank them. All that felt very complicated.

I put Thomas in the seat that strapped to the kitchen table chair, then I secured him and the slotted the tray in.

He banged on the tray.

"Yeah, buddy, I'm hungry too." I hustled to the fridge, found some sliced cheese, and gave that to him in pieces. Not ideal, but I needed him to stay quiet so Hallie could sleep. I hadn't closed the door because I didn't want her waking and panicking. She didn't do well with closed doors.

Next, I put bread into the toaster, sliced some avocados, and found cereal. I'd have to feed it to him, but that might give us some one-on-one time. Time to just breathe. I didn't feel like I'd been doing much of that. Everything had just been panic and rush and chaos. Neither of my children thrived in that environment. Especially not Hallie.

I added a dab of peanut butter to two slices of bread, cut up a banana, and sat at the kitchen table with the cereal in a bowl. The next twenty minutes was a little chaotic as I managed to get toast, cereal, banana, and avocado into my son—without him smushing too much of the stuff in his face—and I consumed toast and an orange juice. I didn't drink coffee. Hadn't for years. Gerard forbade it for me, for reasons I'd never truly understood, and I'd never defied him.

"Papa?" Hallie emerged from the hallway and offered a sleepy smile.

More than I expected, and it warmed my heart. "Good morning, sweetheart. Would you like to eat or would you like to get dressed first?" Gerard always insisted the children be dressed to eat—which often meant I was changing them again after meals if they got messy, but whatever.

"Dressed. I have to pee."

"Okay."

She headed to the bathroom, and I concentrated on eating and getting as much food as I could into Thomas. Once I had him cleaned up, I put him in his playpen with some toys and stuffies. Then I set about making Hallie's scrambled eggs and toast. She also liked cereal, but—irrationally—I felt that if I made her something, she'd see how much I loved her. And, by the time she arrived, ready for food, I had some for her.

As she ate, I cleaned up the high chair, did the other dishes, and tried to figure out what we'd do for the next few meals. The fridge was full of wonderful foods, and cooking was one of the few things I could do well. I found a slow cooker as well as a pork roast. I chopped some vegetables as Hallie poked at her food and Thomas babbled. "Just a little bit more, sweetie?"

She shook her head.

"Okay. Why don't you get your brush. Do you want your hair in a ponytail today?"

She bit her lower lip. "Pigtails."

"Deal."

After sliding off her chair, she headed back to the bedroom. As I put everything into the pot, she returned holding two elastics and her brush.

I set the food to cook, then guided her into the living

room. I sat on the couch, then started brushing out her hair. It tended to tangle at night, often because she got soaked during her nightmares. Once I was finished, I patted her shoulder. "Do you want to play with Thomas? Or watch television?" I hadn't checked out the cable situation, but I was working off the assumption someone had arranged for us to have kids' channels. Everything else seemed to have been organized. It both humbled me and blew my mind they'd arranged everything so fast. Or maybe some of it had been in place when James lived here.

Which reminded me that I hadn't thanked him yet.

Damn.

"Thomas wants out of the playpen."

I glanced over at my boy as Hallie said the words. He actually appeared perfectly content, but Hallie didn't like to be restricted, and she often assumed Thomas felt the same way. "Okay. Will you play with him?" I disliked always putting her in the position of watching when she was so young herself, but she'd do it anyway. She never took her eye off her brother. Almost like she was afraid if she did that he'd disappear. He never did, but that didn't alleviate her vigilance.

She nodded.

"Sure, sweetheart. Let's set up a blanket and some toys. Do you want the television on?"

She considered, bit her lip, then shook her head. "I'll read to him."

My mind was always blown that Thomas would actually sit still while Hallie read to him. She couldn't read, but her imagination allowed her to create fantastical stories that kept him enthralled. Or maybe it was just her.

After I settled them on the floor, I did a quick survey of the room. As far as I could see, the house was babyproofed.

I closed the bathroom and bedroom doors to minimize where kiddos could wander.

Then I did what I'd dreaded doing since yesterday.

I sat at the kitchen table and eyed the laptop computer that sat there—plugged in and charging. James had left a small pile of papers for me to go through along with some things Anthony had given me. I hadn't had the courage to tell the men that my computer skills were limited to what I'd learned in high school. And that I'd never had a machine of my own. No computers or televisions in our household. Tablets weren't a thing, and neither were smart phones in Missouri.

Then the same situation in LA. Gerard claimed to be exposing me to books and art, at first. Teaching me culture and literature. I tried to live up to his standards, as a gracious partner. He said TV was gauche. That social media was a cesspit. He said he'd help me be so much smarter than the people who wallowed in that *shit*.

We had a big-screen television, of course. But I didn't know where the remote was. When the social worker did home visits and discussed online forms, Gerard was there with both his laptop and phone. He showed how he had all the security programmed. Gerard carried on about all the books we read to the children. All the nature walks we took. He made it sound like we were the perfect family.

The social worker never realized how controlling my husband was. At first, neither did I.

He'd given me a phone that I was expected to have with me at all times—so he could communicate with me. And also track me, although I hadn't realized that until after we adopted Thomas. Learned the hard way when I'd gone for an extra-long walk one day. Gerard had come home that night in a right royal temper and made it clear what my boundaries were. Basically, the neighborhood. I told myself it was for my safety, all the while understanding this was a control thing. And that fighting it was pointless. I had a roof over my head, food in my belly, and a man who claimed to love me.

What else could I need? Especially when we added a daughter for me to care for. Except her constant anxiety worried me. Which probably fed into her anxiety. I'd spoken to her pediatrician about it. She'd recommended getting Hallie evaluated, but I'd known Gerard would never agree. He thought our daughter needed to be tougher.

To keep the peace, I acquiesced. Instead, I tried to find books on parenting in the library. I should've probably tried to use their computers, but with one—and eventually two—kids, the challenge of managing them was just too great. I kept the books hidden, of course, but I did my best to be the parent Hallie and Thomas deserved.

I eyed the computer again. I needed to do this. It couldn't possibly be *that* difficult. James had given me login credentials as well as a temporary password. He said I'd be prompted to change it. Except I didn't know anything about passwords. Or what I had known, I'd long forgotten. How insane was it to have been born early in the twenty-first century and yet know so little about computers?

And Colin had said something about getting my GED and eventually taking college classes. I was able to read, but school? I hadn't been in a classroom since I was sixteen. Which felt like a million years ago.

I pulled my phone from my back pocket and pulled up the contacts. James or Colin would be the logical choices. Unlike Anthony, they didn't have kids. They lived nearby.

Yet I couldn't do it.

My finger hovered over Danny's name. I couldn't remember what he said he'd be doing. For that matter, I couldn't even remember where he said he lived. Gaynor Beach?

I glanced at the time. Eight o'clock wasn't too early, was it? Before I lost my nerve, I shot off a quick good morning text.

Moments later, my phone rang with an incoming call.

"Hello?"

"Hey, Rob, it's Danny. Obviously. I'm glad you texted. I mean, I could've texted back, but I thought you might want to speak to an adult. I mean, not that your kids aren't amazing. And maybe you've got someone over. I mean, not *someone* someone, but I don't know, like James or Colin? Did you call them first? I mean, it's cool if you did because they're awesome, but it's also cool if you didn't, because I think Colin was a little tired after yesterday. I mean, that wasn't your fault…the guy can overdo it sometimes, which is way more than you need to know." He drew in a breath. "I mean…I'm happy you texted, and I hope it's okay I called back. I prefer talking."

A laugh bubbled up from inside me. "I didn't think anyone talked anymore."

He sighed. "They don't. Except Mama and Daddy. We've taught them about technology—and they love their smart phones—but they also just love to talk your ear off. Especially if you're supposed to be studying for something." He let out a breath. "What's up?"

I'm lonely. I'm scared. I can't do this alone. I need help.

And I wasn't going to say any of those things. I cleared my throat. "James is the computer guy, right?"

"Yeah. Cybersecurity. Real high-level stuff. Way over my head."

Somehow that made me feel marginally better. "How about regular stuff?"

"He can do that as well." Danny paused. "But so can I. How can I help?"

I took a deep breath. "I was wondering if you could talk me through the login process. James has left a paper with my…" I searched the document. "…credentials."

Danny laughed. "Okay, that sounds way too complicated. It's your login information. I can try to talk you through this, but why don't I just come over? The kids would be okay with that, right?"

Hallie was intently drawing in a coloring book and Thomas had a little car he was pushing around. Clearly he'd had enough of her *reading* and they'd moved on. "Yeah, the kids won't mind. But are you sure? You must have something—"

"Look, I wouldn't offer if I couldn't make it work. Give me two hours?"

"Uh, sure."

"I'm in Huntington Beach at my parents', so it'll take a bit of time for me to get up, showered, dressed, and on my way down."

"Oh God, did I wake you up?"

He chuckled. "I had a late night watching hockey with my dad then talking about…stuff. And I was looking up some medical stuff on the internet."

"Yeah, but—"

"I'm on my way."

"Can I at least make you food? Or do you need to eat before you come?"

"Mama's made breakfast burritos, so I'll eat here. But do you like specialty coffee? I can pick up some before I make my way over to you."

"I, uh, don't really do coffee."

The hesitation was noticeable. "Okay. Right. I just

forget there are people in the world who aren't caffeine addicts."

That was me…being all weird. "I could try—"

"Nope. I have something else in mind. See you in two hours."

Before I could say anything else, he disconnected.

And although I spent the next hour staring at the phone and trying to find the courage to tell him not to come—that I'd figure this computer thing out on my own —I never did call back.

CHAPTER 7

DANNY

I DIDN'T SPEED DOWN THE 5.

Well, not much.

I did stop in at Nice Buns to get some cinnamon rolls and an herbal tea from Ambrose who seemed extra cheerful today. Or maybe that was because I was extra happy today.

Rob called me.

And yeah, I should've been at the library in LA studying for my final…but Rob called *me*. Not James the cyber-geek. Not Colin the money guy. No…me. Who didn't have any discernible computer skills. *Is he comfortable with me or intimidated by the older men?* Hard to guess—so I didn't try. I just grabbed the cinnamon rolls and tea after I parked in his driveway and headed up the front steps.

He opened the front door and gave me what I interpreted to be a nervous smile.

"Hey."

I handed him the box of buns, gently pushed my way inside, toed off my shoes, closed the front door, and gestured to the laptop. "That it?"

He blinked. "Yeah."

You're being pushy because you're nervous. Just…chill… I pointed to the cinnamon buns. "They're fresh. If you're hungry. And an herbal tea." Suddenly, it occurred to me that he might not even like sugar. He was lanky. Slender. While I was…solid. Not to put too fine a point on it, but I maybe should be eating fewer cinnamon rolls. "Damn, I forgot *my* coffee." I held up my finger, handed him the tea, shoved my shoes back on, then hustled outside and back to my car. I grabbed the travel mug I'd refilled at the bakery and headed back inside.

Rob had disappeared—presumably into the kitchen—and I found Thomas toddling toward me as I managed to shut the door just in time. "Hey, little buddy, you move fast."

"He walks good." Hallie's quiet voice came from across the space. She stood by the couch, gripping the arm, and eyeing me.

"He walks great." As Thomas grabbed my leg, I debated whether or not I should scoop him into my arms. Whether that was a level of familiarity I hadn't earned. Judging by Hallie's gaze, I decided not to risk it. Again, I toed off my shoes. I pointed to the books. "What are you reading?"

"*Goat in a Boat.*" She glanced toward the kitchen.

I stayed where I was, not wanting to spook her.

Moments later, Rob returned. He had two plates. The first he held out for me, with a fork to go with it. "Heated it up. That's the best way, right?"

"Yep." I offered a wide grin as I took the plate from him, still balancing my coffee mug.

He walked to the couch and sat.

Thomas immediately released me and followed his father.

Carefully, Rob put a piece of roll on the fork, and he fed a piece to each of his children before taking one for himself. He repeated the process several times over until they'd shared the entire thing.

Hallie brushed at his hair. "Thank you."

"You can thank Danny." He pointed to me. "He brought the treat."

She met my gaze for just an instant. "Thank you." Then she looked away.

"My pleasure." My roll was getting cold, but watching the intimacy of the scene had hit me in the chest. My siblings and their kids were always…so chaotic…when I saw them. I was never privy to the moments of quiet sharing. Tranquility.

Rob held my gaze, his hazel eyes conveying something I didn't quite grasp.

I figured gratitude, but I couldn't be certain.

"Oh, you need to eat that before it cools." He rose, dislodging Thomas, who promptly went over to the mat on the floor.

The toddler plopped down and started playing with a toy car.

Slowly, while occasionally glancing at me, Hallie joined him.

Once she was settled, I made my way over to the table. I placed the plate and coffee mug down, then eased my knapsack to the floor. Two chairs sat next to each other, one with the laptop in front of it. I assumed the other was for me, so I dropped into it. "Okay, let's do this."

He ran his hands through his hair. "I feel like I'm asking too much—"

"You didn't ask. I offered." I cut a piece of roll. "Those the credentials?" I pointed to the top page.

"Yes." Slowly, Rob took the seat next to me. He was

barely settled before he shifted the chair away from me a couple of inches.

That's not a good sign. I did shower… Then I gave myself a good kick. I was some strange guy. A big, strange guy. He was being brave just inviting me over. Hardly a surprise he didn't want to get too close.

"Okay." I sipped my coffee. "Do you know how to turn a computer on?"

He rolled his eyes.

I held up my hands. "We had to drag Mama into the twentieth century kicking and screaming. She only *just* got a smart phone. I don't want to make any assumptions."

Slowly, he nodded. "I know how to turn a laptop on. I used the school computers back in high school. But…" He cleared his throat. "I dropped out at sixteen and haven't used one since."

I blinked. "Okay." I hid my wince. Barely. Who didn't have a computer these days? Which was incredibly snobby of me because lots of people couldn't afford them. That being said, phones were basically just mini computers. "Do you have favorite websites you like to visit?"

He ducked his head. "I don't, uh, go on the internet."

Another slow blink. I pointed to his phone.

"No data." He shrugged. "This is where I pathetically say that my husband did everything."

Confirmation things were even worse than I'd imagined. And I'd gone to some pretty dark ideas over the past day. "Okay. Well, we can set up your phone to get a Wi-Fi signal here so you can have internet access on your phone right away. Then you're not tethered to the computer. Helps when you're chasing little ones." I scanned the papers. "Ah, here's the Wi-Fi password. Let's get your phone set up first. And I'll make certain the settings are such that you can login to other WiFi networks as you come across them. I know Nice Buns has access. Surely other businesses do as well. And the library."

"Oh, I liked the library." Rob smiled. "Anthony's husband Scott works there as a librarian. They have twins who are Hallie's age."

"Really? That's great." I was a little distressed to find Rob's phone didn't have a password, but not entirely surprised. I made a note to set one up when I was finished connecting everything. "Do you think Hallie would want to play with the twins?"

Rob bit his lower lip. "Anthony is, like, my caseworker."

"Ah. Professional relationships." I configured the Wi-Fi and used the password. "Oh, hey, do you want to change this password?"

"Why would I?"

"Well, James knows it. I'll know it—"

"I trust you. I trust James." Said with such innocence. He shouldn't, of course, trust any of us. We were all strangers. Except, in his life, I got the idea that the people who hurt him were the people who were supposed to love him. Perhaps that was why strangers didn't trigger him the same way.

"Okay. Well, it's an easy password to remember, but hard to crack, so that's good. You shouldn't have it written down."

"Do you have yours written down?"

"Not exactly. I have a password manager."

"What's that?"

I hesitated. "Okay, let's finish getting your phone set up properly."

"I don't know how long I'll have it."

"He's going to take the phone back?"

"What? No, he doesn't know where we are." He scratched his nose. "But he pays the bills."

"Okay, so he can cut off your phone, but he can't disable the device. You can still use Wi-Fi even if the cell phone part of it isn't working." I handed him the phone. "You want to enter an eight-digit password. Don't make it your birthday or either of the kids'. Ideally, don't make it a mashup of that either. Something that's truly unique."

"That I'll remember."

"That you'll remember."

"What's your birthday?"

I blinked. Okay, not what I was expecting. Like, at all. Without thinking, I rattled it off.

He grinned. "That's next month." He swiped and typed and grinned. "I added it to my calendar."

For some reason, that made my insides light up. I wasn't huge on birthday celebrations—although Mama was. Regardless, I had something to look forward to in January. Thinking about my textbooks and the studying I *wasn't* doing, I realized a text from him might be the best thing that happened all next month.

"Okay, what's yours?" I yanked out my phone. With a little coaxing, I got his as well as the kids'. Three more excuses for contact. More importantly, I got the sense he didn't often celebrate things in his life. Not something specific he said…just the vibe he gave off.

"Okay." I indicated the laptop. "Let's do this."

He glanced over at the kids.

Thomas lay on the floor with his head on a pillow and a little blanket over him. His eyes were closed, and he had his thumb stuck in his mouth.

Hallie sat next to him, a book on her lap.

Their utter stillness struck me. Leticia and Felicia's kids were never still. Being unknowingly sexist, I'd assumed

Leticia's three girls would be calmer than Felicia's three boys.

Nope. All six children were chaos incarnate.

Are kids supposed to be this quiet? Are they this way because they'd get in trouble if they weren't? Questions I was dying to ask but wasn't certain I wanted the answer for.

At the login screen, Rob entered his credentials. He quickly glanced at me, then back at the screen.

"Okay, so you know about search engines?"

"We had Google." He winced. "Sorry, that came out wrong."

I gently nudged his shoulder with mine. "Not coming is wrong. We'll figure this out together."

As I'd hoped, he got the innuendo and turned a nice shade of pink. *Is teasing him the right thing to do? Am I being too forward? I mean, this can't be anything more than an innocent flirtation...* Somehow, though, I wanted him to see me as a good guy. A safe guy. A potential friend. Which meant putting a lid on flirting.

"Okay, so I'm going to assume you don't have email."

He shook his head. "That's where I get stuck."

"Easy to fix. Let's set you up with a Gmail account to start with. It's free. There's a mailbox size limit, but I suspect it'll take you a long time to get to that point."

He blinked.

I smiled.

We got to work.

A while later, he took a break to prepare a snack while I created a list of all the websites I thought could be helpful for him. Anywhere that might have loyalty points, coupons, or any other discounts. He was going to wind up on some mailing lists, but I'd explained how to just delete the emails that weren't relevant and to not get sucked into buying something he didn't need.

He'd commented he didn't have money for it anyway. Then ducked his head.

I'd resisted the temptation to tip his chin toward me, hold his gaze, and say he didn't ever have to worry about me judging.

Apparently, he didn't even have a bank account. Anthony was taking him to the credit union in town on Monday to set up an account. I would've stayed to help, but my exam demanded I head back to LA soon. Coming south to Gaynor Beach had been an impulse I should've checked, but I was really bad at ignoring a request for help.

Which reminded me I needed to call the doctor tomorrow.

I eyed Rob. *What happens if he gets sick? Or one of the kids gets sick? Does he have insurance? Does he have cash in his wallet?* Questions I wanted answers to but had no right to ask.

"Papa?"

Rob glanced up from the computer, his eyes a little unfocused.

We both turned to find the kids watching us.

"Yes, Hallie?" Rob cleared his throat. "You okay?"

"We're hungry."

"Sure, I can get you a snack…" He glanced at the computer. "Damn. Uh, darn. It's lunchtime." He turned to me. "You'll stay?"

I wanted to. God, I was so tempted. "I really need to head back to LA. I've got an exam coming up and some other stuff to arrange."

He offered a smile. "A sandwich for the road?"

"I won't refuse that." I didn't like the idea of taking food from him, but I sensed he felt obligated because of the substantial help I'd offered this morning. I still couldn't believe a man in his mid-twenties was so clueless about the internet. I didn't spend a lot of time on social media, but I had ways of communicating with friends. With his permission, I'd added my email as well as James's and Colin's to Danny's contacts. And told him to use them as well as our phone numbers.

He'd balked.

I'd pointed to the kids and suggested having people he could reach out to would be a good thing.

After a bit of clear consideration, he'd agreed. Forcing friends on someone who'd never really had them was tough. I didn't know if he'd email me. Or text me again. I was trying not to be overbearing while, at the same time, trying to make him see he wasn't alone anymore. I didn't know Gaynor Beach well, but from the little I'd seen, I knew he'd be okay.

As long as his ex doesn't find him. Pushing that thought aside, I sat on the floor and played cars with Thomas while Danny made my sandwich. Hallie watched, but kept her distance. I couldn't blame her. Stranger in her space. Big dude too.

"I've wrapped it." Rob held out my sandwich.

With no grace, I managed to stand. I took the sandwich from him with a grin. "You're a good man, Rob."

His gaze dropped to the floor and, I supposed, his children. "I try." Finally, after a long moment, he looked at me. "I'm going to make the effort, Danny. I promise."

At a loss for words, I simply nodded. "Whatever you need. I'm just a text or a phone call away."

"Right." He made a weird gesture I couldn't interpret.

"Okay." Reluctantly, I made my way over to the table and grabbed my knapsack. I walked over to the front door and shoved my feet into my shoes. "Bye." I waved to the kids.

Thomas waved back enthusiastically.

Hallie merely watched.

Rob placed a hand over his heart. He looked...forlorn.

If I could've stayed, I absolutely would have. Even if I didn't have a role to play, I could see a man in need. Still, I waved, made my way to my car, and headed back to LA.

CHAPTER 8

ROB

"You're certain you're up for this?" Anthony eyed me as I squirmed inwardly. I'd made it through the visit to the credit union. Thanks to a very kind staff member who watched over Hallie and Thomas while I signed a million pieces of paper, I had a bank account.

"Yeah, I am." I said the words with more confidence than I felt. Anthony's husband, Scott, had invited the kids and me over for a lunch and playdate. Today was his day off from the library. Their older daughter, Laura, would be in school, but Scott was home with the twins and thought they should meet and hopefully connect with Hallie. Scott also mentioned missing those simpler moments from when they were younger and made it clear he'd love to spend some time with a toddler.

I thought he was nuts.

But my kids were also in desperate need of socialization. If they didn't get out and meet people, they'd never cope in daycare. Because I had to go out and get a job. Something that paid enough so I could afford childcare. Which, frankly, overwhelmed me. Still, Scott's generous offer wasn't something I felt I could turn down. So Anthony dropped me and the kids off at his home before heading back to the office. To my mind, some lines were gently being crossed.

And I didn't give a damn. I was being presented with an opportunity to expand their world. I'd be a fool to turn that down.

Anthony helped me unload Thomas from his SUV while I got Hallie out. She wore a pale-blue T-shirt, blue jeans, and a light coat. The weather was warm, but a breeze blew off the ocean. The Wexler-Rodrigues residence was in the Conway Park neighborhood. A step up from Riverside, but not as prestigious as Marina Park. Personally, I thought their two-story house was beautiful. The coral stucco siding coaxed a smile from me. So welcoming compared to the gray concrete of Gerard's mansion. I guessed the second story held the bedrooms and, as we walked into the front entryway, the smell of tomato sauce hit me.

My stomach rumbled.

"Well, perfect timing." Anthony nudged me inside. He put Thomas on the floor. My child immediately barrelled into the living room as two nearly four-year-olds came to greet him.

Hallie stood behind me, grasping my leg.

The little redheaded girl leaned down and pressed a kiss to Thomas's cheek.

He giggled.

"Uh, Alicia, remember what we said about kissing strangers?" Anthony closed the front door and headed toward his daughter.

"Hi, Daddy!" She held her arms open, clearly expecting a hug from her father.

He didn't disappoint as he scooped her up and gave her an embrace.

She smacked her lips against his cheek, then pointed to me. "Who's that?"

"That's Daddy's friend Rob, his daughter Hallie, and his son Thomas."

Anthony let her down and then ruffled his son's hair. "Hey, Zayden, how goes?"

"Okay." The boy glanced over to me. Then he appeared to notice Hallie. He waved. "Come play."

She clung to me.

Scott chose that moment to wander in. He pressed a kiss to Anthony's cheek, then pivoted to me. "Perfect timing. We've got spaghetti cut into little pieces, yellow pepper slices, and cheese. Any allergies?"

I shook my head. And admired how calm the man was. Of course, I'd never had three strangers visit my house like this, so I could only imagine how panicked I'd be. "Can I help?"

Anthony leaned down and pressed a kiss to Scott's temple. "Gotta run." He pivoted to me. "I'm in the office doing paperwork all afternoon. Just call when you need a ride home."

Scott chuckled. "We could manage in the minivan."

"True. But Rob and I have a few more things to go over once I deliver him safely back to his place. Just as easy for me to run him over. Then we're not trying to cram four car seats into the van." He offered me a genuine smile. "It'll be fine. Call anytime you need an escape." Then he was gone.

I faced Scott. "I hope you've got a bib." I'd packed the knapsack with everything I thought we might need, but I hadn't thought to include a bib.

"I've got four." Scott held out his hands. Each of his children grabbed one.

We all made our way into the kitchen where five seats and a high chair sat around a large table.

The next hour was…enlightening. Yes, the six of us managed to consume food. We also laughed. Even Hallie spoke up twice. I was bursting with pride and wanted to hug her, but I knew calling out the unusual behavior would be embarrassing to her.

Zayden and Alicia were hams. They made messes with their food, to be sure, but they also just had fun. Scott encouraged them to enjoy themselves, pointing out he had cleaning supplies.

Supplies I was happy to use after we'd cleaned the kids. The little ones tromped as a group into the playroom—led by Alicia. Scott had pulled out an old playpen, and Thomas was happy to go in there with a pile of toys he'd never played with before. Hallie insisted she would watch over him while Scott and I attempted to put the kitchen to rights.

"Hallie is really protective of Thomas." Scott scooped the leftover spaghetti into a plastic container.

"Too much?" I swept all the straggling pieces of spaghetti into the compost bin.

"That's a parenting question I can't answer." Scott wet a cloth with some soap and handed it to me. "Our older daughter, Laura, is incredibly protective of the twins. But she came from an…well, a bad place."

I swallowed hard. "I did my best, Scott, but Hallie's life hasn't been all sunshine and roses."

His eyes showed empathy, and I hated myself for the emotion welling within me. "He never hit her. He never hit Thomas." I pointed to my taped nose which, amazingly, no one at the bank had commented on. Of course, they all knew Anthony, and there I was, opening my first ever bank account. Pretty clearly, I was fucked. "This was the first time."

"And the last. Good for you." Scott grabbed a broom. "You sweep and I'll mop?"

Way too much spaghetti sauce had landed on the floor. Although Thomas often made a mess with his highchair tray, he rarely sent food over the side. Hallie ate meticulously, never spilling a drop. That level of vigilance scared me.

Often everything about her scared me. "I think Hallie needs to see a counsellor."

Scott scrubbed at the floor where I'd just swept the last of the noodles into a dustbin. "You probably need to see someone as well." He met my gaze. "I'm no therapist. I just…sometimes people come into the library and I can see them hurting and I want to point them toward getting help. Anthony, of course, sometimes shares nonspecific details about things that he's seen."

"That must be tough to hear."

"Sure." He leaned back against the counter. "My parents rejected me because I was gay. I came out here, found a way to pay for school, and did my best."

"You have two beautiful children. Well, and your other daughter."

"Who you might yet meet." Scott gave me a long look. "My route to parenthood was…untraditional. But we don't hide it from people. Well, maybe some parts."

My ears perked up, and I tried to be nonchalant. People never confided in me. That just wasn't a thing.

"Anthony showed up on my doorstep one day with two nine-month-old babies."

I blinked.

"Yeah. Said they were mine. Since I'd never had sex with a woman, I had my doubts."

"And yet…"

He offered a small smile. "I used to donate sperm. Helped pay for college. Unbeknownst to me, a friend of mine figured out which was mine and used it. That…didn't go over well with her husband."

I winced.

"Yeah, pretty much. I won't go into the details, but she needed me to take care of them. For what turned into forever. And I have zero regrets. I've made my peace with my friend. She writes. I send her pictures. She's in a better headspace. Out of that marriage, thank God."

I flashed to my marriage. *Will that ever be over? Will I ever get free?* I just didn't have answers to those questions. "And then…"

"Well, Anthony was helping. He practically moved in because I knew nothing about babies. They became attached. I became attached." He grinned. "My future husband became attached. The next thing I knew, we moved into this place, got married, he adopted the twins legally, and…we started fostering Laura." He chuckled. "I make that sound like it all happened in a day. It didn't. But…" He looked around. "This is the life I was meant to be living. If you'd told sixteen-year-old me that I'd wind up married and with three kids, I never would've believed it."

"Yeah. Sixteen-year-old me wouldn't have believed I'd wind up where I am. I love my kids." I had to say that. He needed to understand.

Slowly, he nodded. "I get it. I really do." He snagged the broom from my hand and tucked it aside with the mop. "Would you like a hug before we go and try to wrangle our kids into taking a nap?"

I blinked rapidly. "Yeah, that would be really nice."

And for the first time in longer than I could remember, someone held me. And for the first time in forever, I let go —allowing myself to have a good cry.

CHAPTER 9

DANNY

Dr. Patton's incisive blue eyes cut right through me. "You're certain?"

I nodded vigorously. *Hell no, doc, I'm not certain. I've never been less certain of anything in my life. But you've just told me I can save a life. How could I ever not do it?*

"There are risks, Mr. Reynolds."

"I know." I tapped my knee. "You and the team have spent the past three days explaining them all to me." The process was usually crammed into two days, but I'd needed to take time off to take my exam.

The exam I'd bombed. "How soon? Because, like, Colin's getting sicker all the time. And so's the other guy, I assume. Do I get to know his name or will he always be *the other guy?*" I knew the gentleman was Black, in his forties, and healthy other than needing a new liver. That might've been more than I needed to know, but I got the feeling they wanted to assure me that my recipient had the best shot at surviving and thriving.

"You'll have the option of meeting your recipient. If he wants."

"And Colin won't know I'm donating. Anonymous, right?"

She continued to eye me. "Your insistence on being anonymous is vaguely concerning."

I shifted in my seat. "I'm an adult. I can make the decision for myself."

"Yes."

"And I'm perfectly healthy. A great donor—your words."

"True."

"Psychologically healthy and fully cognizant of the ramifications of donation including all possible outcomes."

She arched an eyebrow.

"So why should it matter if my family knows or not?" I leaned forward. "I know you're not Colin's doctor. And maybe you haven't met my brother, who is, like the best guy in the world. Yeah, I could die. I'm not making light of that. I can also get taken out on I5 anytime I run down to see them."

Her lips pursed.

"But they'd try to talk me out of it." When she began to speak, I gently raised my hand. "*Try*. They're not going to. I mean, even if the other guy's boss wasn't a perfect match for Colin, I'm kind of invested. There's a life I can save."

"You want to be a doctor. Doctors save lives."

I met her gaze head-on. "If I pass biochem, it'll be a miracle."

That damn eyebrow shot up again.

"Well…" I squirmed. "I passed, but barely. Certainly not good enough to even consider applying to med school. And yeah, I could try again…" I broke eye contact with her to look out the window. LA lay before me, in all her chaotic glory. Excitement, adventure, a quest I'd embarked on three years ago when I'd left Huntington Beach and had moved north.

I was miserable. This fast-paced lifestyle wasn't for me. Even if I somehow made it into medical school, the thought of all that studying for the next however many years was, frankly, depressing. I was on the wrong track, and I needed to get off. Here was the perfect excuse. I turned back to her. "Six to eight weeks of recovery time?"

"This is major surgery."

"And my sister Whitney can take care of me?"

"Certainly. You say she's responsible and competent."

I loved my sister, but those were not the two adjectives I'd pick first.

"So I'll need to take the winter semester off?"

Slowly, she nodded.

"And I can make up the classes in the summer." I shrugged. "I need a break. I'm only seeing this as a win-win."

After a very, very, very long moment, she handed me the paperwork.

Two hours later, I sat in Mama's kitchen as she put the finishing touches on the turkey, gravy, stuffing, cranberries, green beans, mashed potatoes, fresh-baked buns, and roast corn. "Mama, they're three people. Well, one person, one child, and one infant. They can't possibly eat all that." The plan had been for Gracie to take the food hamper down to Rob and the kids. But she got a last-minute audition for a shampoo commercial and, given how much she'd get paid, she'd had to nab it.

When Mama'd heard about the family moving into James's house, and their circumstances—although not the particulars—she'd clucked and said she'd prepare something for Christmas for them. Given her heart wasn't great, I was worried. Surprisingly, Whitney had helped out.

Mama would have two days' rest before she tackled Christmas dinner for the entire Reynolds clan.

"Leftovers, my dear." She wagged her finger at me. "You need to eat more of those."

I cocked my head. "Mama, I always eat your leftovers. Martin's the one who won't because he's so picky."

She eyed me, as if considering. "I could bluster through, but I honestly thought you were the one who didn't like them." She pressed her hand to her forehead. "It's not a good sign that I'm confusing my children."

I stood, made my way over to her, and took her in my arms. She was tiny…in comparison to me. "Mama, I get confused and I'm only twenty."

"Soon to be twenty-one." She swatted at me. "Don't you think I don't remember your birthday is coming up."

I snickered. "The one advantage to being so close to the holidays." Despite the fact my birthday was just after the holidays, Mama always made a big fuss about it. Leftovers were gone by then, and she'd insist on another big feast. So diets in this family—new year's resolutions, anyway—didn't begin until after my special day.

"Now, I'm going to make you a sandwich—"

"I ate before I left LA. That was just over an hour ago."

"Well, you might get peckish. Although you shouldn't eat while you're driving—"

I guffawed. "Yes, Mama."

She swatted my ass. "Help me pack up this food."

As we worked, the scents enveloped me and my stomach rumbled.

"You said you ate." She glared at me.

"I said I ate before I left LA." I put the buns into a container and sealed it. "Did you do your honey butter?"

She pursed her lips…reminding me very much of Dr.

Patton. And how I was holding back something super important from my family.

"If he invites me to join him." I scooped the green beans into another container. "No cheese sauce?"

"I've included a recipe card on how to make it. I wasn't certain it would travel well."

"The cooler is pretty stable." I eyed the thing which we often used for camping when we were younger. I missed those trips. We hadn't gone in years—not since Mama's heart got worse.

"If he wants to keep the cooler, he's welcome to it. Your sisters don't want it and, frankly, can you see Martin camping?"

We met each other's gazes and laughed.

"Uh…no. I don't know if Rob's in a position to start collecting things." I still didn't have a read on Rob's situation. How permanent things were. How soon before he would be moving on.

Whether or not his ex-husband is still in jail.

I hadn't searched. Even from LA, I didn't want to leave a computer trail. James had taught me how to be incognito, of course, but nothing was ever one hundred percent safe. Well, if James did the search then I'd trust it to be untraceable…but I wasn't going to put him in that position.

"And I don't want the containers back." Mama sealed the turkey I'd sliced into another container. "There's both dark and light meat."

Of course there was. "That's great, Mama. I'm sure he'll be thrilled." I considered asking if she'd checked about allergies but, knowing Mama, she had. Plus, the foods were pretty innocuous. And, naturally, everything was labelled with a list of ingredients. Oh, and recipe cards were tucked in the side of the cooler.

"Don't forget the gifts." She patted my arm as I secured the lid of the cooler.

I cocked my head. "And I'm sure you absolutely did *not* go overboard." My parents weren't wealthy by any stretch of the imagination. Their house was paid for, but they'd also helped put seven children through college. Well, since Gracie dropped out after just a few months to pursue acting, maybe it only counted as six children. Most of us had scholarships of some kind—athletic for Felicia and Martin—academic for Leticia, Whitney, James, and me.

Still, I couldn't fault her for buying gifts. With so many grandchildren, she would've known what to get Hallie and Thomas. Or she would've consulted with Leticia and Felicia because, well, Mama was smart.

Twenty minutes later, my car was packed with way too many things, and I waved to Mama as I backed out of the driveway. I hadn't told her about the liver donation. I hadn't told her about biochem or about taking a semester off. I'd thought not blabbing would be difficult—in the end, though, my decision had to be my own. Maybe she wouldn't have tried to talk me out of it. Maybe she would've. Either way, I couldn't take the risk of her interfering.

The miles passed in a blur as I maneuvered around slower cars. Speeding a bit. Not too much, though. Would that change? If I had a family of my own? Not Mama, Daddy, and that crew. No, if I had kids. A husband. Or a wife. Someone who counted on me to come home every night.

Soon, I took the off-ramp to Gaynor Beach and headed into town. I really wanted a coffee, but I didn't want to stop. Weird that Rob didn't drink coffee. Although he'd never been a college student. Everyone I knew mainlined coffee.

I parked on the street in front of the little house. I could've parked in the driveway—given there wasn't a car—but...I always felt that was presumptuous.

Well, except at the Reynolds family home. Whomever arrived first got the primo parking spaces.

I got out, nabbed the cooler, and headed to the door.

Only after I rang the doorbell, did it occur to me that Thomas or Hallie—or both—might be asleep.

Damn.

When no one answered the door, it occurred to me that maybe James hadn't actually called Rob to warn him I was on my way.

Well, shit.

I could leave a note, and head over to James's. But that would be a glaring notice to everyone that the family wasn't home. Oh, I could text him. I was grabbing my phone just as the door opened.

A clearly sleep-rumpled Rob opened the door. His hair stuck up in all directions, his eyes were bloodshot, and he yawned.

Thomas, who'd been tucked against him, suddenly threw himself toward me, tilting half out of Rob's hold.

I caught him under the arms, and suddenly Rob and I were inches apart.

Rob said, "You got the wiggle monster?"

"Yep." I took a better hold on the toddler as his dad let go.

Thomas giggled.

Rob sagged against the doorframe.

"Are you okay? Are you sick?" Kids were forever bringing home viruses. If one of the kids was sick and made everyone else ill—

He shook his head. "Thomas is teething." He wiped

some saliva off his son's chin before it landed on my sweatshirt.

I wouldn't have cared. All that mattered was helping in any way I could. "Well, I brought the Christmas dinner."

Rob blinked.

"James told you we were giving you a full turkey dinner with all the stuff that goes with it, right?" I eyed Thomas. "And gifts for the kids?"

Rob blinked, sniffed, and a tear rolled down his cheek.

That just about broke me. I never cried. Not because I was macho, but because I found tears hard. That they came so easily to Rob made my heart ache. "Okay, can you lift the cooler? Then, if you think Thomas won't mind being with me alone for a moment, you can run out to the car and grab the four garbage bags of gifts. I know it's silly, but we don't have a red sack with white fur trim that Santa might use."

"I..." He visibly faltered—again using the doorframe. "I can't..."

"Can't...?" Thomas grabbed my earlobe. "Hey, buddy, that actually hurts."

He cocked his head, as if trying to understand.

"Can't...?" I repeated the question to Rob. I suspected I knew, but I needed to hear it from him.

"Take all these wonderful gifts." He winced. "I can't afford—"

"Afford?" I scoffed. "The meaning of gift is that it's free. Given from the heart. And, trust me, Mama's got a big heart." I moved in closer. "I suspect some of these things are lightly used—Felicia's three boys are grown out of most of the stuff." I considered. "Felicia and Leticia are both pregnant, but I'm sure they're eager to shop for new things."

"Leticia and Felicia?"

"My twin sisters. Leticia's a few minutes older, and boy, is she bossy. Anyway, she has three girls, and Felicia has three boys, and Leticia got pregnant again and, I think out of the competitive spirit, Felicia felt the need to do the same. And both are pregnant with twins." I winced. "I haven't done the math on all those odds. Astronomical, I'd say. Especially because twins don't run in the family—"

"Papa?" Hallie appeared, glancing up at her dad. Her ponytail was askew, with little wisps of her white-blonde hair escaping. She was rubbing her eyes.

"I interrupted a nap, didn't I?" Another wince. "Sorry."

Rob snagged Hallie and settled her on his hip. Despite her slender and petite size, she was clearly heavy. Rob wasn't a big guy, but he seemed to manage. He turned to me. "We needed to get up anyway. Too much sleeping during the day and we won't sleep properly at night." He eyed the cooler.

"We'll figure everything out."

And we did. Rob got the kids settled in the kitchen with Thomas sitting in his high chair and eating little pieces of melon while Hallie snacked on a granola bar. Rob and I alternated runs to the car and pretty soon we had everything inside. I organized everything for the fridge while Rob put the gifts under the artificial tree in the living room that he'd decorated. *Hopefully that was a good time and Hallie has some good memories.* I worried about her. Always so somber, solemn, and almost sad. Compared to all my nieces and nephews when they'd been her age, the difference was stark.

Rob nibbled on some crackers as I set about laying out the instructions for reheating the feast.

I assumed he could read—although that was a big

assumption. Plenty of people couldn't, and they just sort of got by.

He asked some questions and, at the end, said he understood. "How do I thank your mother?" He rubbed his eyes. "Likely your entire family?"

"I could send a message through the family group chat if you'd like."

His eyes widened. "For that?"

I yanked out my phone. "Oh, they'd love that. Sort of the reason we have it." I popped off a message, and by the time I laid the phone down on the kitchen table, it buzzed several times with incoming messages.

Rob gaped. "That simple?"

"Well, Martin turns his notifications off since he's a teacher. And Gracie's auditioning today, so she might not—"

I glanced down. "Nope, she sends her love."

"She…" Rob swallowed. "She doesn't know me."

"She doesn't have to know you to care." I grinned. "It's a Reynolds thing." I eyed him. "And no one told you I was coming? Because I generally don't like showing up unannounced."

"No one told me you were coming." Rob offered what I thought was a shy smile. "But you're welcome to show up unannounced anytime. With or without gifts." He winced. "That came out wrong. I don't want you to bring gifts again, okay? You've brought so much—"

"Well…" I eyed Hallie. Then I mouthed the word *tricycle* to Rob.

Slowly, he nodded. And looked panicked.

"With training wheels, my friend. We always take things slowly." Even as I had the thought, I flashed to my nephew's broken arm. "Helmet and pads included." I glanced to see if Hallie was paying attention.

Clearly she wasn't as she was coaxing her brother to eat a cracker.

Thomas gave her what I'd describe as a mutinous expression. "Well, he'll be hungrier for dinner tonight, right?" I turned back to Rob. "You don't have to wait for Christmas to have that dinner. I mean, Mama's made enough so you'll have leftovers for days. Heck, you'll still have food Christmas Day." I made a show of eyeing the kids. "Unless these two eat excessively…"

He offered a small smile. "We do okay, but definitely not as much as what all your mother sent." His smile turned weary. "I'm not used to…you know…"

I longed to reach out and hug him, but that felt inappropriate. If he needed physical comfort, I'd be happy to offer it. I came from a touchy-feely family. Although, admittedly, that often came in the form of punching one another in the shoulder. "Why don't we do something fun before dinner?"

"You're staying?" Rob's shocked expression had me wincing yet again.

"No, of course not. I just—"

"We'd like you to stay." He tried for a smile. "If you want."

"Only if I'm not in the way." Something in his expression spoke to something inside me that I didn't understand.

"You're not." He glanced at his children with such loving affection that my heart seized. "I wouldn't mind some…"

"Adult company?"

He met my gaze. "Yeah."

"Okay…I'll stay." I straightened, trying to suck in my stomach. "What would you like to do in the meantime? Play? Walk?"

"I'd love a walk." He eyed me with an expression I couldn't read. "I've never seen the ocean."

Don't react. Don't say anything. But...who the hell lives in LA and has never seen the ocean? I didn't like the potential answers to that because I suspected they had something to do with the controlling ex-husband. Unless Rob had some weird phobia about the ocean. But if he did, then he wouldn't have suggested it. "I'd love to show you the ocean."

"Great." He beamed.

I smiled back with genuine contentment.

CHAPTER 10
ROB

I loaded Thomas into the stroller Anthony had so generously loaned us.

Hallie grabbed my hand, and we started out walking, with me trying to grasp her as well as steering the stroller.

"Can I help?"

Danny's warm laugh washed over me.

Hallie pointed to another couple walking down the street. The man had his son on his shoulders while the woman pushed the stroller. The guy looked way stronger than I thought I was, and I doubted he was as fatigued as I was.

Before I could speak, though, Danny knelt before Hallie. "I would love to carry you on my shoulders. But only if you want." He cleared his throat and winced for, like, the twentieth time.

I wish he didn't feel so uncomfortable around us.

"Uh…and if your papa says it's okay?"

Hallie gazed between the two of us. I trusted her to Danny's care, but I didn't want her to feel like she had to agree. "Do you want to, sweetheart? Because you don't have—"

"I do." She nodded slowly, turning to watch the other child laughing and waving from his high perch. "Yes, I do."

No missing the bravado. But I'd be within a foot at all times, and we'd done this when she was younger, so she understood she needed to balance carefully.

Danny's face broke into a wide grin. "My nieces love doing this." He considered. "Not so much the boys."

I could offer no explanation. I only knew my children. Hopefully Thomas would enjoy this when he was older. When I carried Hallie that way, before Thomas had come along and my time had split, she seemed to enjoy that connection. At the very least, she liked gripping my hair. I eyed Danny's short hair. Not really enough to grab, but I couldn't be sure. "She might pull."

He winked. "No worries." He pivoted, putting his back to Hallie.

I helped her and, within moments, she was secure. He had his hands on her knees and she balanced easily. "Oh, Papa, I can see blue water."

Danny cut me a glance. I swallowed the lump in my throat. "A first for all of us."

He grinned. "You're going to love it." We sauntered down the street. Hallie's view came from between the houses as the land gently sloped downward in this area. Soon we found a paved path that led us down to the boardwalk.

And the ocean.

Thomas sat in the front-facing stroller and clapped his hands as we went, as if urging me forward faster.

When we arrived at the junction of the path and the boardwalk, Danny stepped to the side.

I did as well, maneuvering the stroller out of the way so

we weren't blocking the path. Below us stretched an expanse of beautiful sand and then, lapping gently along the shoreline, the Pacific Ocean. My breath caught. As I looked to the right, I could follow the boardwalk along until I spotted first, the pier that went a fair distance into the water, and then the lighthouse on the far horizon. In the other direction, I could see the marina where, clearly, all the boats were stored. Looking outward, I spotted a few boats and then…just blue ocean.

"It always blows my mind." Danny's voice held a note of awe. "That it's thousands of miles until you reach Hawaii, then Japan, and other parts of Asia. Because you can travel the distance so fast in a plane, you almost forget just how vast the ocean is."

"It's a little intimidating." I tried to play it cool, but the vastness of the water overwhelmed me. The simplicity and yet the inherent beauty.

"Yeah." Danny glanced down at me.

We'd all put on sunscreen, and the adults wore sunglasses while Hallie wore an adorable sunhat with a sunflower planted right in the middle. Prepared for the weather, which was warm today.

"Papa, can I go into the water?"

"Not today, sweetheart. We didn't bring your bathing suit." *In fact, we don't have bathing suits here.* Our house back in LA had a pool, and both my children were water babies—in the water from a very young age. I wanted them to be able to swim, should they ever find themselves in the water and without assistance. I planned to always be with them, of course. That being said, having their father tagging around when they were thirty-five to ensure they didn't drown was, perhaps, a bit much.

Danny grinned. "I think Santa might bring you a suit. If you don't have one."

"Santa's not real." Hallie said the words in a matter-of-fact way that broke my heart.

"What? Of course he's real." Danny cut me a desperate look.

Gently, I shook my head.

He winced for the umpteenth time.

"But we don't tell people that," I reminded my daughter. "If someone wants to believe, that's okay."

She sighed. "Right. Sorry."

I blinked back tears, grateful for the sunglasses. Gerard had done this. Insisted the children never believe in anything magical. That they always be grounded in reality. We hadn't fought often, but that had been a bone of contention with me. Despite all my parents' faults—and there were many—they had at least given me Santa Claus, the tooth fairy, and the Easter Bunny. Dragons had been a step too far, though, and no magical fantasy movies for me. When Gerard wasn't home, though, in those first few months of marriage, I'd watched as many films as I could fit around my chores, on the small television with DVD player he allowed me. I wanted to watch everything. The Lord of the Rings trilogy was, of course, my favorite. Thank God I could borrow things from the library and Gerard wouldn't know about it. Later, when Hallie came, Gerard allowed her to watch a few things he vetted for appropriateness. But never more than a couple of hours a week. I didn't dare do more, even when we were home alone.

"Don't be sorry." Danny tapped her knee. "Everyone's different. I kept believing for as long as I could because I thought I wouldn't get as many presents if I didn't believe. My brother James explained things to me." He gave me a grin. "My very logical and smart brother."

"Aren't you the one headed to medical school?" I

seemed to recall James or Colin saying something about that. All the conversations kind of melded together. Or maybe Danny had said it himself—

He cleared his throat. "Do you want to walk along the Boardwalk? Might be easier with the stroller. When we get to the pier, we can take our shoes off and walk in the sand."

"Yeah." Hallie sounded…almost enthusiastic.

I could've kissed Danny for doing this. Everything felt less daunting when he was around. Making even small choices felt weird, though. Gerard had been gone most of the day, with working so much, but he'd always told me what to do…so I hadn't ever really thought for myself. Now, though, I had to make decisions that affected the three of us. That daunted me pretty much all the time. What if I made the wrong decision? What if I did something that hurt the kids even more? What if I chose the incorrect path, and we wound up back in Gerard's clutches?

"Hey, are you okay?" Danny had walked about ten feet, while I'd stayed rooted to the spot. He turned and came back. "We don't have to—"

"Yeah, we do." I offered my best smile. "It's all good, Danny. I promise."

"Okay." He bounced Hallie gently.

She giggled.

Everything felt possible again.

And so we walked down the boardwalk toward the center of town. School was out now for the Christmas break, so there were plenty of families wandering around. I spotted two gentlemen and a teenager and two dogs. I gently nudged Danny. "Wow, that sure looks like Widget."

"Yeah, but it…" His voice trailed off. "Okay…that's either her doppelgänger or the girl herself."

Even as he said the words, the dog spotted him and started dragging the man.

Danny strode toward them, still gripping Hallie. "Hey, slow down." He held out his hand toward the dog.

The slim, dark-haired man gripping the leash chuckled ruefully. "She seems mighty determined. Apologies. We're walking her for a friend. She's usually better behaved."

"I know she is." Danny smiled. "Hello, Widget."

The bulldog wagged her butt so hard she vibrated.

"You know her?" The teenager restraining the big, furry dog glanced up at us, snub nose wrinkled. "You look kind of familiar." The dog wagged her heavy, white-tipped tail but kept her distance.

"I'm James's brother, Danny." He gave a big grin.

Almost more than the situation called for, in my opinion. Although clearly he was glad to meet new people, and couldn't wave or shake hands while keeping Hallie safe on his shoulders. Danny seemed really social.

Another difference between the two of us.

"Oh, wow." The boy grinned back. "I'm Kevin. These are my dads."

The gentleman holding Widget's leash waved. "I'm Alec."

"And I'm Joe." The other gentleman pointed at the dog. "And that's Zelda."

Danny crooned at the dog, "Unlike a certain Widget, you're very well-behaved." She was, although she pushed herself against Kevin as if not quite certain what to make of all of us.

I don't blame you.

"This is Hallie." Danny tilted his head upward. "And that's Thomas."

Widget again pulled on her harness.

Alec held steady.

"Oh, she knows the kids." Danny's grin didn't diminish.

"Maybe so…" Alec didn't look certain. "I'd prefer to keep her away from small children, if that's okay."

"Yeah." Danny's smile diminished a little. "You're right. I'm surprised you're walking her."

Joe cocked his head. "We do sometimes, when we're doing a long route and James isn't around. Colin says he appreciates it."

Danny blinked. "Oh yeah, James is in San Diego for the day with some client visits. I totally forgot. I never thought to offer to take Widget out for them."

"Well, we get to, so we don't mind." Kevin's smile radiated. "Widget's a cool dog. Did you know artist Toulouse-Lautrec painted French bulldogs? Widget looks a lot like this really famous one, Bouboule."

"I did not know that." Danny mock frowned. "I'll just have to have a word with my brother."

Kevin's face fell.

Joe nudged him. "He's teasing."

"Oh, yeah, sorry." Danny chuckled. "My family's…a little over the top. We just assume everyone's teasing and no one takes anything seriously."

I filed that tidbit away. Danny sometimes felt like…a lot. It would help to remember he was used to a big family and teasing everyone.

Danny met Joe's gaze. "Except Colin's illness, of course."

"Yeah. That's why we're happy to help." Alec gazed at me. "You've got two great kids."

Suddenly, I realized they might think Danny, and I were together. Two men. One Black, one white. Two kids. One Black, one white.

"Rob's new in town." To my relief, Danny spoke first.

"He met me when he moved in. I'm still up in LA. You probably didn't know that."

Alec cocked his head. "I seem to recall James saying something about a large family, but I didn't pry."

Danny laughed. "Oh, feel free to pry. Nothing more we love than talking about my six siblings, seven nieces and nephews, and the five on the way."

"Oh, wow, that's cool." Kevin grinned. "I like being an only child, but I wouldn't mind a brother or sister. Maybe not six though."

"Five on the way." Joe frowned, clearly trying to work that out in his mind.

"Each of my twin sisters are pregnant with twins. And my brother Martin and his wife Shondra are expecting as well."

"Wow." Alec's eyes widened. "That's…"

"A little over the top?" Danny leaned in. I held my breath as his shoulders tilted but he held Hallie safely and she actually smiled. "I think so, but I get to spoil them all like crazy. I love kids." He said the words conspiratorially.

Kevin laughed. "Oh man. That's…a lot of presents."

"Kevin." Joe's voice held just a touch of admonishment.

"Oh, he's right. I'll need to get a job just to pay for all the gifts." Danny laughed. "And I couldn't be happier."

Thomas, who'd been amazingly quiet to that point, pounded on his stroller.

Danny, Joe, and Alec all turned to smile at him.

I managed a smile too, though it felt fake. This was so overwhelming. And I hadn't said…anything. I just didn't have anything to contribute to the discussion.

"Well, Widget, I think the little man wants us to get a move on." Danny tipped his chin at Thomas. "And I've learned to do what the little ones want."

"True," Alec said, with a smile I'd call wistful. "They're only young for such a short period of time." He glanced between Hallie and Thomas. "You're so lucky."

I cleared my throat. "Yeah, I really am. Lovely to meet you all." I glanced down at Widget. "Another day, okay?" Thomas adored her, but Hallie was still uncertain around the pup for reasons I couldn't clearly understand. Usually my daughter loved dogs, so her reticence around Widget confused me. I hoped she wasn't heading into a new phase because of all the surrounding chaos.

Joe put his hand on Kevin's shoulder. "I'm sure we'll see you around. Welcome to town. You've picked a great spot."

Being polite, I didn't point out that the spot had been picked for me. "Uh, thanks."

Danny encouraged Halley to wave and she actually lifted a hand as the family, with the two dogs, moved on. He fell into step beside me. "Too bad Thomas couldn't have said *hi* to Widget."

"Alec was right to be cautious."

"Sure, I guess. Oh, there's a good spot." He pointed to a small patch of sand where no one else was around. "Would you like to get down?" He glanced up at Hallie, twisting his neck in a way that couldn't have been comfortable.

She nodded solemnly.

He lowered himself and I helped her off.

Unsurprisingly, she stayed close to me as I got Thomas out of the stroller.

Danny hefted it over to the spot he'd chosen while I followed behind with the kids. At his encouragement, I'd brought a blanket, a couple of Thomas's toys, and drinks for us all. Danny spread the blanket and laid out the toys as I plopped my son onto the ground.

He popped back up and made a run for the water.

Danny was closer—and faster—and managed to scoop up my little man before he made it too far. He pivoted and came back to the blanket. "We could take off his shoes and pants, right? He and I could dip our toes in."

"Sure." Nothing against propriety there. Hallie, however, couldn't take her pants off. "Hallie, do you want to roll yours up? We could walk along the shoreline."

She eyed the water for a long time before she shook her head.

"Next time." Danny grinned. "We'll all wear our swimsuits." He patted his belly. "Better work on this."

Before I could comment, he had Thomas's shoes and pants off, had toed off his own shoes, and was down the beach. Well, I could've commented…I just didn't know what to say. Despite Danny making several disparaging remarks, I didn't have the words to respond. He wasn't, to my eye, unhealthy. Maybe a couple of pounds over what some people would consider *perfect*.

Like Gerard.

Yeah, my husband would've made negative comments. He often put people down, and everyone who wasn't their ideal weight garnered his biting remarks— usually only audible in my direction, of course. I never had much of an appetite, so I fit within his definition of acceptable. He worked out daily and liked to show off his body. I'd, once upon a time, thought he was handsome. That he took care of himself. When I discovered that was at the expense of other people—in the form of negativity and derision—I came to see him very differently. That *perfect* body was a weapon he wielded. It, to his mind, gave him permission to be cruel toward others.

I couldn't abide by that, and I'd become worried our

kids would either get an eating disorder or, just as bad, make cutting remarks.

Danny rolled up his jeans a few inches and walked into the water while holding Thomas's hands.

My son laughed in delight.

In turn, my breath caught. Much to my frustration, Thomas had very little exposure to people of his cultural and ethnic background. I'd tried to include a variety of people in my circle, but there just weren't that many Black families on our street and, thanks to my controlling husband, I never left the neighborhood. Thomas's pediatrician was a brilliant Black woman who kept assuring me that everything would work out. She knew my worries. I didn't want my son to grow up disconnected from other communities. Just like I worried Hallie's worldview would be seen through the narrow lens of the neighborhood Gerard had chosen. Of the friendships he chose to cultivate. Of the people he purposely excluded from our little world.

Breathe. He can't hurt you anymore. He can't hurt the kids anymore.

Gaynor Beach was clearly an inclusive community in many ways—confirmed as I looked up and down the beach and spotted plenty of color. And diversity of relationships. Not just hetero white families. That alleviated some of my stress.

But not all. I hadn't found a job. I hadn't found childcare I could afford. Anthony had arranged to put some emergency funds in my new account at the credit union, but I needed to figure things out. I'd worried about Christmas presents but, thanks to the Reynolds family, that appeared to be taken care of. Hallie would never have said anything, of course, but I liked the idea of having something for her. And we'd had Thomas with us last

Christmas, but he'd only been a few weeks old. This was his first real Christmas, as far as I was concerned.

At least I could take pictures with my phone. To commemorate the event. To start to build a life without Gerard. I was worried about losing them, but I'd upload them to my cloud account as soon as I got home.

Hallie curled against me as we sat on the blanket, watching the giant man with the tiny toddler.

"Papa, you okay?"

I gazed down at her. "Yeah, Papa's okay."

If I wanted that to be the truth, that was good enough. Right?

I didn't have an answer to that question either.

CHAPTER 11

DANNY

Rob had been subdued the entire time I'd been with him, and I couldn't help thinking I should just take off, but when we got back to his house, he was adamant I sit at the table while he set about heating plates of food for the four of us.

Who was I to argue? If it meant spending more time with this wonderful little unit of three, I was happy to do it.

As we dug into Mama's delicious meal, however, I finally cracked. "What's wrong?"

He dug his fork into the mashed potatoes—slathered in gravy—and hesitated. "I need a job, Danny. Really badly."

"Is it money?" I didn't have much, but I could give him something. I could definitely help get more for him. Even if that meant hitting up every family member I had and—

He shook his head. Then winced. Then nodded. "I get some money from the state for a bit, but that's going to run out." Finally, he met my gaze. "I've never had a real job before. I want to feel like I'm contributing. I want to show my kids—"

I waved my hand in the air. "Hang on a second."

He stared.

"You've been taking care of two beautiful, amazing, brilliant children for four years?"

"Well…" He eyed them.

Hallie sat watching us, while Thomas nibbled on the turkey I'd cut up for him.

"What's brilliant?" Hallie blinked.

I'd have to remember to watch my words. She was very smart, so that was true. Just…she apparently understood more than I gave her credit for.

Rob feathered her hair. "Smart. You and Thomas are smart."

That appeared to satisfy her as she ate a green bean.

"Maybe we can take up this discussion later?" Rob's gaze was pleading.

Later? I should be getting on the road soon—back to either Huntington Beach or LA. I could crash with James, of course, but I didn't like to drop in unannounced. If Colin was having a bad day, then that wouldn't be fair. "Sure. I, uh, have some news to share with you. But you have to promise not to say anything."

Rob chuckled. "And who, precisely, would I tell?"

"I don't know." I cut a piece of turkey. "You might feel an obligation to run over to tell James and Colin."

He laid down his fork and, after a long moment, placed his hand over mine.

The contact shocked me. I'd been so careful not to touch him. Not to spook him. But here he was the one initiating contact. I had to be respectful of that.

"If you tell me something in confidence, I'll hold it to my heart and never share it, okay? You can trust me." He blinked several times. "I've only ever said that to two other people. Two women." He gazed at his children. "God, I hope—wherever they are—they're not regretting their decision. I don't ever want to let them down. To let my children down." He added that in a whisper as Hallie gazed at him.

"Papa?"

"I'm thinking we should read one of those wonderful books from the library." He gave her a smile. "We didn't have much of a nap today."

I'd noticed Thomas was nearly falling asleep in his food. "I'll do the dishes."

"And help me put them to bed?" Rob gave me a look I struggled to interpret. "It's good that…"

That someone else do this as well? I wasn't certain I was filling in the blank correctly, but I understood. He'd probably been the only one taking care of the kids for four years. If something happened to him… "Happy to help." I slowly rotated my hand so our palms touched.

He grasped my hand.

Our gazes held.

The man was so stoic that I struggled to interpret his expression. But I understood he was asking for help.

We finished eating dinner, then had some of Mama's homemade apple pie. She'd even made the crust, and Rob was clearly impressed.

I made a note to try to learn myself so I could impress him on my own. That was what I wanted—that he saw me as competent. Not just a college student living in a dorm who never did anything for himself.

In the end, I read a book for Hallie as, in the other room, Rob sang quietly to Thomas. The song broke my heart because it took me back to my childhood. Mama had sung to each of us. James, who shared my room, had said he was too old. Yet he'd never left the room as Mama enjoyed that nighttime ritual. I vowed to tell her how much that had meant to me the next time I saw her.

Hallie was asleep by the time I finished the story. Slowly, all day, she'd been less wary around me.

Finally, as I pulled her door closed, but not shut, I breathed a sigh of relief. I wanted her to like me. Rob had enough shit in his life. If he let me help—which was a big *if* —I needed the kids to be comfortable around me.

I made my way back to the kitchen and did the last of the cleaning up. Mama was going to be so happy to know how much everyone enjoyed her dinner. In fact, I decided to text her that moment. I shot off the text of gratitude.

Moments later, she said she was pleased and asked if I would be home that night or if I was going to LA.

That made me think. LA made more sense. I needed to pack up my dorm room and move my stuff to Whitney's. Thank God I didn't have much, so her storing it wouldn't be a big deal.

I told Mama I'd head back to LA.

She admonished my decision—clearly thinking I should be home in her nest—but said she'd see me Christmas Eve. An entire two days from now.

After sending back an *I love you* text, I put my phone in my back pocket.

"Hey." Rob appeared in the kitchen, offering a smile. "You didn't have to clean up."

I waved him off. "Of course I did. You think Mama wouldn't lose her mind if her baby didn't do everything in his power to make life easier for someone…"

"In need?" He wrapped his arms around himself.

"That wasn't what I was going to say." I stood a little taller.

Rob arched an eyebrow.

"The dishwasher should be turned on. I just didn't know if it would bother the kids."

He shook his head as he moved to the cupboard

under the sink. He had some doohickey thing that ensured darling Thomas couldn't get into the space. After pulling out the dishwasher soap, he loaded it into the dishwasher and set it to run. "Thomas can sleep through anything, and Hallie…" He put the soap back under the cupboard, breaking eye contact. When he straightened, having put the soap away, his eyes were bleak as they met mine. "She sleeps heavily at first. Then, often, the nightmares come." He blinked. "Most nights she winds up in my room."

His bed was a decent size, having been James's—who was huge—but something about the crib, the bed, and three beings in that one small room felt overwhelming. Still… "They need you, Rob. I know you feel you have to be strong. It's okay to falter with me, though, okay? I can hold you up when you need it." *What the fuck are you saying? You barely know this guy. This is* so *presumptuous.*

Yet, as soon as the words were out, I didn't regret them.

Especially because, slowly, he moved toward me. He held out his hand.

I took it.

"You're very kind, Danny." He offered a slightly crooked smile. "But you said we could talk about you. About this secret you're holding in that's about to burst out."

As much as I wanted to keep the closeness and create a space for him to open up about his life, I didn't have the qualifications to help him emotionally. I saw his pain. For all his stoicism, moments flitted by when his pain flickered across his face. Still, I did need to unburden. And maybe helping me would be the best thing for Rob, would even the scales a bit. Best for me, too. I'd told Whitney, obviously, but no one else. "Maybe we can sit?"

"Sure." His gray eyes flashed compassion as he

indicated we should make our way to the living room. If we were quiet, the kids wouldn't hear.

To my surprise, he didn't let go of my hand. Instead, he tugged me down next to him. He turned his body toward me, open in a way he'd never been before. Part of me acknowledged that level of trust. He had no reason to believe I wouldn't hurt him. Yet he clearly did. And that warmed something inside me. I drew in a deep breath. "You know Colin's sick."

He nodded. "Everyone being protective of him was a pretty good clue…but he doesn't look well. I take it that the situation's serious."

I winced. "Yeah. Close to critical. He needs a liver transplant. As soon as possible." I let those words sink in.

"And James is donating…" He cocked his head. "You're donating."

"Yeah, I am. It's complicated, but I'm donating to someone who needs a liver, and their friend is donating to Colin. Well, half a liver. And it'll grow back. The risks are pretty minimal—"

"But there are risks." He gripped my hand. "All major surgery involves risk."

"Pretty much."

"When?"

"The first of January."

He held my gaze. "What does your family think of this? Mama? James?" His eyes flashed. "Colin? They don't know, do they? Because they'd try to talk you out of it? Hell, if I didn't know you as well as I do, I'd try to talk you out of it."

If I didn't know you as well as I do… Did he know me that well? As I pondered the question, the answer of *hell, yes* came up. We'd spent little time in each other's company, yet I felt like I knew him and I was certain he knew me. I was mostly an open book—I didn't try to hide who I was. Except... I cleared my throat. "Colin would try to talk me out of it. The rest of the family would fuss and smother me. Plus, I'm also taking a semester off school. That's not likely to go over well."

"That makes sense." Rob tilted his head. "But the transplant's not the only reason, is it?"

"Nothing gets past you."

"Lots get past me." His voice held a tinge of bitterness. "Otherwise I would've seen the monster I married before we brought two kids into the mix."

No one today had commented on his still-purple nose. Joe, Alec, and Kevin had been respectful. Plus, not everyone who had a broken nose had been hit. Things happened. People really did walk into walls and doors. That was a thing.

"We can all be deceived."

He looked away.

"Rob." Said quietly.

Slowly, after what felt like an eternity, he met my gaze again. I had to offer the truth as I saw it. "What's going on?."

"He didn't touch the children." Clearly, he needed me to understand.

Understanding dawned. I saw it in his eyes. "But he was about to. And that's why you intervened."

He blinked several times then, finally, nodded. "Yeah." He cleared his throat. "But we were talking about you. When are you going to tell your family? Christmas is—"

"Never, if I can avoid it."

"Danny." His chastisement was clear.

"Why? Why do I have to tell them? Colin's going to get his new liver. I'll stay with Whitney until I'm better."

"And tell your parents what, exactly? Don't you visit

them regularly? And won't they notice if you're not in school?"

"I, uh, plan to lay low until I'm feeling a bit better. Then tell them."

Rob barked out a laugh. "And you think your parents aren't going to notice you're not in school?"

"Hey. You sound like you know my family." Because yeah, if they thought I was in trouble they would totally do that.

He arched that damn eyebrow again.

"Well…by then it'll be too late. Colin will have his liver. I'll recover. I'll go back to school for the spring semester, and everything will be as it's supposed to be."

"That sounds awfully neat and tidy."

I shrugged.

Still, he held my hand. "I might be naïve about a lot of things. I might not have seen much of the world."

"Okay…"

"But I've learned that things rarely go as planned."

I gulped.

Rob offered the couch that night, but I really did need to get back to LA. I resisted the urge to hug him goodnight. I waved goodbye and headed my car north.

Have I just made a big mistake or is saving Colin's life worth it?

CHAPTER 12

ROB

I hadn't expected to be invited to Christmas at the Wexler-Rodrigues family celebration but, as I sat and enjoyed eggnog while Alicia and Zayden played with Thomas, I was able to breathe. Just like when I'd been with Danny, I felt weirdly secure with these near-strangers.

Gerard was out on bond but, with lawyer Wynn Cavanah's help, I'd secured a restraining order. I worried Gerard might figure out Wynn was from Gaynor Beach and come after us here, but Wynn used a lawyer friend in LA to file the formal paperwork. No chance, he promised, that I could be tracked here.

Anthony had helped me disable the tracking on my phone in LA that first night and, last week, had helped me acquire a new one. I'd migrated my meager few contacts, then carefully texted James, Colin, and Danny with the new number. Anthony had a friend in the police department who was happy to recycle the old phone. My ex had always been prodigiously careful about what he put in writing—so I didn't have incriminating texts or emails from him. He always issued his threats in person. He was efficient that way. And paranoid. Which stood him in good stead. I could attest to his vicious verbal attacks and threats in the last few months—but I had no witnesses or anything in writing. I could point out he'd broken my nose—but he maintained I'd walked into a door and was blaming him so I could take his children away.

So far, it appeared the cops in LA—including Officer Greenaway—weren't buying what he was selling. But it was only a matter of time, as far as I was concerned, before someone bought his story. He'd acquired a lawyer, after all. Someone who would back him up when he said he'd never laid a finger on me or the children. Hallie's bruises, he maintained, were my doing. Not his.

"Hey, you okay?" Scott's concerned voice reached me. "I asked if you wanted some cider or hot chocolate. It's a mild day, but I'm from Oklahoma and used to freezing my nuts off at Christmas. So a hot beverage is kind of a tradition."

"I'm from Missouri. Not a tradition in my family. Uh, hot chocolate would be nice."

"Great, let me—"

"I'll come with you."

Hallie and the twins were absorbed in a building-block game of some kind—one only they understood.

Thomas was fast asleep in Anthony's arms.

Laura, Anthony's nine-year-old, read a book she'd gotten for Christmas while leaning against Anthony. Periodically she would stroke Thomas's leg. She clearly adored the little ones.

Anthony offered me a broad grin, making it clear he was happy and had everything under control.

Today, I was breathing more easily. The constant panic had abated a little while being here. We were three grown men, and although two of us were on the smaller side, we had enough might to deal with any threat from Gerard. I just didn't feel I had that same protection when I was alone with the kids.

Scott gently pointed the way to the kitchen, and I followed him.

Heavenly scents assailed me as I walked in. "You're certain there's nothing I can do?"

He shook his head as he got the milk out of the fridge. "Those rolls you brought are perfect." He gave me a sheepish grin. "I might've tried one."

"I brought a dozen. They're Danny's mom's recipe."

As he poured milk into mugs, Scott cocked his head.

"What?"

"Interesting that you refer to her as Danny's mom instead of James's." He put the milk back in the fridge and took out some sweetened cacao powder.

"I could've said James." Heat slowly crept into my cheeks.

He stirred the chocolate into the milk. "And it's okay that you said Danny. I just…" He stopped. "You've mentioned him a couple of times today. You probably don't even realize you're doing it. Of course, I'm hoping something might come of your friendship. That Danny might…" He scrunched his nose. "I want to say heal, but that's wrong. Anthony would give me a stern talking-to about that."

"Oh?"

"I hope you can each give the other some support. I'm not sure what's going on with Danny, but I think he needs a friend, and you do too. Someone to be there while you do the hard emotional work ahead."

"Work?" I was pretty sure I knew what he meant, but I didn't really want to hear it. I needed to, though, which was why I stayed.

And because I really wanted hot chocolate. Although I sensed if I shut down the conversation, he'd take the hint —he seemed like that kind of guy.

"Like…" He put the mug into the microwave. "I can tell you, without breaking confidence, that Anthony had a tough time with how his brother, sister, and mother died. And when his past caught up with him, he had to make some horrible, difficult decisions on how to deal with things. Whether to move forward or stay stuck in the past." The microwave beeped, and he removed the mug. "Let it cool." He placed the mug before me.

"Sure." I met his green-eyed gaze. "And?"

"And he had to choose whether to hold on to past angers, and past regrets, or to move forward. It helped that, by then, he had me and the twins to consider. I was prepared to give him all the space in the world, but…" He put the other mug in the microwave and turned it on. "I was able to offer him a home. A safe harbor. I had my own shit to deal with—my family and all that. I was, ironically, in a better place than him. And once I was able to deal with the twins' mom—a good friend no less, but with some rough choices of her own to figure out—then I had my future set. I was lucky he chose to be part of that."

"I can't see either of you alone."

"God willing, we won't ever be." He laughed. "I don't believe in my parents' God. Just that there's something more powerful than me in the universe. Nature?" He pointed to his beautiful and lush backyard. "We sure didn't have this beauty during the winter in Oklahoma."

"Snow can be beautiful."

The microwave dinged. Scott removed his mug and put it on the counter. "Sure. When it first falls and it's pristine white. Then you have to shovel it. It turns mushy, dirty, and slushy. Or it freezes and turns to ice. I've fallen on my ass more than a few times over the years—but not once since I arrived in SoCal. I'm never going back." He held my gaze. "For any reason."

"That's fair. It's, uh…" I ventured a sip and broke into a wide grin. "This is delicious."

"For a powder mix, it really is. I've done the whole melt-a-chocolate-bar thing, but that's tons of work, and I just don't have the patience." He cocked his head. "What were you going to say?"

"Just…how similar our backgrounds are. I mean, I don't know yours exactly, but we both came from the middle of the country and wound up out here."

"And we've both found happiness with beautiful children." He ventured a sip. "You're a great dad, Rob. It's so damn obvious how much you love those kids. They're damn lucky to have you."

I swallowed, trying to rid myself of the lump in my throat. "I don't always feel that way. I wonder…"

Scott held my gaze.

"I mean…their moms, although great people, couldn't care for them. But I wonder if they might've found better people to adopt their babies. People more…stable. I worry about what these first years have done to them."

He waved off my concern. "That's valid, but you love them. They've always had that love, whatever else was going on. You'll get things sorted, and everything will be fine."

"You don't *know* that." I persisted because I was all about pessimism these days. I didn't have his optimism.

"Well, when do you see Danny again?"

I cocked my head. "I don't know. He's…going to be very busy for the next little while."

"School?" He took another sip.

Fuck. "Something like that." They weren't my secrets to

share. "Anyway, I need to get my problems solved myself. Like getting a job. And finding a babysitter."

Anthony walked into the kitchen at that exact moment. "I've changed his diaper, but I think he wants—"

I had the hot chocolate set down on the counter and Thomas in my arms in an instant. I met Anthony's gaze over my son's head. "Thank you."

He tossed the folded used diaper in the garbage under the sink. "I'll remember to take that out shortly." He met my gaze. "My pleasure. I remember what the twins were like at that age. My favorite thing was just to have them lie on my chest."

"Because that was the only time they stopped moving." Scott rolled his eyes. "Holy terrors. Both of them."

"They seem so well-behaved now."

Even as I said the words, a howl came from the living room.

Scott grabbed his hot chocolate. "I'll get that." Within a moment, he disappeared.

I watched as Anthony opened the fridge, grabbed a jug of water, then closed the door. He found a glass, poured some water, then put the jug back in the fridge. After all that, he leaned against the counter and regarded me. "You said you need a job?"

I shifted uncomfortably. "Uh, yeah. I need to be independent, you know?"

"Sure…" He appeared to consider. "I was talking to Oscar the other day. He's the vet tech at the Gaynor Beach Animal Hospital."

"I don't know anything about animals." I loved them, but they also scared me. Zelda and Widget were okay, but unknown animals? Not my jam.

"Well, you wouldn't be dealing with the animals." He took a long pull of water and swallowed. "He was saying they've had trouble finding reliable help to clean the clinic after hours. I know it's not glamorous—"

"I'll take it."

"—work." He held my gaze. "It's tough work. The pay's decent, but you can't do a half-assed job. Otherwise, I can see if Hugh, Oscar's husband, knows of anything at the hospital. Orderlies get paid a good salary, but that's hard work as well."

"I can do hard work." I stood a little taller. "Just because I've never had a job—"

"You've raised two kids." He offered a smile. "That's a job, Rob. Don't ever doubt that. They're happy and healthy. That speaks to dedication and hard work. The only problem is the job is in the evening and Corey doesn't run Charmers Daycare after hours. I can see if she can recommend someone…"

"Could you?" I scratched my head. "But I don't see how I can pay someone a decent childcare wage and cover everything else."

"Oscar said they pay a good wage." His deep-brown eyes held my gaze. "James isn't going to raise your rent. So you need to make certain you have enough to take care of your kids. The clinic will offer benefits after your probationary period, so you'll have good insurance coverage. Dr. Louisa's a great boss, and I think you'll really like Oscar. His daughter Marilee is just a year older than the twins. And he and Hugh have a foster son as well that they're looking at adopting."

"Another gay couple." I shook my head. "I've never met so many."

"Oh?"

I winced. "That sounds bad. But…" I swallowed. "I didn't know anyone back home, and Gerard didn't let me meet anyone. There was one guy on our street. Well, a couple. But I really only knew Jake. He worked from home and did much of the child rearing because his husband travelled a lot. He didn't mind, right, because they were so happy. And they had two great kids, and you did not need to know all that."

"Maybe not. But knowing where you've come from isn't a bad thing. You'll find tons of gay and lesbian couples in Gaynor Beach. You don't have to feel isolated anymore."

"And you can help me with getting this job?"

"I can definitely get you an interview. And I might have a lead on a babysitter. Oscar's sister, Lacy, does that sometimes. Let me ask him if she can help out, even if just temporarily. And she's attending the high school, so she might know other students looking for a bit of pocket money."

"That…" I floundered. "Sounds so easy." I pressed a kiss to Thomas's head even as he drowsed against me.

Anthony cocked his head. "Because sometimes things can go your way. Sometimes people who need help can reach out and it's there. And I don't just mean you. Oscar and Louisa are desperate. They need someone diligent and reliable. The last company charged them a huge amount and didn't do a good job. The salary they're offering is competitive. I've seen how spotless you keep your house, even with two little kids. You'd do well. Cleaning isn't glamorous—"

"It's what I know." Heat flushed my cheeks. "It's what I'm good at."

"Okay. And, when things are more stable, you might consider babysitting other people's children. You'd have to do a background check." He pointed to my healing nose. "And you need to be recovered…but there are never enough daycare spots. I'm not suggesting you open your own, but taking in a kid or two a couple of hours a week or more could boost your resources. You're already watching your two." He shook his head. "But you're going to be working on your GED."

"I can do both. It's a great idea." The GED felt so damn far away. But babysitting another child—especially one who could play with my kids—sounded doable.

"Well, we might keep you in mind." Anthony grinned. "I've been trying to talk Scott into a weekend away. We each get a couple of days off for Christmas, but it's never enough. And, all that being said, as the supervisor of social services in town, I'm on call if my social worker who's working needs help."

"You never really get a break." Paying me would probably be a conflict of interest, but I could definitely offer to do it as a thank you for all they'd given to me.

He shrugged. "Sometimes. But if I spirited my husband hundreds of miles away, we might actually be able to breathe."

"Funny...I've been saying that to myself a lot lately— that I need to breathe."

"Well, think about it. Laura would be here, and as much as I say she needs to just be a kid, she also derives a lot of her self-worth from helping with the twins. She's mostly healed from her injuries, but her recovery was aided by the incentive that the sooner she got better, the more she could interact with the toddlers. We didn't let her push, but we didn't hold her back either."

"Ah, tricky balance. I get that."

"Yeah. She's thriving."

"Did you get her counseling? Or did you handle that yourself?"

Anthony shook his head. "I'd never attempt therapy with my own child." He smiled. "Your kids have an appointment with Dr. Coral Llewellyn after Christmas, right?"

"Yes. It'll be their second appointment. She saw them two days after we came to town, and she wanted to see them again. Do you think she could recommend someone?"

"For certain. I can as well. Also…" He took another drink of water. "If it comes down to some kind of dispute about what happened that night, the courts might want Hallie to speak to a psychiatrist. We have a good one in town—Dr. Xavier Martin. He's in general practice, so he's dealt with kids and adults. I've never hesitated to encourage a client to seek him out."

I felt lightheaded. "They won't make her testify, will they? And her memory's probably getting fuzzy, if not completely gone."

Anthony gave me a long, level look. "She's traumatized, so it's entirely possible she'll have recall issues. Or she remembers everything and hasn't processed it. Let's see what Dr. Llewellyn says, and then we'll find someone for Hallie to talk to."

Maybe we should've done it sooner. Even though I wanted to forget the whole thing and pretend like it never happened. Maybe that was unrealistic wishful thinking. As we finished our visit, though, I pushed all thoughts of that from my mind.

CHAPTER 13

DANNY

"I'm fine. Stop fussing." I glared at James.

Who glared right back. "You just fucking donated, like, half your liver."

I winced. I did *not* need to be reminded of that fact, lying here in a hospital bed a couple of hours after major surgery.

Even though my brother wore a mask, his displeasure was clear. The mask was more for Colin's sake than mine. With his weakened immune system, he was way more in danger than me. "Look—"

"Are you seriously going to try to justify your actions? Lying to Mama, to us?"

"You wanted Colin to die?"

James eyes widened, and he pressed a hand to his chest.

In return, I pressed my advantage. "Yeah, some other donor might've died, and he might've gotten an organ that way. But I was healthy. Another guy needed a donation I could provide. His buddy had part of one to spare for Colin. Pretty decent fellow, I'd say—"

"Danny—"

"—and I had half to spare as well. Look, we both know I was happy to do this. As long as I take it easy, I'll be fine. I have Whitney to look after me."

"Jesus Fucking Christ, Danny, she's had three fish die."

"Well…" I'd known this would be an uphill battle. "I'm not incompetent myself, James. Darling brother. I'll take my pills and rest. She can feed me. If not, I can do takeout. There are healthy options—"

He waved his hands in the air. "No way. No fucking way."

I squinted. "You realize that you don't swear, right? That you're always afraid Mama will wash your mouth out with—"

"Mama's not fucking here." He pointed to the phone on the bedside table. "But she will be in just over an hour. Make the call, Danny, or I will."

"Aren't they coming tomorrow to see Colin?" I was certain they'd wanted to come today, but Colin needed more time to recuperate. Just like I did before I faced the wrath of the two people I pretty much loved most in the world. I carried on about Mama, but Daddy was just as important. And as capable to flare to anger. We were…a passionate family. "And anyway, there's a big rainstorm. They shouldn't be driving in this weather. I promise I'll call in the morning." I yawned. "Or you can."

James scratched my scalp—something he'd been doing practically since I was born. Much the way Gracie did. Less as I grew older, and not when I'd gone through my afro phase. But clearly he needed the contact.

And apparently so did I.

He left, and I drifted off.

Several times I woke in the night. Usually when a nurse was checking on me.

In the morning, Whitney flitted in, gave me the once-over, then pronounced she had some video she had to watch and she'd do it in the cafeteria so as not to disturb me. Then she vanished.

Great. No nagging about calling Mama and Daddy.

At least I'd been granted a reprieve.

I was eyeing the gelatin the hospital had given me for breakfast when Gracie breezed in. I dropped my spoon back on the tray.

She glared.

Feeling like self-preservation was important, I shrugged. "Where's Widget?" She was babysitting the dog while Colin was in the hospital.

"With my neighbor. Don't change the subject."

"Uh…okay."

She advanced toward me. Aside from James, she was the sister I was closest to. And probably the one I should've approached to take care of me. But Whitney said she'd do it, and…that had just felt simpler. Better than having to deal with Gracie's ire.

"I'm fine."

She pressed the back of her hand to my forehead—as Mama had done a million times before when she thought I was coming down with something.

I swatted her hand away.

"You call Mama yet?" She glared.

"No." I nabbed the spoon and poked the orange gelatinous substance. At least they'd picked my favorite flavor. Because lime was just gross.

"Daniel."

My gaze shot to hers. No one in the family called me Daniel. That just wasn't a thing. Which was why it'd been weird for me to tell Rob that was my name. On my birth certificate, certainly, but nowhere else in the family lexicon.

Thinking of Rob gave me a pang.

And reminded me that I hadn't texted him yet. I'd been out of it last night and dealing with sisters this morning.

"Grace Ann."

She glared.

Yeah, another name never mentioned. She loathed her full name.

Wearily, I pressed a hand to my forehead. I couldn't tell if I was getting a headache because I needed more painkillers or if the stress of dealing with her was pushing me over the edge. "I'll call them."

Her eyes flashed triumph.

"Can you go see how Colin's doing? I don't know where he is."

She waved her hand. "He's in the room next door. They told James and me that when we arrived. He had a good night." She placed her hand on her hip. "You'll call."

"Only if you leave."

After harrumphing, she left.

I breathed. Then, instead of calling, texted Mama.

While I waited for the explosion, I texted Rob.

Who shot back a request to call me.

Since Mama hadn't yet, I said sure. Seconds later, my phone rang. "Hello."

"Oh, Danny, I was so worried. And then I told myself you'd just had major surgery, and you didn't need to think about calling me." His voice quavered.

"I'm sorry." I winced. "James figured it out last night, and I had to deal with him. Then I fell asleep. I meant to text you first thing, but then Whitney arrived. Gracie just left and I texted Mama and then you—"

"How'd your mother take it? Because you didn't tell her, right?"

He'd suggested, in a text two days ago, that I should really reconsider that stance.

I hadn't listened.

And I didn't regret my decision, but I was also keenly aware my parents were going to be hurt.

My phone buzzed with an incoming call. Along with that, my heart sank. "I have to go."

"Of course. Call me later. If you're not too tired. Or text or…"

"I will. Bye." I'd almost said I loved him. Which would've made no sense to anyone except a Reynolds. We always told each other that we loved each other. Because that's what families did. And, somehow, I felt Rob was connected to our family. Through living in James's house. Through Mama sending him a care package for Christmas. Through me—

The phone buzzed again. I swiped to answer. "Hey Mama."

And so, the interrogation began.

A few minutes later, totally exhausted, I offered a smile to the nurse who precipitously arrived.

She eyed my food.

I shrugged. Then I tried to swing my legs out of bed.

"Whoa. Hold up. Where do you think you're going?"

"To see Colin. I need to know he's okay."

"He's fine. My co-worker is caring for him. Just like I'm caring for you."

I met her gaze. "Please. I just…my family's going to be here soon, and I won't have time with him. I need to know he's okay. I mean, I can just walk—"

She bit her lower lip. "All right. In a wheelchair. But only because Dr. Milson said you're doing well."

Dr. Milson was Colin's hepatologist. Since Dr. Patton, my surgeon, had been called into an urgent surgery, Colin's doctor had checked me out this morning. She was pleased with my progress.

The nurse offered a smile. "I'll get a wheelchair. Don't move."

I didn't…but I did shoot off a quick text to James. If Colin wasn't up for company, he'd let me know.

Two minutes later, as the nurse helped me into the wheelchair, James stepped into the room. "Oh, no. No way. He had major surgery yesterday. This is completely—"

"Oh, shut the fuck up, James."

His jaw snapped shut as he met the nurse's gaze. She broke the silence stare-off. "He said he'd walk by himself. I don't want to tie him to the bed, so this is the safest alternative."

"I'm fine. Honest to God, I'm fine." I watched as my nurse fussed with my IV.

"You might be fine…" James started to speak.

I held up my finger. "Do not make me regret doing this."

His eyes went wide, likely with hurt.

I grunted. "Sorry. That was uncalled for. I just…had a bad phone call with Mama and Daddy."

He snickered. "You think that was bad? Wait until they show up."

"Which is why I want to see Colin first. Then…I'll deal with the fallout."

James offered a smile to the nurse. "I can take him."

She nodded back. "Ten minutes. No stress. I'm counting on you." She gave him a stare.

He nodded vigorously.

Yeah, he'd care for me. He might also kill me for putting him through this—but we'd come out the other end. We always did.

He rolled me into Colin's room, and my resolve to be

strong broke. He was sitting up in bed and...looking good. So much better than I'd ever seen him.

I did that. I helped save his life. I couldn't find the words. So when James pushed me close enough, I took Colin's hand.

Our gazes held for a long, long time. He was, as far as I'd ever seen, a stoic guy. He didn't express feelings easily. At Christmas, when my family'd given him a scrapbook with photos from our past, he'd nearly broken. His resolve crumbling in that moment had been clear to me. Because he'd understood we saw him as an honorary Reynolds. One of us. No matter what happened between him and James, we'd claimed him.

I blinked back tears.

Then, to ruin the moment, James smacked me on the arm—our family thing. Although lightly, given my health status. "Taking a semester off school?"

I managed a watery laugh. "If you saw last semester's grades, you wouldn't be surprised. Things aren't going well for me right now."

James perched on Colin's bed, holding my gaze. "What are you saying? That pre-med isn't for you?"

I winced and shook my head. "Even this—" I pointed between Colin and myself. "—isn't enough to motivate me. It's the science classes. They're destroying my soul. Biochem is the worst. I got, like, sixty-six or something. That's not going to get me into any med school in the country. Or, at least in California."

"If you want to go to an out-of-state school," Colin said, "just let me know where to send the check. And living expenses and money to travel home for holidays, of course."

I balked. "That's...beyond generous. And not why I donated." He needed to know that. Judging by the SUV he

drove and the area he lived in down in Gaynor Beach, I'd
suspected he had some money. But that wasn't why I'd
given him the chance to live. If he'd been poor, I still
would've done it. I was doing this as much for James as I
was for him.

"Of course not." Colin grinned. "Because I doubt
James told you how rich I am."

James stuck his fingers in his ears. "La la la la la. I don't
want to know."

I laughed. Then winced as a pang shot through my
stitched-up middle. *Fucking ouch.*

"Okay, and on that note, I'm taking you back to your
room." James started to rise.

"Can't I just have one more minute?" I might've
whined that.

James shook his head. "Hey, at least you'll be out of the
hospital for your birthday."

"Yeah, but no alcohol." I didn't grouse the words,
though, I grinned. I didn't care that I couldn't drink again.
Well, a sip now and then would be okay, but serious booze
would endanger me in a way I wasn't willing to do—I had
too much to live for.

"You're going to be legal."

I laughed at his expression. Then put on a somber
expression. "I have to take care of my liver, so no alcohol."

"I'm sorry for that." Colin winced.

"I'm not." I grinned. "I always wanted a legit excuse
not to overindulge." I squeezed Colin's hand. "You've
given me one."

"Thank you." Colin blinked several times. "I can't—"

I blinked. Then waved him off. "Do good in the world.
Make an honest man out of my brother. Then we're even."

Colin's gaze shot to James.

Have I overstepped?

After a moment, though, he smiled. "I can promise to do that."

"Good." I glared at James. "Take me back to bed so I can look weak and done in when Mama and Daddy arrive."

James groaned. "Do that, and I'll be in even more trouble."

I cocked my head and blinked.

"I'm sure they'll think I knew about this." James's mouth drooped dejectedly.

I released Colin's hand to grasp his. "They won't. I'll set them straight. Dr. Milson will set them straight. I did this of my own accord and on my own terms."

"Speaking of Dr. Milson…" James grabbed the handles of my wheelchair and pushed me toward the door. "Have I got a story to tell you."

As he pushed me out of Colin's room, I glanced up at him. "What?"

"You know Dr. Milson?"

"Yeah." I scratched the back of my hand, near the tape holding my IV in place.

He smacked my hand. "Don't."

"Right." I glared. "Dr. Milson…"

As he pushed me back into my room, he chuckled. "I think…"

"Oh my God, bro, just spit it out."

He locked the wheels in place and held a hand out for me. I appreciated he wasn't bothering a nurse for this. I could certainly be careful and they were always so busy.

"Yesterday Daddy showed Dr. Milson a photo of Gracie and Widget." James helped me slip onto the bed and then pulled the covers up to settle on top of me.

"So Dr. Milson got to see Widget. She is, truly, the cutest dog ever."

James grabbed a jug of water and poured me a glass. "I don't think Dr. Milson even noticed Widget."

I took the glass from him and was about to sip, then the meaning of what he said sunk in. "You're saying…?"

"Well…" He grinned. "If the looks Dr. Milson and Gracie were giving each other this morning in Colin's room were any indication, I'd say there was definite interest."

"Is that…" I sipped, considered, and then continued. "Like a patient code violation or something?"

"Colin pointed out that Gracie's not *his* sister." James fluffed my pillow even though it didn't really need fluffing. "If it is, I know Gracie will back off. Colin's health comes first."

Naturally. But our sister also liked to push up against, or even break, rules. "You might want to just make certain." I met James's gaze. "This is too important. Gracie's a flirt. She's never taken anything seriously. Well, except her acting career." Our sister enjoyed dalliances—much like I did. James was the opposite of that. I'd once told him I thought he was demi. I still did…and, to me, his intense relationship with Colin was proof of that. He'd just needed to meet the right guy.

Would Gracie settle down if she met the right woman?

Would I settle down if I met the right person?

And why did that question not scare me as much as it used to?

"You little shit." Mama's voice carried from the door as she bustled in, Daddy hot on her heels. She advanced toward me with anger in her eyes. Anger I rarely saw. Flames shot out of her ears.

"I can—"

"Explain? Oh, I bet you can. You're always good with all your *explanations*. Dropping out of school. Major surgery…" She blinked several times. "Are they taking care of you? Who's your doctor?" She gazed around as if she could magically make someone appear.

And someone did. My nurse strode in. "What's all that noise?" She put her hands on her hips and looked at me. "I told you to take it easy."

Mama moved to my side and placed her hand on my head. At least she didn't scratch my scalp—although undoubtedly that would come later. "I apologize."

She didn't look the least bit contrite.

Daddy slowly advanced toward the nurse. "We're Danny's parents. You might or might not know that he didn't tell us he'd…chosen to…" He sniffed.

"Be a hero?" The nurse gazed back and forth between my parents. "He said his sister Whitney would take care of him. Although I haven't seen her lately, and—"

"What nonsense." Mama waved the woman off. "He's coming home with us."

"Yeah," Daddy gave me the side-eye. "Because his mother would never forgive herself if something happened because he wasn't getting the best care."

Well, shit. As much as I loved my sister, Mama and Daddy were probably better choices.

By the end of the discussion, I'd agreed to come home and let her spoil me while I recovered. Hey, the cat was out of the bag, so it came down to Whitney's not-so-tender care, or Mama's love and cooking. Not a hard choice at all. Even if I'd have to listen to her praise my self-sacrifice and complain about my stubborn ridiculousness together in one breath for weeks.

CHAPTER 14

ROB

LANDING THE JOB AT GAYNOR BEACH ANIMAL HOSPITAL proved easy. Oscar, the amiable vet tech, introduced me to Dr. Louisa Blair, the veterinarian, as well as her nephew Dr. José Blair, the newest vet to join the practice. Christa was the receptionist and Marisol was the office manager everyone spoke of, but people rarely met. She poked her head out of her office, welcomed me to the team, reminded me to submit my paperwork, and disappeared again. Oscar said usually the office manager was in charge of hiring, getting references, setting up the hours—pretty much everything that didn't involve vet work. With my not having references to provide—except Anthony—Dr. Louisa was more concerned about the fit with the rest of the staff. As long as I did my job, everyone would be happy.

And relieved.

Oscar assured me I'd never have a problem with a paycheck or a reimbursement claim—but if I did, Marisol would fix it immediately.

My head spun at all the new people.

In the clinic, working my third night on the job, I shook my head as I mopped the floor. Now I was about to sanitize and clean all the other surfaces thoroughly. I liked this. Being self-supporting for the first time in my life. Gerard had made it clear I'd never be able to do this. But I was. And I felt damn good about it. Even proud, although I knew pride was not always a good thing. *Pride goes before the fall.*

I also worried about failing. Some disaster was right around the corner. I could feel it. That always happened. And what would Gerard say to my kids about me being a janitor? That job might be looked down on by some people, but I was damn happy for the great paycheck, fabulous coworkers, and potential raise and benefits if I did a good job.

So I'd do a fucking good job.

Still, I was lonely. I wrung the mop out, let the dirty water run down the drain, and contemplated my life as I looked at all the cleaning left to do. When my cell phone rang, I yanked it out of my back pocket. *Danny.* "Hello? Is everything okay?"

"Yo."

I laughed. "Seriously, that's my greeting?"

"When I know it's you." His low-rumbled chuckle came through clearly. "What are you doing?"

"Cleaning the autoclave."

"The whata what?" He yawned.

"It's the machine that sterilizes all the equipment. Seriously, does so much work in just a few minutes. But it needs to be cleaned as well, and that's part of my job." I had Danny on speaker so I could keep working."

"Cool. I know what an autoclave is. I was just…" He yawned again. "How are things working out with Nai?" Oscar's sister Lacy wasn't able to fit babysitting for me into her jam-packed schedule, but she recommended her friend, Nai.

"She's great. Although I don't like keeping a high school senior up so late, she insists she's a night owl and does her best studying long after dark. She also has a spare period first thing in the morning, and so she can sleep in." I sprayed disinfectant on the counters and got to work. "I met her parents in person, wanting them to know me. Also, in a stroke of pure luck, she lives just a block away from me." I sighed. This was harder than I'd ever thought possible.

And I wasn't talking about the cleaning.

"Hallie took to her right away, the first time we did a trial run. She was fascinated by Nai's intricate braids." I blinked. "Then I realized Hallie has almost never spent time with a woman. She doesn't have any fear to unlearn. Thomas, of course, loves everyone."

"Talk about fearless. Yeah, he's a good guy."

"Anyway, I'm not happy having Nai walking home in the dark when I'm done with work, but it's Nai's preference —complete with a lecture about saving the environment— and her parents said a block in a quiet neighborhood was fine. She keeps her phone on and talks to me as she walks so I can be sure she always gets home safe." I scrubbed the cupboards. "The pay I offered her isn't great, but she wants to become a teacher and so, by tutoring Hallie, she'll earn a glowing reference from me."

Tutoring my four-year-old.

"How did things go with the DA?"

"Huh? Oh, right." I'd forgotten telling him about this. "Uh, the assistant district attorney from LA, Carlin DiFrancesco, drove down to meet with me." I checked the autoclave to make sure it had enough distilled water. "She's a smart, no-nonsense woman, and she admitted her department is hoping for a plea that includes jail time—but that Gerard's lawyer is aiming for a dismissal as my ex continues to maintain I walked into a door and am using the abuse allegation as an excuse to keep the children away." Every time I heard about his lawyer claiming a door broke my nose, I had a flash of Gerard's fist coming at my face. The burst of pain, and then the burst of clarity that the time to run had come. Gerard could tell the judge I was trying to take *his* children. Well, maybe I'd ask them to have him demonstrate changing a diaper in the courtroom. Something he had never once done for *his* children. And yet, he had the money, the fancy representation, the big house with the pool. Would the court pay more attention to those than who loved the kids?

"That's such bullshit." Danny's anger rang through the phone clearly.

"Well, she swore she hadn't been followed, and I tried to believe her." I held back the rest, not wanting to upset him. But after she left, I kept expecting Gerard to burst in. I jumped at every noise outside and was continually checking windows and doors.

"Okay…that sounds rough. How's Hallie handling this?"

"That's another thing." I sighed because things just kept moving forward at breakneck speed. "I agreed to allow Hallie to see a psychologist. A guy who's new to Gaynor Beach, Dr. Josiah Braithwaite. He's been assigned by the courts to determine Hallie's ability to be a witness—should that be necessary." I grabbed the phone and moved into the exam room where I started scrubbing the sink. "I haven't seen his report, but he suggested he wants to see Hallie periodically. Not to talk about the events leading up to Gerard's explosion, but just to ensure she's doing okay. I worried about the cost, Danny, but he said something about it being covered by the state."

I didn't believe him.

But his motives seemed to be about caring, not the money. He said Hallie was one of the most extraordinary children he'd ever met.

"Well, stuff like that can be sometimes. Take it for the gift it is and see that she gets whatever help she needs. This is all good, Rob. Moving forward."

Echoing the sentiment I'd just had. "There's more. Turns out I've truly been blind to my daughter's talents. While I believed she was just making up stories to match the pictures in her books, she can actually read many of them."

What kind of father doesn't realize his daughter can read basic words, for fuck's sake? How can I keep her safe when I don't even understand her?

Danny whistled. "I didn't see it either."

"I should have." I wanted to call myself a bad name, but I was really trying not to. When the sink was clean, I moved on to disinfecting the exam table. "Jesus, Danny, I haven't even asked how you're doing."

That low rumbly chuckle again. "Because nothing ever changes." He sighed "Mama's babying me—"

"As she should."

"And Daddy's finding movies and sports we can watch together. I swear, by the time I'm well enough to leave, I'll have watched everything on every streaming service that has ever been made."

I doubted that greatly, but his frustration was clear. "You have my sympathy. And my…I don't know. I want to say gratitude, but that's Colin's line. Just…I'm super proud of you. Which is also *super* cheesy." I grabbed the phone, the cleanser, and the cloth and headed into the second room and started disinfecting this one. "Speaking of Colin…" I was always scared to ask.

"He's fighting a scary postoperative infection. Nasty thing. But the liver's holding—for now."

"You're worried."

Another sigh. "Man, I'll worry forever about him. He and James are…"

"Are…" I prompted.

"I see Colin like family. We gave him a family album. We make one for every partner when it's clear they're staying. Rashon and Bryan were a little confused—as was Colin, I think. Shondra bawled for, like, twenty minutes. I don't want to stereotype…but those reactions seem pretty gender-specific."

"I've never heard of that tradition."

"It's a Reynolds thing." He yawned.

"You should be in bed."

"Naw, I'm a night owl. You almost done? What other gross things are you cleaning tonight?"

"Well, I found something nasty in the garbage—"

"Oh my God, I do not need to know."

I laughed. "You asked."

"Yeah, I did." His smile came through the phone line clearly.

My heart seized. I hadn't realized how important he was becoming to me.

Had become to me. "I need to say goodbye. I'm almost done."

"Yeah, okay. Take care on the way home."

"I will. Goodnight."

"Night." He cut the connection.

I finished that room, ensured I'd restocked the drawers and spray bottles properly, made certain the runs were clean, checked that the garbage cans were empty, did a last check of everything, clocked out on my timesheet, set the alarm, and headed out into the inky blackness. I locked the door, pocketed my keys, and began my walk home. Riverside wasn't far, and I couldn't afford a cab. I also still didn't have a car. Well, or a driver's license. Anthony had added that to the long list of things I needed to do. I pointed out I'd never be able to afford a car, gas, repairs, insurance, and everything else.

He said that might be true today, but my life could change.

I didn't believe him. Still, I planned to ask Nai to watch the kids one morning when she didn't have school, and I'd go down to the DMV. I'd been studying the manual for several weeks and almost felt ready to take the test. I had, when I turned sixteen. But that felt like a million years ago —and I'd lived in another state. Everything felt different in California.

Arriving home, I put the key in the lock and, with great weariness, turned it. As I stepped into the house, Nai rose from the couch to come over to greet me.

She grinned.

I smiled back. A brutally difficult thing to do, but I was obligated, as far as I was concerned. "How did it go?"

"Hallie wants to move past the reader Miss Agnes suggested."

Miss Agnes was the former grade-one teacher in Gaynor Beach. She was also an honorary grandmother to Oscar and Hugh's children, and she lived with them. When I'd spoken to Oscar about my fears with Hallie's intelligence—and how that might make her stand out—he brought Miss Agnes over. She did several informal assessments of Hallie and devised a plan to keep my daughter occupied.

"She's four," I whispered. Hallie still slept lightly and

often woke when I arrived home. I glanced down the hall and found her bedroom door almost shut and no sign of her.

Nai smiled. "There are plenty of appropriate books for her to read. Miss Agnes put together a list. She has some herself, and Dr. Hugh dropped those off on the way to the hospital. Most of the rest are available from the library, and Scott's going to drop more off tomorrow. We'll have at least a month's worth of reading."

My head spun. Dr. Hugh was an emergency medicine physician and Oscar's husband. Scott was the librarian, of course. Everyone kept stepping up and helping—all without me having to ask. I felt guilty at not being able to reciprocate…but also incredibly grateful Hallie was getting the support she needed. Support I couldn't offer.

"Thanks, Nai."

She nodded. "Do you want me to stay over and handle the kids in the morning? You look exhausted."

I could've wept at her offer.

But I also declined it. My children weren't her responsibility.

And, as much as I needed to sleep, I couldn't afford to pay her overnight.

I held up my phone.

Understanding my gentle refusal—and likely the gratitude that went with it—she packed up her schoolwork, saluted me, called me on her phone, and headed out.

As she carried on chatting about how great my kids were—which only made me tear up more—she walked the couple of blocks and, soon enough, I heard her unlock her door, step inside, and lock it. "Goodnight, Rob."

"Thanks, Nai."

This method wasn't foolproof, of course. But Gaynor

Beach was a safe town, and I could sprint and be out of the house and down the street within moments.

But then the kids would be alone.

My mind conjured up Gerard hiring someone to grab Nai. While I was racing to her rescue, he somehow got into the house and took the kids. The scenario was massively improbable…but not impossible. *I should find a way to pay for a cab for Nai.* It couldn't possibly be that expensive. Maybe I could get a discount since we did this six nights a week? She could've driven her dad's car, but it was the only one the family had, and the family needed it for any activities of her many younger siblings as well as for emergencies. If something happened at my house, her mom or dad could be over quickly, but both went to bed way earlier than I got home. Asking them to stay up wasn't fair either.

And I kept offering her a night off—figuring I could ask Scott for a favor—but she insisted she loved doing this. She had her Sunday nights off, so she planned to drag her friends out for something or other. She'd also confided she needed the money for college. A scholarship would only take her so far.

I, of course, panicked when I realized she'd be leaving in August. In fact, her schoolwork would be done in June and she might get bored with just hanging around and babysitting. Although she'd said something about getting ahead in her university studies…?

Most of the time I saw her, I was either racing out the door to get to work or coming home completely exhausted.

As I made my way to the kitchen, I contemplated a snack. I used up precious time while cleaning at the clinic to heat up and quickly eat a meal so I could keep up my strength. Anthony maintained I'd had a job for four years —caring for my kids—but I'd never done this kind of labor. At the mansion in LA, I'd organized cleaning so I did a bit each day—usually while the kids slept. I'd known exactly how to prepare all of Gerard's favorite meals, and had a timetable laid out. I could cook while I did other things. I multitasked.

In my current job, I just had to work hard and fast.

"Papa?"

Hallie caught me off guard, and I pressed a hand to my chest as I spun. I crouched. "Yes, sweetheart? Couldn't you sleep?"

"Bad dreams."

"Ah." I scooped her into my arms and settled her on my hip. She felt heavier than she had when we arrived. Part of that was just she was a growing child…but her appetite seemed to have improved. I spent less time bribing her to eat her food. That felt like a small victory. "How about some warm milk? I think I'd like some myself. And maybe a cookie?" I'd baked a couple of batches that morning while the kids watched a television program. I hated to use the TV as a babysitter, but I needed to keep the house spotless and always have plenty of healthy food on hand. Home-baked oatmeal and raisin cookies counted, as far as I was concerned. Anything to show authorities I could take care of my kids.

Hallie tucked her head against my shoulder as I moved us into the kitchen. If I could've made the warm milk with one hand, I totally would have. "Papa needs to put you down."

She yawned. "Okay."

I put her on a kitchen chair, then hustled into the living room, coming back a moment later with a fleece blanket to wrap around her. Then I moved to the fridge and pulled the milk out, steadying the jug while I unscrewed the tight cap. "How was your day? Did you read to Nai?"

"Yes." She drew patterns on the tabletop with her fingers. "Nai's nice."

"She is. And very smart." I put a small mug of milk in the microwave and turned it on. "You're smart too." I glanced over to her.

As I'd expected, she scrunched her nose. Somewhere along the way, she'd absorbed that girls weren't smart. I wanted to claim I didn't know where that assertion came from…but I also knew who her other father was. I thought he'd made the sexist remarks out of earshot but, as I learned every day, little ears heard everything.

The microwave beeped. I took the mug out and tested the temperature before gingerly giving it to Hallie. "Sips, okay?" The milk wasn't too hot, but it was warmer than she was used to. When I gave her chocolate milk, I tended to make it cold.

She sipped.

"Okay?"

She nodded.

I put my own mug in. "Lots of girls are smart. Nai's smart. You're smart. Miss Agnes is smart." To my frustration, Hallie still didn't have many women in her life. I hoped eventually to introduce her to Dr. Louisa down at the vet clinic. The amount of schooling required to be a vet blew my mind. And she still did continuing-education courses and stuff. Oscar said she was busy all the time. He had classes to do as well. I didn't want to be a vet, but I envied them for all the education stuff.

My phone buzzed in my back pocket as the microwave beeped.

As Hallie was absorbed in sipping her milk, I checked my message.

From Danny. Asking if I was home safe.

I popped off a quick reply and said I'd send something longer later on.

Pondering his claim that he'd become a night owl since his surgery, I smiled. Sleeping until noon and then staying up super late. Drove his mother nuts, but she also acknowledged he was an adult. I'd asked if he was preparing to go back to university in the spring semester, but he was evasive about that. I respected his silence on the topic. I also restrained myself from asking when he might come down to visit James and Colin. James looked harried when we'd run into each other at the grocery store, and said he'd only left Colin for a few minutes—at Colin's insistence. Apparently James was hovering.

I could see that. And I suspected Danny would've been doing the same for any partner of his. Just like I would have if my partner was ill. It was a good thing Danny did his recovery down in LA.

You don't have a partner.

"Papa?"

"Mmm?"

"Are you going to drink your milk?"

I blinked. "Of course, sweetheart." I did. Then I tucked Hallie into bed next to me, given she was still shaken from her *bad dreams*. In the end, I forgot to text Danny back.

CHAPTER 15

DANNY

"What do you mean, *do you want to move in with us?*" I stared at James and Colin.

Colin, who had some true color in his cheeks, sort of leaned against James as they sat on their couch. My brother just grinned.

"Uh…" I scratched my chin, regretting not having shaved. "You guys are pretty tight here. I mean, I get that it's a three-bedroom house—"

"In our new house." James offered the words smoothly.

Absently, I stroked Widget who'd decided I would be the human at her beck and call today which meant she sat on my lap and preened. I'd driven down from LA that morning, at James's request, and I wasn't going to show how tired I was. This recovery thing wasn't going as fast as I'd hoped. "What new house?" All of a sudden, I blinked. "Are those…wedding rings?"

James made a big show of getting out his wallet and handing Colin a twenty.

I cocked my head.

Colin tucked the cash into his jeans pocket. "I bet him

you'd notice in under an hour. He figured you'd leave without piecing it together at all."

I glared at my brother.

He grinned. Whether from the fact I'd damn nearly missed them—and cost him twenty bucks—or because he was…

"Married or engaged?"

"Engaged. February 14th." Colin got a sappy look on his face.

My jaw went slack as I was absolutely gobsmacked. "It's the eighteenth."

James nodded slowly as if to say *yes, dumbass, we know that…*

"You've been engaged for four days and didn't tell us?" My voice might've gone a little high on that. And I'd nearly said *me*, but realized Mama would've kicked my butt for not making it an entire Reynolds family thing.

"You knew I was going to." Colin stroked James's hand. "I asked their permission and Mama helped me arrange—"

I waved him off. "And you told us you were planning to…but…"

"But what?" James cocked his head "You, Gracie, Mama, and Daddy knew."

"That Colin was planning to propose…sure. But…" I pointed to the rings. "When were you going to share the news?"

"We wanted to tell everyone all at once. The next family gathering isn't until next weekend." James held my gaze.

When we were finally going to officially welcome Leticia and Bryan's twin girls to the family. They'd been born Christmas Day, premature, and had been in the hospital for several weeks. Then Martin's family had caught some virus, and then Whitney had taken ill, and… we just hadn't had a full family event in more than seven weeks—practically a new record. Oh, and Colin couldn't risk being exposed to some nasty virus or bacteria. He and James had visited us last weekend, but it'd just been them, Mama, Daddy, and me.

"And you're telling me first because you want me to move in with you?"

"In the new house." James snagged a piece of paper off the coffee table and handed it to me.

I whistled because the first thing I saw on the real estate spec sheet was the price. I eyed Colin. "This has to be you because, as successful as my cybersecurity business brother is, he hasn't made this kind of money."

Colin laughed. "I came into my inheritance in January. Plus, I made quite a lot of money in my old job as an investment banker. Most was tied up in long-term securities. I couldn't access it when I first came out here." He swung his hand around the house. "This is a great place—and we have plans for it—but we're ready for something bigger." He smiled at James. "We have plans."

"Plans?" I might've squeaked that.

"Like…" James eyed Colin.

Who shrugged.

"It's okay, you don't have to tell me." I almost joked about them getting another dog, but I couldn't help wondering if they meant kids. With Colin's still-precarious health, that had to be a weight on their minds, and any kids would be a ways off. I wouldn't add to the stress of revealing something they weren't ready to share. "So… why me?"

"Well…" Colin met my gaze. "We figured you might want…a fresh start. You said you want to take the online psychology program."

"Yeah. Which I really appreciate you being willing to pay for. I promise I'll pay you back—"

Colin cut off my verbal gush with a wave of his hand. "In case you haven't figured it out, I'm not short of money. And James contributes a bunch as well," he was quick to add.

"We have a basement suite," James added. "Which sounds less appetizing, but when you see it, you'll realize it's not like my old bedroom in Mama and Daddy's house." He yanked out his phone, swiped a few times, then handed it to me.

I slowly scrolled through the pictures of what appeared to be a spacious area. "This is a basement suite?"

"It's a walk out. So you'll have your own patio under our deck. There are plenty of windows as well. Lots of light."

"You don't have to sell me on it." I handed James back his phone. "This is incredibly generous—especially since I won't be able to pay much rent. I'm going to get a part-time—"

"No you're not." Colin scowled. "You're going to be a full-time student. Isn't that what you said?"

"Well, yeah, but…" I thought of all the little things that still needed to be paid—car insurance, gas, health insurance, books…

Colin visibly bristled, shifting in his seat.

"You okay?" James glanced at his future husband.

Oh my God, my brother's getting married.

"I'm fine. Just annoyed I didn't make it clear to Danny that he's getting a monthly stipend to pay all his expenses. Everything." Colin glared. "Don't argue. You want to study this program…that's great. I did the research. It's super intensive. A four-year undergraduate degree and a

Master's degree in just three years. You'll be going to school year-round and doing practicums."

James cocked his head. "That's…"

"Nuts," Colin supplied. "And I suspect you're doing this because you don't want to be dependent on me any longer than you have to." He directed that comment at me.

"Well, yeah…" I didn't want to take a penny from him. But I'd lost my scholarship to UCLA when I'd quit. I likely would've lost it at the end of the next semester because of my crappy grades, but this highly specialized program didn't have scholarships. At least none that I qualified for.

Colin again waved his hand in the air.

James snagged it and tucked it against his heart. "I think he gets the point. He donated a liver. You feel you owe him. He doesn't feel that way because he would've done it anyway. Okay, so you're both noble people. Great." He snuggled into Colin. "At least Colin's taking money from me, so I'm sort of helping my brother." He aimed a glance at me. "You're going to do good in the world as a psychologist. If you want to pay Colin back so badly when you've got your own practice, you can take pro bono patients."

For a moment, I was stunned. That had never occurred to me. I just hadn't made it that far in my reasoning. I wanted to help people. That was a no-brainer. Being a medical doctor was beyond me, but I felt like being a therapist was something I could do. I'd done tons of reading and research about it over the last six weeks— including some quizzes to see if I had the right temperament. Everything I'd read said I did. I believed, in my heart, this was the right course for me. "I feel badly taking money from you two."

"You're not taking money." Again, Colin bristled.

James pressed a hand to his chest. And glared at me.

"You're letting me contribute to society in a new way." Colin flashed those green eyes at me. "I used to make tons of charitable contributions. I intend to start doing that again now that I've got access to more money. In fact, Arthur—James's friend—was at the city council meeting a couple of days ago. He's fighting to get an animal shelter set up. I intend to be a benefactor for that project." He smiled at James. "I'll have him name a kennel after you."

My brother swatted him playfully. "You will not. Oh, name the kennel after me, I mean," he added quickly. "If you want to make a contribution to the shelter, I'm all for that."

Seeing these two together—so happy and with Colin looking so healthy—made my heart soar. "Okay, I accept your offer. Although..." I scratched my chin again. "I'm not clear why you want me living in your basement."

Yet again, they shared a look.

James nodded slightly.

Colin met my gaze. "You know...back-up. In case we go out of town. You can watch Widget."

I called total bullshit. They could run her up to Huntington Beach and my parents would spoil her. Gracie, in LA, would treat their little pumpkin like a queen. Hell, I figured even Whitney would step up. *Still glad she didn't take care of me after the surgery after all.* I really had needed Mama's TLC. "Really?" I arched an eyebrow.

James cleared his throat. "Well..."

Colin laughed. "Danny, every email you send to me ends with *have you heard from Rob?*"

I blinked. I hadn't realized that...but he was likely right. "Well, just neighborly concern."

James nodded. "Of course. I happened to run into him the other day at the grocery store."

"You did?" Whoa…I sounded way too eager. "Oh, like, cool. He didn't mention it."

"How often do you talk?" Colin cocked his head.

Shit. "Like, I dunno, a couple of times…"

"A month, week, or day?" James issued the challenge.

"Whatever." I swatted away his question like I would a pesky mosquito. "How was he?"

"Honestly?" James held my gaze. "Looking tired. He works at the vet clinic six days a week and never takes time off."

"I know." And I'd pushed about that. He said they wouldn't be able to replace him, but I didn't buy that. More likely, he couldn't afford it. "Having kids is expensive."

"Yeah, it is." Colin tapped his thigh. "I've arranged to get some money to him through Anthony, but he's wary about it being too much for Rob to accept. I'm donating to a program Anthony runs that gives grants to all the single parents with a child under two in his caseload, and some of it goes to Rob, but it can't be too much. Well, he doesn't want to take money from the government anyway, but that feels a little less…"

"Desperate? Pathetic?" Feelings I experienced when I took scholarship money. That meant someone else, likely as deserving, wasn't getting it. "You're thinking I can help him out?"

"We don't know." James gripped Colin's hand, which he still held against his chest. "We don't know how close you and Rob are, but I'd bet he needs a friend even more than he needs money. We try, but he's still wary of us, if we push too hard. You're both around the same age, but from very different backgrounds. And I don't just mean the racial thing," he added quickly. "Rob's been through hell—"

"And I come from a loving family who'd do anything for me." I didn't need to say the words, but I did anyway because I needed both men to see how much I appreciated my family. How much they meant to me. How I'd never take any one of my relatives for granted.

"Well, yeah." Colin took a deep breath and let it out slowly. "I came from a family of bigots who only showed their true homophobia when I got sick. They were happy to throw me out, along with their *imperfect* dog."

I gripped Widget tighter. Colin had shared this story with me. How his parents had rejected both him and the dog. How he'd come west looking for something better. How he'd found love and acceptance with my brother and, by extension, our family. He'd wanted me to understand the depth of his gratitude. Sure, he appreciated the liver. The chance to grow old and all that. But he also appreciated being surrounded by people who loved him. Who accepted him for who he was and not who they thought he should be.

"Rob's family, from what little he's shared, was even worse." Colin frowned.

"He told me."

Colin's furrowed brow lessened a little. "I didn't want to speak out of turn."

"He's…" I considered. "He can talk about what happened before LA. But his two years on the streets and then his six years with his dipshit scumbag ex-husband are…off the table. And I respect that."

"Have you heard how the criminal part is going?"

"The guy got bail. Rob's terrified he's going to show up in Gaynor Beach. He's talked to the prosecution about testifying. He's concerned they might make Hallie say what she saw, even if she's not ready yet. What that asshole did to Rob that night." I indicated my nose. "But she's really too young. She's seeing a counsellor, though. And she's an incredibly smart child. Poor Rob feels badly that he didn't notice. Which I think shows how bad things were for him. Anyway, Hallie's taking reading lessons."

"She's four?" James snickered. "You were barely reading at ten."

If Widget hadn't been on my lap, I would've gone over to smack his arm. "Ha ha."

"That's...amazing."

"Yeah, but Rob's worried. That she might get singled out in a negative way. That she might turn out to be smarter than him—"

"He's working on his GED though, right?" Colin tapped his thigh. "And I won't tell him, with how touchy the money thing is, but you should know there's money for college if he wants to go."

"That's..." I considered. "Really generous. His GED studies are going slowly. Between work and the kids, he's got his hands full."

"Understandable." James scratched his beard. "I can't even imagine being a single parent."

"And you'll never have to," Colin said, gripping his hand. "Well, unless something happens to—"

James pressed a finger to his fiancé's lips. "Nothing's going to happen to you. And don't start with the *transplant recipients live shorter lives*... You're going to live forever."

A shadow passed in Colin's eyes.

I'd known this, of course. Only half of all transplant recipients made it to twenty years out. Colin was only in his early thirties. I couldn't imagine him dying when he was barely into his fifties. Of course, he could be hit by a bus tomorrow. Which always felt incredibly morbid except my friend's mother did get hit by a bus when she was just forty-one.

Life could be super shitty like that.

My life might also wind up being shorter. Shit happened. Didn't mean I had a single regret about donating half my liver to save Colin's life. I rarely thought about the man who'd received it. I was grateful to him because if he hadn't needed one, I might not have had someone to donate to and there wouldn't have been the other guy to donate to Colin. Really, though, I looked at Colin and saw my donation. I'd done it for him. And for James. And for me. If Colin had died and I could've prevented it, that would've dogged me. "Rob worries about something happening to him and leaving the kids with no one."

He'd never said those words, but they'd been the subtext several times when we'd spoken. He'd talked about how Colin was lucky that he had James to care for Widget, in case something happened to him. Implicit in that was his worry that he didn't have anyone.

"Speaking of Rob…" James offered up a smile, obviously trying to push away the solemnity of the past few minutes. "We're asking him to move in here when we move out."

"Uh…what?" I frowned. "He's already got a house."

"With one bedroom and a den," Colin pointed out. "This is a three bedroom with two bathrooms. And a large closet that could easily be converted to a den or computer room. Hallie and Thomas could each have their own rooms. They won't all have to share a bathroom—"

"I'm certain Rob doesn't mind sharing a bathroom with his kids." *Why am I arguing this?* Perhaps because I could see Rob objecting as well. "He can't afford this place. He has to know that."

"It's not just about Rob. Yeah, it started out with a queer young man in a bad spot, and wanting to help. Then meeting Rob and he's such a sweetheart, and the kids are adorable, so we wanted to do what we could. But I had an idea for the small house that's a win-win." Colin shrugged. "I coordinated with Anthony. There's a young woman… she's been homeless for about six months, but she's ready for help. With proper support, she's got a good chance. She just needs a roof over her head. I want to help her too, and if Rob moves in here, then the small place is perfect for her."

My mind whirled.

"So if Rob gives up my old place and moves in here, then she's got the perfect-sized home to move into." James grinned. "See, it all works out. We told Rob the rent would be the same here."

"Uh…" I considered. "He might not be highly educated, but he seems like a pretty swift guy. What did he say? He really doesn't like handouts and this feels like a big one."

"He's doing us a favor," Colin quickly added. "I don't want to sell this place, but I also don't want to have just anyone in here and be a landlord."

"If Rob's renting from you, I think that makes you a landlord." I didn't try to keep the sarcasm from my words.

"Rob…" Colin hesitated. "He doesn't feel so much like a tenant. I mean, we haven't interacted with him much, but I'd go so far as to call him an acquaintance. Someone I feel like I know."

"A friend." James gazed at me. "Through his friendship with you."

I couldn't argue that. Rob and I had met precisely three times in person—but we'd kept in touch, talking regularly. I considered him a friend. Hell, he'd been the first person, aside from Whitney, who I'd confided in about the transplant. And he'd been right in his advice to me that

I should've told my parents ahead of time. Mama said she forgave me. But, for her, that kind of hurt ran deep. I'd been wrong. She wouldn't have tried to talk me out of it—she would've been there holding my hand and respecting the fact I was an adult who could make his own decisions, and I could have dealt with any smothering like an adult, too. "Okay…so, friend. Yeah, that fits."

"And we think being in closer proximity might be good for both of you." Colin offered a sheepish smile.

Suddenly, everything came into sharp focus. I wagged my finger. "You're matchmaking."

"We are not." James stuck his nose in the air. "I would never—"

"Oh, you so would." I pointed. "You're as bad as Mama."

He frowned. "I'm quite certain you're mistaking me for our sisters. I lived in the basement and kept my nose out of everyone's—"

"Yeah, but now you're hooked up, and you think everyone should be."

His jaw dropped. Then he snapped it shut.

Colin stroked his beard. "I think he's got your number."

James scrunched his nose. "I'm mostly worried about Rob, and you're always asking about him. Seemed to me…" He waved me off. "I don't know what I was thinking."

"That you might be right…" I tapped my thighs. "Okay, I guess I need to get going."

"You're not staying for dinner?" Colin's brow furrowed, and he looked genuinely hurt.

"When am I moving into your basement?"

"Two weeks?"

"Then I'm thinking I need to get home and get

packing." Plus, honestly, my emotions were all over the place. I was in Gaynor Beach. Rob's house was just a short drive from here. "Hey, how far between here and the animal clinic?"

"Not far." James nodded. "Yeah, we had the same thought. Him moving here's going to mess with his babysitter, though. She'll have to take a cab home every night."

"Another expense." I winced. Rob didn't like to talk money, but I could read between the lines. "Still, they'll be closer to the ocean." The Pacific was just a short stroll away. Either Colin or James—or both—took Widget to the boardwalk and the beach every day. "I'll, uh…think if there's something I can do to help. Oh…" I picked up the discarded spec sheet. "Where's Marina Park?"

"Other side of town." James grinned. "So it's a good thing you've got a car."

"And also near the animal shelter," Colin added.

James snapped his fingers. "Right. Arthur's new baby. Assume you're going to be helping out with all the furry friends."

"I can't wait." Truthfully, I adored James's friend, Arthur.

Although not as much as I was coming to care for Rob.

CHAPTER 16

ROB

"I can't thank you enough." I rubbed my elbow. I'd lost track of how many times I'd thanked Colin, but I'd do it again a thousand times if it somehow drove home to him how grateful I was. He was basically giving me the perfect home for my kids to live in. Sure, I was paying rent. But an appallingly small amount. I'd done my homework because I'd known I couldn't stay at James's house forever. He'd meant that for someone who was in desperation, and now I had a job, I was trying to pretend that I wasn't desperate.

Even though I kind of still was.

But the thought of having a room to myself—and a bit of space to breathe—overwhelmed me. Anthony implied I'd be doing Colin and James a favor. That they wanted to hang on to the house but were moving shortly, and wouldn't it be easier if I moved at the same time…? And then there was the woman who would move into James's place. I knew exactly what a lifeline that would be for her.

I was dubious. On the other hand, if they wanted to help me, help my precious kids who deserved the best, how could I turn it down? Being prideful while also needing help didn't work. Sure, I hated being beholden. Every fiber of me was terrified of depending on someone else again, even this kind of benevolence of strangers. I wanted to stay in the small place where I had the illusion I was self-sufficient. But I couldn't stand in the way of that woman's safety, and I wouldn't let my fear keep my kids cooped up in one small room. I'd take the gift and say thank you. And I'd pay it forward. Someday I'd find someone who needed help, and I'd be the one to help them.

Danny had accompanied James, Gracie, and their friend Arthur who helped move Thomas's crib into one room, Hallie's little bed into another, and the boxes carrying our meager few possessions into the various places. I still needed to unpack, but we'd put the foodstuffs away. I noticed Danny kept to the lighter items and I assumed that was because he'd been cut open not that long ago.

Colin had decided to leave most of the furnishings behind, opting to buy new for their new home together. Which meant I could leave the furniture behind in James's old home, and Vanya, the young woman moving in, had everything she needed.

All neat and tidy. But it was a surprising wrench to leave things behind again, even if they'd never been mine. I was glad the kids would have their beds and the changing table and toy chest. Some familiarity, as we moved one more time.

James's friend Arthur headed our way. "I'm going to head out. I'm meeting with the property guy again this afternoon." He rubbed a hand over his curly red beard. "I still can't believe someone's making the animal shelter a reality. I keep thinking I imagined it all, or there'll be a hitch. His dad showing up at the town meeting and claiming the deal was off almost gave me a heart attack. But Theo's following through."

"You sure you don't want me there?" Colin nodded. He looked tired, but I had no idea what was going on.

"No. I appreciate the offer. I may have you look over the financial stuff. Wynn Cavanah's doing the legal stuff."

Colin nodded. "Well, we're a phone call away. Thanks for pitching in with the move."

Arthur offered a small smile as he waved Colin off. "Easiest thing I've done in a while." He held out his hand to me, and I shook it. "I think you've got a great family. I wish you all the best." Then he headed off to his car.

How much does he know? Does it even matter? He helped. Be grateful.

I surreptitiously glanced between Colin, Gracie, and Danny. Of everyone, Danny had heard the most from me. Didn't mean the others didn't know.

James stepped out from the house, holding a sleeping Thomas in his arms. "This kid can sleep through anything." He whispered the words with genuine admiration.

Hallie, who held my hand, stared up at the giant of a man carrying her brother. "He's a good boy."

"He's a very good boy." James grinned, nodding his approval.

"But I'm not a good girl."

Oh Jesus.

I crouched down before her, panic sweeping through me. "Sweetie, I told you that you're a good girl. You're the best girl in the whole wide world."

"But Daddy left because I was bad."

Jesus fucking Christ. How had I not seen this coming? We so rarely talked about Gerard. I left that up to Josiah. If the psychologist thought I needed to know something, he'd tell me. Sometimes we had sessions with the three of us, but occasionally he liked to talk to Hallie alone. I'd be on the other side of the glass, worried, but trusting the psychologist knew what he was doing.

"Daddy left because he had to go away." I glanced at Danny before turning back to Hallie. Embarrassment swamped me. *He must think I'm a horrible father.* "You are the most important thing in my life. You and Thomas. If we have each other, we'll be okay, right?"

I willed her into my arms, but I wasn't going to press the issue—especially in the midst of strangers. Still, eventually she threw herself into my arms. She whispered something in my ear, but I couldn't make it out. Now wasn't the time, but I promised myself I'd make it. Glancing over, I saw Gracie had put her arm around Danny and a lone tear streaked down his face.

God, can I do nothing right? I'm making other people cry as well.

"Hey!" James's startled comment had us all turning our attention to him.

Thomas had awoken and had a strong grip of the man's beard.

Colin untangled Thomas's little hand before I had a chance to intervene. "Hey, buddy."

Thomas took one good look at Colin and started crying in earnest.

Someone please rescue me from this hell. Great. My son was crying at the man who was basically our savior.

James, Gracie, and Danny laughed.

I squeezed Hallie and kissed her cheek, then rescued Thomas from James's arms. "I'm so sorry. Let me rock him. He'll settle."

James pressed a hand to my arm. "He's a baby. Babies cry. Hell, most people would look at Colin's ugly mug and want to wail."

Everyone laughed. Colin most of all. That allowed me to relax. A fraction.

Danny clapped his hands. "You folks need to get settled." He turned to Hallie. "May I show you your new room?"

She had her arm wrapped around my leg. Did she even remember Danny from his visit all those months ago? "Only if Papa comes."

Danny met my gaze. "I insist on Papa coming."

I positioned Thomas on my hip so I could hold Hallie's hand as we walked inside our new home with Danny.

Only belatedly did I realize we'd left Gracie, Colin, and James standing on the front lawn.

Part of me wanted to run back and thank Colin yet again. The other part of me realized Hallie needed to feel settled before night came or she'd be sleeping in my bed again. As she still did most nights. Getting her into a routine of sleeping in her own room was critical.

Danny stepped into her room and swung his arm in a warm, welcoming arc.

Hallie stepped in. And gasped.

I'd known, of course. Colin and James had asked me more than a week ago—once my moving in was confirmed—what they could do to make Hallie's transition easier.

Balking hadn't worked.

They said if I didn't give my input, then they'd just do it themselves. Colin said something about having a horrible sister back east and James mused about his sister who loved stomach-medicine pink as a color. Whitney?

I was being manipulated...and didn't care. If Hallie wound up with something that suited her, who was I to complain?

A week ago, they'd moved the spare bed out of here and hired a mural designer to paint a wall for Hallie. I'd felt this was over the top, but James said something vague about kids and something else I didn't entirely understand. I'd agreed because this was, after all, their house.

Even knowing that, my breath caught. Yeah, over the top. But so welcome.

The woodland scene was unlike anything Hallie would've ever seen in real life. She'd never left Los Angeles or, now, Gaynor Beach. The ocean was the closest she'd gotten to nature. There were forests east of the town—out near the air base—but we'd yet to venture out that far. Being without a car hampered our adventures.

Not that I was complaining.

Thomas, now fully awake after his nap in James's arms, reached out toward the mural. I eased him to the ground, and he toddled right over, putting his hands against a family of rabbits.

I panicked.

"The paint's dry." Danny caught my gaze. "They would've never let you move in if it wasn't. This was finished days ago."

"I know." I bit my lower lip. "I'm worried he's going to damage it."

Danny cocked his head. "How? It's paint. I suppose he could use a crayon on it and you'd have to wipe it down. Or I guess he could try to paint over it…but something tells me you don't leave him alone with gallons of paint."

"No." Quick confirmation he clearly didn't need.

"Papa?"

I knelt down to Hallie's level. "Yes, sweetheart?"

"Is this for me?" Her wide blue eyes made my heart stutter.

"Yes. Colin and James did this for you."

Her brow furrowed. Damn, had I introduced her to them? Sometimes she remembered everything and sometimes she remembered nothing. I pointed to Danny. "James is his brother."

She turned to him, peering up. "Thank you."

I bit my lip.

Danny lowered himself. "On behalf of my brother, you're welcome." He pointed to her bed. "Is that in a good place?"

She nodded. "That's my blanket."

"Yes, it's your bed, same as always."

"It's a new room, but it's my own bed."

"Right. We wanted you to be comfortable in your new home."

I held my breath. She'd asked several times over the past few months if we'd be going *home*. Obviously she meant LA. Somehow, I hoped she might see this place as home…as long as we stayed here for a while. So much upheaval—

"Hey, little man." Danny held out his hand to Thomas, who grabbed it. "Want to see your room?"

Thomas threw his arms around Danny's neck.

Danny grabbed him up and swung him around. "Okay, buddy, let's go."

My son giggled as they headed out. I wanted to follow them. Not that I didn't trust Danny, but I still clutched when someone took one of the kids out of sight, and despite a hundred phone conversations, seeing Danny made him feel new and uncertain. But Hallie was still looking around her room, and she needed me here.

"Papa?"

"Yes, sweetheart?"

"Who's that man?"

"That's Danny."

She gave me her patented *duh* look that had me

dreading her teenage years. How could a four-year-old already the ability to give attitude when she wanted to?

"He's our friend. He's James's younger brother."

She eyed me.

I held my hand up way above my head. Then I scratched my chin. "The guy with the beard."

"Okay." She moved closer. "Is Danny Thomas's father?"

My world shook. "No, sweetie. I'm Thomas's father." I nearly added that Gerard was as well because, in the eyes of the law, he still was. To me, the moment he'd hurt Hallie emotionally, and physically, he'd lost the right to be called a father. Hurting me just sealed his fate—at least in my mind.

My daughter pursed her lips.

"Danny's a friend," I repeated. "Colin and James—the two men from before—are friends."

Finally, after a long while, she nodded.

Through her early years, I'd carefully curated lots of stories about blended families. Tried to show her that not all families looked identical. For her to somehow understand that Thomas's father would likely be black...? Or perhaps he'd been mixed race. Or even white. Cantrice was dark-skinned. I hadn't asked her background. I'd wanted to—if only so I could answer Thomas's questions, should he have them, when he was older. But she'd not been in the right headspace for that. She wanted to know her baby would be cared for. I gave her that assurance. Beyond that, there hadn't been the opportunity for more.

Of course, I wondered if one or both of my children would sign up for one of those ancestry websites. Whether they'd seek out biological relatives. I wanted to believe I was enough family...but I understood curiosity. I'd always told my children they were adopted. That I chose them.

That I loved them. Until today, I wasn't entirely certain Hallie understood what that meant. Now, pushing down the panic, I decided I needed to speak to her psychologist.

"That is the best big-boy bedroom ever." Danny's words carried down the hallway.

"Do you want to go see?" I brushed Hallie's hair back from her eyes. Usually she wanted her hair up. Today she'd chosen down. The mass of curls was totally full of tangles, so I wasn't looking forward to brushing it out tonight.

"Yeah, Papa." She grasped my hand and held my gaze. "New home."

With a little prayer in my heart, we headed out to join Thomas and Danny.

CHAPTER 17

DANNY

After a huge lunch shared with all the helpers, Rob thought the kids needed to get out of the house. We headed out to the boardwalk and the beach. I loved how close they were to Rob's new house.

I loved how I already thought of it as *Rob's house.*

Maybe I shouldn't have been so presumptuous as to just stick around, but I caught flashes of panic coming off Rob all morning and I just…needed to be close until he settled.

He'd told me walking often calmed the children. That it helped when Rob tried to put them down for their naps. In fact, he was sort of hoping Thomas might fall asleep right in his stroller.

No such luck.

With great indignation, the little one demanded to be let out of the contraption. For a toddler who was pre-comprehensible language, he certainly had the ability to communicate exactly what he wanted and why he felt he deserved it.

Oh, and Hallie tugged on Rob's jeans and whispered, "Thomas wants out."

Before Rob could move, I squatted facing Thomas. "Let me get him?" At Rob's nod, I unbuckled him and gently removed the toddler from the stroller. I tried to sneak in a hug, but he was already twisting and angling for the ground.

With a chuckle, I put him onto the boardwalk and on his feet.

He made a beeline for the nearest stairs.

Chuckling yet again, I sprinted after him. Apparently he wanted the beach.

Even as I was darting to snag the little guy, a cry of, "Gracie," caught my attention.

I expected to see my sister, but a streak of white-and-black fur passed me, and as I scooped Thomas in my hands to ensure he wasn't bowled over by anyone who might be following, I glimpsed the mass barreling into Hallie. My heart seized in absolute panic as I envisioned her being mauled.

Rob, who'd been fussing with the stroller, abandoned it and sprinted for his daughter.

I hustled as well. *Please let me not be too late. I can call 911. Maybe we can get her to my car…I don't know where the hospital is. How do I not know where the hospital is? I'm around kids—*

Hallie's giggles had me slowing.

Rob, however, did not. He swooped in and snagged her up, lifting her above the husky who started to jump up, trying to reach her apparently new friend.

"Papa, put me down. It's a good doggie!" Hallie's indignation was as clear as Thomas's had been.

A young woman jogged up, carrying a leash with a collar attached. "Gracie!"

The dog paid her no mind, still trying to lick Hallie's

skin where her pant leg had ridden up as Rob held her tight.

"Oh my God, this is so bad." The young woman elongated the *so* in an adorable way.

Now I could see the dog meant us no harm, I could better take in the situation.

Every time the woman advanced, Gracie danced out of her way. Obviously, to the dog, this was a game.

I turned to the woman. "Trade?" I indicated she should take Thomas. I wouldn't normally just hand a toddler to a stranger, but Rob's panic was increasing exponentially with every second that passed.

Clearly understanding my meaning, she scooped Thomas into her arms and handed me the leash.

I undid the collar and tried to assess how to best approach the situation. Getting it around the dog was key. I could tighten it once it was secure.

"Rob?"

"Yeah?" His voice shook.

"It looks like Gracie's not going to hurt Hallie."

"You don't know that." For just an instant, he looked away from the dog and at me.

Crowds had gathered on either side of us. I pointed to two very steady-looking women who indicated at each side, at least with their body language, they might be willing to help. "Try to nab her if she heads your way?"

Both women nodded.

Gracie could still jump off the boardwalk, but I'd take the chance I'd get to her first.

"Rob?"

"Yeah?" If anything, his terror was increasing.

"Have Hallie call to the dog. But keep her out of reach. That'll entice Gracie and while she's distracted, I'll grab her." I had no idea the extent of the dog's vocabulary, but I used a sing-songy voice so she wouldn't—hopefully—know I was up to something.

"I don't know—"

"Trust me, Rob."

He met my gaze. Very slowly, he said to Hallie, "Call her name."

"Gracie." Hallie said the name with great enthusiasm.

Gracie again went onto her hind legs to reach the girl. If Rob hadn't been so sturdy, I might've worried about the dog knocking him over. Also, claws on skin were a thing.

I lunged. I looped the leash around her neck, and then held her while I buckled on the collar.

Where I expected indignation—because that was going around today—she turned and licked my face.

Repeatedly.

"Okay. Just give me a second." I pulled and slid straps to tighten her collar so she wouldn't be able to slip her leash again.

Hallie tried to lean out of Rob's hold. "Papa, I want to see the puppy. Danny gets to play with her. I want to play too! She's a nice puppy. Pretty puppy. Soft puppy. She has all the fuzz!"

"Sweetheart—"

"No! Put me down! Puppy!" Hallie kicked both legs.

In any other circumstances, I would've been amused. Instead, I was stunned. Admittedly, I'd spent little time in Hallie's presence. I'd assumed she was as placid in the rest of her life as she was with me. If Rob faced this spitfire on a regular basis, I felt a little sorry for him. She reminded me a little of my own Gracie and how fiery my sister could be—especially if she saw an injustice in the world.

As I clung tightly to Gracie's leash, I snagged the stroller and indicated to the woman with Thomas that we should move to the side so we were no longer blocking the boardwalk.

When I did that, a spontaneous burst of applause came from the onlookers.

I grinned and took a bow.

The young woman, obviously chagrined, said, "Oh my God."

"It's all good," I told her. "No harm, no foul. Now—"

"Papa, I want the puppy now! Put me down!" Then, in a sad tone I'd never heard from Hallie before, "Please."

My heart broke. Shattered right there.

By the obvious look of distress on Rob's face—with the wide eyes and drooping mouth—I could tell she'd bested all of us.

"Really, she's a good dog." The woman continued to hold Thomas, who squirmed so violently, I worried he might try to escape.

"She's clearly an escape artist." I chuckled.

"I swear that's never happened before." The woman winced. "I'm a temporary foster for her. The previous owner—an older woman—broke her hip in a fall. Not Gracie's fault," she was quick to add. "But she had to move into a nursing home. She was my neighbor, and I said I'd take Gracie. But I just got a job in San Diego. My new condo doesn't allow big dogs. I plan to rescue a small dog, but I'm going to have to give up Gracie. I just…" She winced. "I don't want to take her to the shelter in the city."

"Papa—"

"Hush, Hallie, please." Rob's voice quavered. "Let me think."

I pointed to the stairs. "Why don't we all go down to the beach, and Hallie can meet Gracie in a controlled way." I continued to hold the dog's leash. "I have her, Rob. I won't let her hurt your kids."

"She would never," the young woman added. "My neighbor had six grandkids who played with Gracie all the time. Frankly, I think she misses the kids."

"I don't know…"

"Papa, I want to see the puppy!" Hallie struggled to get down.

Thomas struggled to get down.

Rob, meeting my gaze with resignation—and just a touch of annoyance—sighed. "Yeah. On the beach." He eyed me. "You control her or this ends."

"I will." I didn't have a ton of experience with dogs, other than Widget. Every instinct I had, though, said this dog wouldn't hurt the kids. Maybe I was wrong. Maybe the young woman was lying to us, and… "What's your name?" I glanced at her.

"Druscilla." She winced. "Obviously I didn't pick it."

"Nothing wrong with the name." I grinned. "I'm Danny. That bundle of energy is Thomas." I pointed to the wriggling body. "They are Rob and Hallie. Let's move to the sand."

When Gracie and I were partway down the stairs, Rob finally let Hallie down.

She tried to bolt, but he held her hand tight. Somehow, he wrangled her and the stroller.

Druscilla had a competent grip on Thomas, so I wasn't worried. Within moments, I had a corner of the beach staked out. The day had been overcast, and I spotted some darker clouds on the horizon over the ocean. Even though we were close to home, we'd need to be aware of impending rain.

I plopped down onto the sand and pulled Gracie toward me without being too rough.

Clearly pleased with this turn of events, she licked my chin.

"Stop."

She did.

I met her gaze. "Be good." Of course, I had no idea if she actually understood me. Or if she'd continue to do her own thing.

Druscilla stayed back as she waited for Rob and Hallie to join us.

Thomas again lunged, nearly toppling them both over.

"Can you hang onto him? We'll let Hallie take her turn."

The young woman laughed. "I swear, nothing spooks that dog. She's just a bundle of energy who adores children."

As Gracie tried to pull toward Thomas, I winced and pressed a hand over my incision.

"Danny?" A fraction of a second later, Rob was by my side.

Hallie, taking her father's momentary distraction as permission, ran toward the dog.

The two crashed into each other in a tangle of limbs, giggles, and happy barks. Gracie got in a few licks before I managed to pull her back. I winced again.

Rob snagged the dog's leash. "Damn, man." He met my gaze for just an instant before turning his attention back to Hallie. "You need to back up a minute, hon. I had dogs when I was growing up. They can get really excited around kids and sometimes hurt them without meaning to."

Hallie stuck out her lower lip. "I want to pet the puppy."

Thomas clapped his hands.

Rob sighed. He knelt and petted Gracie, running his hands over her ears, her legs, her face, picked up her paws, even opened her mouth. Her tail never stopped wagging.

He rocked her lightly back and forth, while she panted, then eased his grip a bit. "She seems pretty chill. Here, honey, let me show you how to pet her. No hugs. You don't like strangers running up and hugging you."

Hallie said, "I guess not."

"What a dog likes is patting, rubbing, and scratch her neck and her front, like this." Rob guided Hallie in petting the dog's thick coat.

Until Gracie twisted herself in a pretzel to lick Hallie's face.

Hallie giggled.

More pats and licks were exchanged. *Going to have to do some serious washing tonight.*

I sat back down carefully on the sand, trying to hide the ache in my stomach.

"Is it because of your surgery?" Rob whispered the words with both anger and urgency.

"Uh…" Was there a good way to answer that question? James and Colin didn't know I'd had a rougher recovery, with a mild incision infection and more pain than Dr. Patton was happy with. If she'd known I carried a few boxes today, she'd throw a fit. I'd pushed. But I worried that my brother, and especially Colin, would feel guilty if they knew. "It'll pass."

"Gentle, sweetheart. Let the puppy move." Rob gazed over to them.

Hallie had wrapped herself around the dog's front paws while Thomas reached for a handful of fur.

Druscilla gently redirected his hand.

Which Gracie promptly licked.

He's going to put that in his mouth. Did we bring wipes? Did we even bring a diaper bag? This had been meant to be a quick stroll to get the kids sleepy for a nap.

Now everyone was the opposite of ready to rest.

Rob went and took back his toddler, holding Thomas where he could see the dog.

"Gentle." Druscilla motioned petting Gracie gently.

To my delight, when Rob tipped Thomas down close, the toddler mimicked the action.

The dog's tongue lolled.

"Keep the puppy," Hallie declared.

"Fucking hell." Rob's whispered curse could only be heard by me, but I felt it. He didn't swear often. And certainly never around his kids—at least that I knew of.

"The puppy belongs to Druscilla, Hallie." I smiled. "We have to give the puppy back." I stilled. "How old is she?"

Druscilla grinned. "Puppy's almost accurate. She's one. I'm not sure my neighbor should've rescued her—"

"She's a double rescue?"

"Yeah. She was living on a tether on a property just outside of town. Really horrible for a dog with fur like this to be out in the heat." She said the words quietly, ensuring Hallie couldn't hear. "Arthur rescued her."

"Arthur Bjornsson?"

"Yeah." She cocked her head. "You know him?"

"I do. He's a friend."

"Oh, wow. Like, small world. Anyway, he rescued her, but needed a foster, and my neighbor was happy to take her. And usually Gracie's good on a leash. I swear." She looked like she was about to cross her heart. "Your kids...I guess they made her think of my neighbor's grandkids." She blinked. "I'm hoping the shelter in San Diego can place her." She swiped at a tear. "I don't want to leave her. But my job is going to be twelve-hour shifts. I can't be driving back and forth to Gaynor Beach while working those hours, and I can't afford doggy daycare."

The drive was just over an hour. She'd have to be in

bed the moment she came in the door and back on the road so soon after waking up. No, that wasn't a solution. And I wasn't going to suggest finding a condo that accepted large dogs. Such a thing wasn't practical, and I had no doubt Druscilla had tried. Hard.

"Have you talked to Arthur?"

She bit her lip. "He sort of…he got all upset, and I lied to him. I said I had a lead in San Diego to take her. He's such a great guy, and…"

"Do you know if he tried to find a foster home?"

"Yeah, he tried. He said there's nothing and was going to try out of town. But with the economy the way it is, there aren't a lot of people who can foster. No, Gracie needs a permanent home. It breaks my heart I can't be the one to give it to her."

Before I could think it through, the words came out of my mouth. "I'll take her."

CHAPTER 18

ROB

"No, you won't." *Jesus, what is this idiot thinking?* Clearly, he wasn't recovered from the major surgery just two and a half months ago. I'd suspected he'd been lying to me—and everyone else—when he'd said he was *fine*. God, an insipid word if ever there was one. How often had I told those around me that I was *fine*? All the while, both back in Missouri and then during my marriage to Gerard, I'd been anything but.

"It'll be fine—"

"No, Danny, it won't be fine. She might be obedient most of the time—"

Druscilla nodded frantically.

"—but she's still way more of a dog than you should be handling right now. And you're living in your brother's basement—"

"Widget will be thrilled. She'll have company."

"Widget?" Druscilla cocked her head.

"My brother's French bulldog. Real sweetheart. Everyone—"

"I'm a sweetheart," Hallie proclaimed, smiling, still

patting Gracie's shoulder exactly the way I'd shown her. "So is the puppy."

My chest seized. The past few minutes were the most she'd spoken spontaneously since we moved to Gaynor Beach. Hell, probably the most she'd ever said. Certainly the most demanding she'd ever been. While Thomas expressed his displeasure at anything that annoyed him, Hallie would gently ask me to change whatever was bothering her. Or, worse yet, I'd only discover later something was hurting her—emotionally or physically— and she wouldn't speak up. Her demand for the *puppy* was the most she'd ever asked for. And when had I last seen her smile like that?

"If I rescue Gracie, then the kids will be able to see her whenever they want without you having to deal with the hassle of a dog." Danny offered a tentative grin.

"She's not a hassle," Druscilla added. "She's just such a darling. Great with kids. Great with my cat too, which not all huskies are. They're good buddies. I hate to give her up. But a cat can handle my long hours. A dog can't."

Hallie abandoned her lovefest with the dog and leaned against me, even as I held the leash tight in one hand and Thomas on my hip with the other. "I love Gracie."

Danny chuckled. "My sister will be amused."

Druscilla squinted.

"His sister's name is Gracie. Not Grace," I was quick to add. "Gracie." She'd been quite firm about that when she'd helped out this morning. As far as I knew, she'd headed back to LA after lunch. A long way to come…but par for the course with the Reynolds clan. James hinted his Mama and Daddy had wanted to come as well. Mama had sent a pot roast that was in the slow cooker right now. Dinner and fresh rolls waited for me and the kids to celebrate our first night in our new home.

"I could…" I floundered. We had a backyard, so Nia could let Gracie out while I was at work. Or maybe I could bring her with me. Surely Dr. Louisa would be okay with that. I'd have to ask Oscar. I might've asked him to foster Gracie, but he had his Newfoundland Hemingway and a new foster son. He and Hugh had their hands full. I flashed to Scott and Anthony…but Crumpet the cat would definitely not appreciate permanent custody. His fits when Hemingway visited were legendary. Or so Scott confided in me.

"Could…?" Druscilla prompted.

"Take her. Till Danny can." Thomas giggled, clearly enjoying the game of poking toward Gracie's nose. She kept licking his hand. "Be gentle." I held him where he couldn't make direct contact. My son likely wouldn't understand, but Gracie seemed to have a phenomenally good nature. I maybe should've been more worried, but Druscilla's calm demeanor helped. A lot.

"I can't ask you to do that." Danny placed his hand on mine.

I startled. I couldn't remember him ever initiating touch with me. He was always so careful around me. Like I was glass that would shatter under the slightest pressure. I needed to prove to him that I was stronger than I looked. Than I seemed.

And, hell, I needed to prove that to myself as well.

"Why don't we call James? Have him meet us at your house?" Danny squeezed my arm. "I think he'll be happy for me to rescue Gracie. After all, he's always bugging me to be more responsible."

Yeah, I'd call bullshit on that one. Danny was one of the most responsible people I knew. Even with dropping out of university, he still worked damn hard. He'd told me how tough this new academic program was going to be.

The last thing he needed was the responsibility of a dog. Yet even as I had the thought, he was pulling out his phone.

I glanced at Druscilla. Her relief was palpable. I didn't have the heart to cut off this possible route of rescue. Gracie truly was a special dog. She didn't deserve to wind up in a shelter—even temporarily.

Gracie whined.

Panic seized me.

Druscilla chuckled. "She has to do her business. She's good about letting me know. Just give me a minute." Carefully, she extricated the dog from my children.

Thomas wailed and tried to follow by attempting to lunge out of my arms.

"Yeah, I'll text you the address and meet you there. That's great. Uh…thanks." Danny swiped his phone and then tucked it into his back pocket. "James says it's fine I get a dog."

"Does James know you're not fully recovered?"

Danny glared.

I glared right back, squatting to set Thomas down for a moment, since the dog was out of reach.

Hallie pressed her palm against my forehead. "Don't be mad, Papa."

"I'm not…" Frustrated at having a child who saw too much. "We should get organized. I guess we should find out where Druscilla lives…?" I eyed the stroller, my two children in need of washing and naps, as well as the errant man who was slowly enmeshing himself into my life. My friend.

And yet he was so much more than that. How I had come to care so much for someone I'd met exactly three times?

"I'm just three streets over." Druscilla had come back, and somehow, I'd missed her arrival.

Hallie and Thomas approached Gracie who, to my relief, appeared marginally calmer. I scooped Thomas back up anyway, and settled him on my hip.

"Then we'll come with you, and we can settle up with Gracie." Danny started to push up off the sand.

With a firm hand, I pressed him back down.

Our gazes met.

"Let me help you."

"Uh…yeah…" He blinked. "Bossy." He might've whispered that under his breath.

I had to smile to myself because no one had ever, in my entire life, accused me of that. "And don't you forget it."

"Oh, I won't. I kind of like it."

This time, I blinked. We weren't flirting.

Were we?

I straightened and, while keeping an eye on Hallie— who was totally enthralled with the dog—offered my free hand to help Danny stand. Truthfully, he had to do much of it himself. He often made self-deprecating comments about his weight, which bothered me a lot. He was a big guy—although more in height than girth. He was solid and, to my mind, had lost a bit of weight since his surgery. Had Mama noticed? Was she worried?

"Thanks." Danny pressed his hand to my arm. "I probably could've done that by myself, but we'll let you believe I needed it."

"Danny." I used my stern *papa* voice.

He caught my gaze, his dark-brown eyes going wide. "Okay. Just…" He glanced at Druscilla and the kids. "Don't tell James and Colin. Promise me."

I didn't want to agree. He'd be living in their basement. If he wasn't as strong as he claimed to be, then they had a right to know. Hell, if he were mine, I'd want to know. Nothing worse than being kept in the dark. And yet, I still owed him. For helping me move a couple of times. For bringing the Christmas basket. For texting with me virtually every night as I tried to relax enough to sleep.

For keeping the monsters at bay—even if from a distance.

He's living here now. He can keep you safe from nearby.

That thought brought images of Gerard looming over me and I quickly shoved them down.

Focus on the here and now. Don't go borrowing trouble.

Good advice. Too bad I rarely heeded it.

"Rob?" Danny squeezed my arm.

My gaze shot to his.

"It's going to be okay."

Whether he knew where my stress stemmed from or just sensed my general distress, I was grateful, knowing he had my back.

Forty-five minutes later, as five grown men crowded in poor Druscilla's sitting room, I wondered about who had whose back.

Danny had tried to shove me home with the kids, but I wouldn't be railroaded. Now, as he glared at me, I knew I'd done the right thing in insisting I be part of this.

Thomas snoozed in his stroller while Hallie sat quietly in the corner, talking to Gracie. The dog, for her part, appeared completely enraptured with my daughter. My initial panic had abated, but I still maintained that dogs could be unpredictable. Our schnauzer had bitten my brother when he'd yanked too hard on her tail. And yeah, my brother'd had a mean streak that easily followed him into adulthood—he'd said some of the cruelest things to me—but that didn't make things better. What if Thomas hurt Gracie? Wouldn't she fight back? And wouldn't that be my fault for not watching everyone carefully? But how could I cook and do other things while watching everyone vigilantly?

"Normally I vet foster homes." Arthur's blue eyes were troubled.

"I'm James's brother." Danny placed a hand on his heart. "He and Colin will be living right above me. I'll do whatever you need." He pointed to the boxes. "If I don't take Gracie, then she goes to a shelter in San Diego tomorrow."

Druscilla sniffed.

Arthur blinked several times. He turned to her and asked, gently, "I thought you said you had a family for her?"

"I did. But they backed out. I could see how stressed you were, and I didn't want to bother you again—"

"I…" He winced. He'd likely would've said he'd take Gracie, but James had confided, while we waited for his friend's arrival, that Arthur's little house was overflowing, and he couldn't possibly take another dog right now. If he'd known of a foster placement, he would've taken Gracie off Druscilla's hands weeks ago when she first approached him.

Blaming her for seeing his obvious distress wasn't helping.

"So I'll take Gracie." Danny grinned. "I've always wanted a dog. And I've helped take care of Widget—"

"You've never had a dog?" Arthur's distress increased.

James shook his head. "No. Allergies in the family. We always wanted one, but we couldn't."

Colin grinned. "Widget's his first, too."

"Yeah. So now I'm experienced, and I can definitely help Danny."

"You're taking care of Colin," Danny argued.

"Well, but you—" I started to speak.

He glared at me.

I glared right back.

James waved back and forth between the two of us. "What's up with you two? I mean, if Danny's taking Gracie, why are you here?" He asked me the question with curiosity. Not unkindly. Just with confusion.

Danny and I continued to glare at each other. He was going to do it. He was going to take a full-grown dog who needed lots of exercise while still recovering from major surgery. He still wasn't telling me the whole story, either. Of that, I was certain.

Danny's going to get hurt and have a setback and not tell anyone... I couldn't stand that thought. "I want to take Gracie."

Four adults joined Danny in staring at me while Hallie whooped in joy.

In that moment, I knew I'd made the right decision. Four years, and I had never heard that sound from my child.

One I might come to regret...but fostering Gracie was the right thing to do.

CHAPTER 19

DANNY

Mama's pot roast had never tasted better. It even managed to squash some of my annoyance with the man sitting across from me.

Rob studiously cut meat for Thomas into little pieces… all the while ignoring my glares.

Thomas shoved cooked carrots into his mouth.

Hallie used her fork to eat a piece of melt-in-your-mouth roast.

Gracie sat at our feet. Quiet. Yet clearly waiting for something to be dropped. Apparently she was good at that.

Despite Hallie being fatigued, Rob and I had spent over an hour with Druscilla learning all about Rob's new pet.

Arthur had insisted on carrying the huge bag of dog food and her crate to his car and transporting them over here and then putting the food away.

James could've done it easily. So could Rob, for that matter, given how he carried Hallie frequently.

Arthur, though, had wanted to be useful.

When James offered to pay the adoption fee, I'd tried to argue that Rob was only fostering Gracie for me and…

No one in that room believed that once Rob brought her home, she wasn't staying. Barring any catastrophe, of course. At the least, if Gracie went away, Hallie would never recover from the disappointment.

So I'd have to do everything in my power to keep Gracie in their lives—even if that meant not taking her when I was better.

Bitterness churned in my gut. Why couldn't I just be better? Recovery was normally six weeks for healthy adults. Aside from a few extra pounds, I'd be the epitome of health. Dr. Patton had been impressed with all my test results. I should've bounced right back.

Damn incision infection—which I hadn't told anyone except the doctor about—had set me back. I'd spent a lot of effort pretending I was fine when I probably should've been focusing on getting better. And I'd stayed up late every night, waiting for Rob to text that he was home safely. I let him believe I was a night owl.

I wasn't. In fact, I was up at the crack of dawn most days, even if I wanted to sleep in. Mama commented I looked tired, and I'd investigated products that might make me look less tired. I'd asked Gracie's advice, and she'd advised me to actually sleep more.

Damn sister.

"Hey…"

Rob met my gaze.

"Is there…?" I cleared my throat. "Any chance we could change Gracie's name?"

"Uh…" He cocked his head.

"My sister's name is Gracie."

"Oh, right. Yeah, that could get awkward. I'm not going to ask your sister to change her name."

"You're a smart man."

"Papa?"

"Yes, sweetheart?"

"I have a name for Gracie."

I was a little surprised she understood the conversation, but I was quickly learning not to underestimate Hallie. As smart as my niece Mel was, Hallie had her beat at that age.

"Oh? What is it?" Rob cut a glance to me.

Dude, you don't have to worry about me saying something mean. Sheesh, do you not know me by now?

"Drizella."

I blinked.

Rob blinked.

"Uh…who's Drizella?" I wracked my brain, but came up blank.

"Cinderella's sister." Hallie gave me the patented *duh* expression.

I did a little cheer, because that was the first time she'd ever done that with me. Somehow, this felt monumentally important. "Right." I squinted. "Cinderella's step-sister."

"Yes."

Rob glanced between Hallie and myself. "Sweetheart, Drizella's…not really a nice person. But we could name the puppy Cinderella."

I winced inwardly. Right…like I wanted to go around calling the dog Cinderella. That might be cute when Hallie or Thomas—or both—were around. Not so much when it was just me and the pooch. I suspected Rob felt the same way.

But Hallie came first.

I wracked my brain. "You know, James told me about his conversation with Colin to name Widget."

Rob squinted. "Her name wasn't always Widget?"

I guffawed. "Uh, no. Try Chambord."

"Oh God." He winced. "Widget is much better."

"I agree."

"What about Ella? That's short for Drizella, And Cinderella. A compromise." I had to try.

Hallie crossed her arms. "Drizella."

Rob's eyed widened. Was he going to reprimand her?

That tone and attitude would've gotten at least raised eyebrows from Leticia to her daughters, and she was pretty easygoing. *Please don't think I'm offended.*

"Maybe we can sleep on it?" He cast me a worried glance.

I offered the best smile I could. Drizella was fine with me. Cinderella was fine with me—if that would make Hallie happy. Without words, I understood from Rob this was the most engaged Hallie had been for a long time. He'd not just agreed to bring Gracie home, he'd made it clear this was, barring catastrophe, a permanent thing.

Arthur's relief had been palpable.

James was still suspicious of why I'd been so enthusiastic about taking the dog but then had, so quickly, yielded to Rob's offer.

Colin had appeared both amused and fatigued. Soon after everything had been settled, he'd coaxed James to take him home. He'd given me a look, though. That made me wonder if he'd picked up on my own exhaustion. Today had been a damn long day.

Rob tapped my foot under the table.

I looked up and met his gaze.

"You're falling asleep."

"I'm glad I don't have to go back to LA." I rubbed my face. "For a moment there, I was trying to decide between Huntington Beach and LA."

"Then you realized you live in Gaynor Beach now."

I yawned. "Yeah. I even know the way back to my place."

"You could've stayed on the couch."

I almost retorted that his couch was uncomfortable, but I was thinking of his old couch. The old couch in James's house. Which was incredibly uncomfortable.

On purpose.

My brother'd maintained he never wanted guests.

Ha. More fool him. Now he lived in a six-bedroom home with an extra two in my basement suite. I'd joked we could pretty much handle the entire Reynolds clan. He'd winced and said sure. Well, at least the kids. All twelve of them…so far.

James had said he and Colin were considering fostering once Colin was fully recovered. A way to pay forward their damn good luck.

I eyed Hallie and Thomas. They'd fit in with all my nieces and nephews. Mel would pull her into some game or other that little girls played. My three elder nieces were all creative creatures. And they all doted on the babies.

My three elder nephews were holy terrors…who would dote on the twins when Felicia finally had them. Two boys, no less. If I'd been a better math student, I might've tried to figure out the odds of having either five boys or five girls. Plus my twin sisters each being pregnant with twins at the same time.

Voodoo magic, Mama claimed. And since we weren't superstitious and didn't believe in that, I just rolled my eyes.

"Danny?"

I blinked. "Yeah, Rob. Sorry."

"Maybe you should crash on the couch tonight. Or, better yet, you can sleep in my room. I can…" He gazed over at the couch. "Colin swears it's comfortable."

"Colin's not wrong. I've spent a night there myself." I offered a smile. "I'm safe to drive home, Rob."

"Are you tired?" Hallie gazed at me. "You look tired."

"Wow, I must really look bad."

Her mouth went into a little *o*.

Sheesh. "But you're right," I added quickly. "So maybe you can read me a bedtime story?"

At least Rob had today off work since it was Sunday. He'd be back at it tomorrow.

Hallie scrutinized me, her little brow furrowing. "You can read."

"Sure. I could read to you. Or you could read to me."

Thomas pounded the tray of the highchair, clearly finished eating and fed up with the discussion.

"But it's okay if you don't want to," I was quick to assure Hallie, even as Rob removed Thomas's bib and tried to mitigate the damage as much as he could. Mama's gravy was everywhere.

Everywhere.

She would be thrilled.

I whipped out my phone and snapped a photo before Rob could remove Thomas from the high chair.

Rob cocked his head.

"Family chat. Mama's got to see how much her gravy was appreciated."

For just a moment, Rob stilled.

"Oh crap. Sorry, I wasn't thinking. I haven't sent it yet —" *Stupid. He's in hiding. Of course he doesn't want pictures of his kids uploaded…even to a private chat.*

"No, it's fine." He offered me a smile even as he released Thomas. "I just…I don't think I've taken many pictures since I've been here. Even with the new phone."

"You backed up the old ones, right? To the cloud server I showed you?"

"Yeah, I did what you suggested. All my photos are backed up there." He rubbed his forehead as if in pain.

I laughed.

He frowned.

I indicated his temple.

He wiped…and came away with gravy.

To my relief, he chuckled.

"Papa?"

"Yes, sweetheart?"

"Drizella needs to go out."

Both Rob and I turned to find the husky sitting patiently by the door.

"I'll handle the dog and you handle the kids." I winked to Rob. "Somehow, I think I'm getting the better end of this."

Since even Hallie had gravy on her shirt, Rob seemed to acknowledge my point with a sigh. "Take three bags. You just never know."

Fifteen minutes later, Drizella and I were back inside. The rain had come in earnest and neither her raincoat nor mine had kept us particularly dry. Arthur had expressed surprise Gracie came with a raincoat but Druscilla swore she was good with it. I was grateful because she would've been ever wetter.

Rob handed me a towel as I toed off my shoes. He pointed to the dog. Then he disappeared.

I unhooked her leash, removed her coat, and set about trying to dry her as best I could.

Moments later, Rob reappeared with a nicer looking towel. He pointed to my wet hair.

"Well, you could dry me while I do her."

His eyes widened and, for just a moment, he looked like he was going to bolt. Still, after a long minute, he indicated I should duck my head. Then he dried my hair.

Since it was pretty short, it didn't take him long. Still, as he diligently worked away at it, something inside me stirred. No one had taken care of me like this for a long time. Well, aside from Mama and Daddy after the surgery. But someone I wasn't related to…? I couldn't remember. I'd dated plenty of men and women over the past six years—since Mama decreed I was old enough—but I'd never met someone who spoke to me the way Rob did.

I'd spent the past three months trying to tell myself what I felt wasn't real. That, even if it was, one-sided attraction never worked. Rob wasn't interested in me. Would never be. And, even if he was, he had his kids to focus on. I could never, ever allow myself to be a distraction.

He pulled back, and I straightened. This close, he had to tip his chin back a little to meet my gaze. I had the impression he was less slender than when he'd first arrived. Like maybe he'd put on a bit of weight. Still slim, though.

Fucking attractive.

But I wouldn't do anything about it. Because he didn't need complications right now.

And neither did I. "Hallie and Thomas in bed?"

He nodded, offering a little smile. "Hallie didn't even want to read. She was out as soon as her head hit the pillow. Thomas was just behind."

"They never did get their naps."

"No, which is why I was so impressed they were well behaved at dinner."

"Drizella," I deadpanned.

He winced. "I'm going to keep working on that. There's an Ella movie or something, right? Maybe I can convince her to try that."

"It's okay, Rob. Dogs have weird names. Hell, kids have weird names. Anyway, my niece's name is Etta. That's too close to Ella." I eyed the dog. "Are you supposed to be on the chair?" The thing was fabric, so it would dry and therefore wasn't so much an issue—but I didn't want her doing things she wasn't supposed to.

"No." Rob sighed. "She's not. That's what Arthur suggested. Although he also suggested I hire a local trainer as, clearly, she's got some bad habits."

I cast my gaze to Drizella. "We should've kept your name. You're going to be trouble—just like my sister."

The husky held my gaze, with her crystal-blue eyes, and then defiantly tipped up her chin.

"Oh yeah, trouble indeed."

CHAPTER 20
ROB

I cleared my throat. "I'm sorry, Nai, can you repeat that?"

"Pneumonia." She could barely get the word out.

"Okay, take care. Uh…let me know when you might be ready to come back?"

"Sorry. Really." Then she cut the line.

I pressed my phone against my forehead. Tonight was supposed to be the first night of our new arrangement. Her dad was going to drop her off here before taking the other kids to their after-school activities, she'd watch the kids like always, and I'd pay for a cab to take her home. More expensive, for sure, but I needed to work. It'd cut into our food budget, but I figured we could make it work. It had never, not in a million years, occurred to me that Nai wouldn't be here tonight.

Hallie sat on the floor, playing blocks with Thomas. If I brought them with me and…what? Set up the playpen in the staff room for Thomas to sleep there? Make a cot for Hallie on the floor? And then wake them up to bring them home just before midnight?

Losing the shift wasn't an option, though.

Call Danny.

No. He can't think I want him just to watch my kids.

So…Scott said he could help in a pinch. They had a crib and spare bed over at their house. But Anthony would know, and that might affect how he saw me as a parent. I needed his testimony to be perfect if custody came up.

People get sick. It's not your fault.

There had to be a solution that didn't involve calling Danny.

But if there was, I couldn't figure it out.

So I texted him.

And eleven minutes later, he was on my doorstep.

He looked better than he had yesterday. His dark skin meant I couldn't judge based on color—but he had a pep in his step that didn't feel forced. And his smile came easier.

"You're not on painkillers, are you? You didn't take them because you were headed here?" I asked the question as he headed over the threshold.

"Uh…no." He grinned. Then gently smacked my upper arm. Just like I'd seen him do to James and Gracie several times. As they'd done to him. Felt like a family tradition of some kind.

And he'd done it to me. Not just that he'd touched me…but that he'd treated me—in a weird way—like one of the family. That meant more than he'd ever know. Because I wasn't going to tell him.

He winced. "Sorry."

"For what?"

"I shouldn't…you know…"

A moment passed before his meaning registered. "You can touch me, Danny. I know you're not going to hit me in anger. Only one man has ever done that, and you're not that man. I..." I sought the right words. "I trust you to keep me safe."

"I will." His eyes went wide and sincerity came off him in waves. "I'll protect you. I'll take care of you." He gazed upward, then finally back at me. "Too much?"

After a moment—making him sweat—I laughed. "No, not too much. Not too much at all." Tentatively, I grasped his large hands in mine. In comparison, mine were downright puny. Delicate. In a way I didn't necessarily like. *Was this why Gerard hit me? Because, clearly, I'm incapable of fighting back?* Yet another question I couldn't answer.

"Rob?" Danny's deep, dark-brown eyes penetrated my soul.

"I'm okay." I felt like he needed to hear that. "Like I said, I trust you." I indicated with my chin over toward Thomas and Hallie.

Oops.

Hallie watched us intently, her little brow furrowed. Her left hand was sunk into Drizella's thick coat as she petted the dog. The dog who hadn't even come to greet Danny. *Some watchdog.* Yet her gentleness with the kids couldn't be overstated. After a moment, Hallie went back to watching the television. We didn't do that often, but I found sometimes it helped with the transition to the babysitter. Nai said it meant she could gently extract Hallie to do her reading while leaving Thomas with his shows.

Damn. I'd have to be more careful. Hallie's power of observation was legendary. I could get away with very little. Yet I couldn't let Danny's hands go. I shifted my gaze back to him. "I trust them with you, Danny. Not just because I'm desperate, but because you'll take care of them. And they're getting to know you."

"And I have twelve nieces and nephews?"

I laughed. "Yeah, that too." I didn't add that I'd

overheard Colin and James talking about fostering. And that I knew, to the depths of my soul, that Danny would treat those children as if they were blood related to him. Reluctantly, I let him go. "Call if anything—"

He shushed me. "I have your number. We'll call before bedtime."

My eyes stung. That was part of the routine with Nai. That he remembered touched me more than I could express.

So I didn't. I went through the kids' full routines with him, reminded him never to leave Thomas alone with Drizella because unlike Hallie, my toddler didn't understand "Be gentle," and said my goodbyes. Then I grabbed my knapsack with my snacks and dinner and headed out. The walk to the clinic didn't take long as my legs ate up the distance. I was paid a straight amount to clean. If I finished sooner—and didn't cut corners—then I could go home early. That was why I skipped my break. No one was the wiser. And it got me home sooner. If I needed more time—and clearly wasn't dawdling—I had permission to bill it. I never had. I cleaned that clinic so it sparkled and then hauled ass home.

Danny had initiated a video chat with the kids before bed. Thomas was really too young to understand, but Hallie knew. She always frowned a little, asking when I'd be home. I always promised just after she fell asleep. And, thank God, I always was. As I walked back through the dark streets, though, I acknowledged I still hadn't named a guardian for the kids. Might Colin and James be willing? They seemed like amazing men. Clearly were open to having children come into their huge home. I'd snuck a look on the realty website when they'd given me their new address. Wow. Just…wow. And them being there allowed me to give my kids an amazing home where they could have their own bedrooms and we were just steps from the beach. And just a short bus ride to the local school when Hallie was old enough.

If we were still lucky enough to be where we were.

Which was a big *if*.

Then, as I neared my house, I remembered the phone conversation I'd had earlier this evening. The one I hadn't wanted to dwell on. The one whose implications hadn't really set in.

I used my key in the lock and stepped inside as quietly as I could.

Textbooks and a laptop were spread across the coffee table.

Danny lay curled under a fleece blanket on the couch. And, true to his word, his large frame fit. He looked… comfortable. He slept…peacefully.

And Hallie wasn't at the door to greet me, which I always took as a good sign. That meant she'd likely been asleep for a while. After bedtime, Danny hadn't texted me to say she was awake, so I'd believed she'd gone to sleep for him without a fuss.

I toed off my shoes, shucked my jacket, and gently laid my backpack on the floor.

Am I supposed to wake him? And where's Drizella? Shouldn't she be here to greet the newcomer?

Slowly, I crept down the hall. I poked my head into Thomas's room to find him lying on his back in the crib with his limbs spread in all directions. *Big surprise.* Then I advanced to Hallie's room. Gently, I poked my head in. The first thing I'd done when we'd moved in was to oil all the hinges. To eliminate any extraneous noise that might wake my girl.

Drizella popped her head up from where she lay curled

on Hallie's bed, gave me the once-over, snorted, then resettled.

In sleep, Hallie moved her hand to the dog's fur and dropped it there—all while seeming to not wake up.

I withdrew, a grin on my face, and headed toward the kitchen. I wouldn't have thought I'd be okay with a dog sleeping on my daughter's bed. The last twenty-four hours had taught me differently. Drizella—or Trouble, as I now referred to her in my head—had slotted into this family without a single hiccup. She made her needs clear while accommodating the kids and their demands at every turn. Thomas was still a little rough and I had to watch him every second when they were together, but Hallie was patiently demonstrating for him. For her part, Trouble appeared completely unruffled. *Things can't keep going this well, right…?*

"Hey."

I whirled, hand pressed to my chest, to find Danny at the threshold to the kitchen. I'd had my head in the refrigerator and my mind completely elsewhere. "Oh, hey." I pulled the milk out. "Would you like a cup of warmed milk? Or hot chocolate? I don't think there's actually much caffeine in it."

"Shouldn't you be heading to bed?"

Danny eyed me as he ran his hand through his short, curly hair. *I wonder what it would be like if he grew it out. He said something about an afro in high school, right? Would it be like that?* Basically, I longed to touch. To connect. Holding hands earlier had been nice, but I wanted more. "Uh, I always have steamed milk before bed. I don't know if it actually makes a difference, but after the hustle home—"

"You didn't have to hustle tonight." He advanced toward me. "I'm not on the clock."

I blinked. "But I'm paying you."

He reared back and held up his hands. "Uh, no, you're not. A friend needed a favor. I did a friend a favor. I'm not taking your money." He squinted. "If James had come over, would you have tried to pay him?"

"Of course."

He chuckled. "Word of warning—don't. He'd come from the goodness of his heart. So would Colin. So, I suspect, would your other friends." He eyed me. "And you can't tell me that saving tonight's babysitting money won't make a difference. Because I know it will."

I hadn't come out and told him how tight our finances were…but I hadn't held back that information either. He was…a friend. And a confidant. Someone I could share things with. Breaking eye contact, I muttered, "Yeah, okay."

Again, he chuckled. "Grudging much?" He advanced over to the counter and pressed his hip against it. "I'll take a mug of hot chocolate. Before I hit the road."

"You should stay. You were fast asleep."

"Rob, it's a six-minute drive home. If that. I can stay awake for that. Now, two hours on the 5 would be a completely different story. But, as everyone likes to remind me, my home is in Gaynor Beach now."

"That simple?" I pulled the hot chocolate down from the cupboard.

"Yeah, that simple." He cocked his head. "Now, what's on your mind? You haven't asked how the night went, and I can tell something's nagging at you."

Part of me marveled that he could know that…and part of me wasn't surprised at all.

The microwave beeped with my steamed milk. I pulled it out, finished mixing chocolate powder with milk for his drink, then put that in the microwave and set it.

"Rob." He used that exasperated tone that he generally seemed to reserve for this family.

"Danny," I shot back.

He wagged his finger at me. "Don't try that, my friend. I don't put up with that from anyone." Yet his eyes shone and a smile broke through, clearly putting a lie to his words.

"Wynn Cavanah called tonight while I was working."

Danny scrunched his nose. "I want to say that's the lawyer—"

"He is." I sipped my milk, wincing at it being too hot.

The microwave beeped, and I pulled Danny's drink from it. "Watch it, it's super hot."

He took it and sipped. "Perfect. I like my coffee extra hot."

"Hey…" I indicated the kitchen table.

He sat.

I did as well. "We haven't discussed dietary restrictions. To do with your donation. I know booze is out."

"Uh…that's the big one. There's a small list of things to avoid, but it's not significant. You'd never put them all in one meal… or it would be the weirdest meal ever." He laughed. "Honestly, it's not a big deal." He cocked his head. "Why, you planning to feed me a lot?"

I blinked. *Shit. I haven't asked him.* "Uh…" My resolve crumbled.

"Right." He took a sip and grinned. "You need a babysitter until Nai recovers from pneumonia. Maybe even longer if her parents aren't happy with her coming this far—"

"They said they didn't mind."

"And maybe they won't. But you haven't actually done it yet, so you don't know what the reality will look like. Possibly different than you envisioned."

"Danny."

"Rob." He parroted back the same voice. "I told you that tone won't work for me. I'm babysitting every night well into the future, and it's a total win-win. See…I got a ton of schoolwork accomplished. I couldn't turn on the television, so it focused me on getting done what needs to be done. My program runs in the afternoon and evenings back east. I'm done by five since that's eight for them. I'll hustle over here, and you head to work. I watch the kids, then get in several solid hours of studying before you come home. I sleep in—since I don't have early classes—and then I'm fresh for my lessons."

"That coffee table can't be comfortable for studying. You could come in here—"

"I know you've got a monitor for Thomas. I'd want one for Hallie as well." He scratched his nose. "I'd be happy to buy it…"

I thought of the gadgets I'd had back in LA—the nanny cam and the baby monitor. I'd believed I needed all those things to be a good dad. As I'd discovered here, just being tuned in to my kids was enough. Parenting on a basic level. Having the tech as a back-up wasn't a bad thing… but I had bigger priorities. "Uh, yeah, we're fine." Nai hadn't said she had any issues with Hallie.

"Here's the thing…" Danny pointed to the closet that could be turned into a mini den. "You could totally fit a small desk, ergonomic chair, and a couple of shelves. You're not using it for anything else right now—"

Because I don't have anything to put in there. Because I don't have stuff. And was that a bad thing? Again, living a pared-down life wasn't leaving us deprived. "No, nothing else."

"Right. Nai might want to use it and, for sure, Hallie would enjoy the space when she's older and needs quiet. I suspect Thomas will drive her nuts."

"You noticed."

"Yeah, he does not like when her attention is focused on reading books. I did my best to keep him distracted…"

"But he can be unrelenting, I know. Of course we can turn the cupboard into a den." Dollar signs floated in my head. But if I saved the money I would've paid Nai, it wouldn't take long to have the funds.

"Great. Leave it to me."

"Uh—"

"Now, what did the lawyer say?"

Take a deep breath. "That my ex-husband punched the process server when she delivered the divorce papers."

CHAPTER 21

DANNY

I BLINKED.

Several times.

"You're saying…"

Rob nodded.

"Jesus. And you were married to that idiot for…"

"Six years?" He winced as he framed it like a question.

"No, I didn't mean it like that." He took it as an insult while I meant it as awe. He'd managed to put up with that asshole for six fucking years. Sure, he hadn't felt like he could leave. But living with someone so obviously volatile —and stupid—took courage. "What happened?"

"Happened?"

"After he punched her…"

"Oh. Right. Well, the police came and arrested him, obviously. And the poor woman's got a broken nose. He seems good at that. She's not going to sue us, thank God. Wynn warned her employer that my ex was violent. Apparently that employer didn't warn her. Or… something…" He waved his hand. "My ex is considered served. I'm supposed to hear from the assistant district attorney tomorrow." He cleared his throat. "Mr. Cavanah thinks my ex is likely to plead out. Especially now there are two charges. He might've been able to try to talk his way out of the first one. But this one is neatly wrapped up. Mr. Cavanah is thinking jail time."

"Is he in jail now?"

Rob nodded.

"So you can breathe a little easier, right? I mean, I don't want to make assumptions—"

"No, you're right." His smile, though, was forced. "He's going to get out. Eventually he'll see the light of day again. And I can keep the kids, and myself, hidden. But no one's really safe, you know?"

"I'd say the threat of going back to jail is a powerful incentive to behave. But I also know the recidivism rate for violent criminals. He's going to lose everything, right?"

"Mr. Cavanah said I'm entitled to half, and the law's pretty clear about that. My ex will either have to fork over the cash for half of everything or sell the mansion to pay for it. Mr. Cavanah says he's done some digging, and my ex has quite a few offshore bank accounts." Rob winced. "There are hints of tax fraud, so the government will have the first crack at everything. Mr. Cavanah says it's a mess. But he swears there'll be something left at the end. The house is entirely paid for. Unencumbered, I think he said. He said he can arrange for someone to go with me to get my stuff." Rob rubbed his hand across his face. "I don't think I can go back."

"Nothing is worth that kind of stress." I longed to reach out, but still held myself back. "But someone could go for you, right? If you made up a list of what really mattered? There's got to be some of the kids' things…"

"Like their baby books? And their footprints? Yeah, for sure."

"Well, I can go." I grinned. "I've got time on my hands."

"You've got studying and—" He cut himself off.

"Babysitting? You bet. But I can take a day. James will come with me. If we drag Colin and make him sit in the car, and we can swing by my parents' place on the way home. Daddy's promised to make his famous barbecue ribs. Oh, I could bring some for you. Wow. Mama's a great cook…but Daddy's even better when it comes to the grill."

Rob held up his hand. "I can't ask you—"

"You didn't." I shrugged. "I offered. Work it out with your lawyer. Better that I get up there sooner rather than later. Grab the stuff for the kids and anything you want. I agree you shouldn't take anything that's not clearly yours. No sense poking the bear." *The asshole bear.*

"I'd like the pictures. There's an amazing family portrait…" He bit his lower lip.

"Hey, I know a graphic artist up in LA. If I give her the portrait, I'm sure she can erase scumbag right out of it."

Rob blinked. "How did you know?"

Finally, I advanced a couple of paces toward him. "Because I know you. Or I'm getting to, anyway. You'd want the memory of your children when they were younger. But you wouldn't want him in the picture. Leave it with me. My friend is amazing."

"I can't ask—"

"Fucking stop saying that. You didn't ask. I offered. And I'm going to keep offering. See, this is the great thing about being friends. We get to do things for each other, and the other person has to accept them with a smile. Like you took Drizella for me. Now you have to smile while I do this for you."

He let out a watery laugh. "I'm pretty sure that's not the actual definition of friendship."

"Well, it's the definition of being my friend. And of James's. And I'm certain Colin's and for sure Gracie's and if you toss in Mama and—"

He moved swiftly, suddenly putting himself just a foot in front of me.

I had to look down a bit, and I hated that. I didn't want my size—both height and bulk—to intimidate him. I wanted him to trust me. To feel comfortable around me.

Hesitantly, he reached out his hand to lay it on my chest.

Over my heart.

He looked up at me, blinking several times. "You're a good man, Danny Reynolds. One of the best men I've ever met. And I feel like I'm not worthy—"

Oh, fuck this shit.

Having taken him touching me as permission to touch back, I gently laid my finger against his lips. An incredibly intimate gesture. One I never would've considered if he hadn't made the first move.

He desisted. His gray eyes went wide.

"Tell me to stop, if this isn't what you—"

He moved so quickly that I didn't have time to blink. He had his arms around my neck and was cuddling up against me. Clinging to me. Shaking even as I wrapped my arms around him.

I sort of thought this was going in a different direction.

Yeah, you wanted a kiss.

I did.

You don't always get what you want.

As I held Rob, I defied my inner voice to argue the point further. I'd wanted this man in my arms since I'd first seen him—vulnerable, nearly broken, but valiantly holding it together for the sake of his children. I'd wanted to comfort. To offer protection. To nurture.

Now, though, I wanted him in my arms for an entirely different reason as well. To cherish. To make love to. And yeah, also to guard. I was sure as shit glad his scumbag ex was in jail and that Rob didn't need my added protection. I'd still offer it. For as long as I drew breath, I'd keep vigil over this family. I tucked his head under my chin, fitting him in perfectly against me. "I'll be here, Rob. However you'll have me."

He shuddered.

God, was I saying the right words? I'd never been in this situation. Had never had anyone depending on me. Needing me. Not that Rob *needed* me. He could do this without me. He'd survived two years on the street and six years in an abusive marriage—he had inner strength... even if he didn't recognize it.

Finally, he pulled back. Didn't loosen his grip on me. Just angled his head back.

I met his gaze. I thought I saw desire. I thought I saw him asking me to kiss him. But I couldn't be sure and I sure as shit couldn't get this wrong. "I need you to say it, Rob."

He blinked, then touched his lips. "Please?"

Okay, that was good enough. Slowly—so as to give him plenty of time to pull back—I lowered my head to his.

His eyes drifted shut.

I didn't know whether to take that as a good sign or not. My own closed as I pressed my lips to his.

Softness. Pliancy. Gentleness.

He opened his mouth and I read that as an invitation. As if I had all the time in the world, I slid my tongue inside —gently gliding it along his. He shuddered.

I hope that's an 'I'm turned on' thing. I didn't know him well enough. Knew the vulnerabilities, sure, but not what he liked. What turned him on. What would make him feel good. I splayed my hands across his back and pulled him closer…all the while not wanting to crowd him. I wanted to bring him pleasure without panicking him.

After a moment, he pulled back.

Our gazes locked.

He quirked an eyebrow. "I can hear you thinking, Danny."

"Uh—"

"I know you think I'm breakable. I know you think I'm damaged—"

"I don't."

"—and you might not be wrong on that score."

I frowned.

"But I'm also choosing to touch you. And to be touched by you. I don't want to talk about my ex…but he was never violent and vicious in *that* way. He used sex as a weapon, sure. But only psychologically. I've talked to a counsellor."

"You have?" I frowned.

"I don't tell you everything, Danny. I have some secrets. Some things I feel I need to keep to myself."

I shoved down the feeling of hurt because he was absolutely right. Still, I would've preferred to know more. Like if his taking the lead with…whatever this was…was the right course of action. Whether I might say or do something to spook him—even inadvertently. If we even had a future together or if that was just wishful thinking on my part. "Whatever you want to tell me, Rob. I'm here to listen."

"Maybe just…" He grinned. "Kiss me again?"

"Yeah, I can do that."

CHAPTER 22

ROB

Danny Reynolds was a stubborn man.

In so, so, so many ways.

By the end of the first week of him babysitting, the entire closet had been transformed into a fully functioning office space. He argued I'd need a place to go when I was studying for my GED. Which, admittedly, was going slower than I would've liked.

By the end of the second week, he'd convinced me to take the exam to get my learner's permit.

I passed.

He celebrated. Then started making noises about me taking lessons.

Gently, I asked that we take one step at a time. The idea of driving terrified me…even though I'd readily admit it would be easier to get around with the kids.

By the end of the third week, Nai's doctor said that although she was healthy enough to return to school, there was no way she could put in the late nights she'd been doing for me. Regretfully, she tendered her resignation.

Danny celebrated.

Personally, I thought he was nuts. But he insisted this put him in the running for best-babysitter-ever award from Hallie, which Nai had been a shoo-in for until now.

I rolled my eyes.

Then Hallie told me that she'd miss Nai, but Danny was lots of fun. That warmed me and worried me. I was thrilled Danny and my kids were getting along so well. I was terrified for the day he quit and I was back to seeking someone to help. Because he was going to quit. He couldn't keep up with his schoolwork *and* watch my kids six days a week.

Plenty of single parents do. You're practically co-parenting.

A treacherous thought I had to suppress.

Because every night when I got home, there were *glad you're home from work* kisses. *How was your evening* kisses. *Goodnight* kisses.

So much kissing.

I never found the courage to ask him for more. Never found the guts to invite him to spend the night. I could've explained it to the kids. *Danny was too tired to drive home, and he slept in my bed.* The lie would fall easily from my lips…but I never had to use it.

By the end of the fifth week, he announced I was to be his 'date' for Colin and James's wedding in two weeks and Mama was arranging outfits for my kids and I couldn't possibly disappoint Mama by refusing.

Considering we'd eaten dinner at the Reynolds clan home in Huntington Beach the Sunday before and I'd met the formidable Mama, I knew resistance was futile. My kids had played hard with all Danny's nieces and nephews. His sister had even let Hallie sit on my lap with little baby Keyla in her arms.

I couldn't remember my two ever being that tiny. But the premature twins were thriving and, according to

Danny, getting bigger every day. He'd sat next to me with Malaya in his massive arms.

Arms I liked to remember holding me with the same exquisite gentleness…

The babble of the wedding crowd broke through my memories. Here we were in those fancy clothes, in the middle of the Reynolds family.

Gracie poked me.

"Hey." I attempted indignant. I'd learned, at the family dinner, to watch my back with this Reynolds sister.

"You're getting that dreamy look again."

We sat next to each other in the second row. Hallie sat to my left, while I managed to keep Thomas on my lap. Gracie held Shanice…Leticia's middle daughter.

See? I could keep track.

Sort of.

Hallie tugged on my sleeve. "Soon, Papa?"

Even as she asked the question, the music changed.

To my surprise, James and Colin walked to the front of the gathered crowd together—hand in hand. Danny and Arthur stood at the front by the minister. Danny was Colin's best man while Arthur was James's. I'd been surprised…until Danny gently reminded me that Colin didn't have family he was in contact with. That he was a Reynolds now. And with the donation…he'd asked Danny. But only after he'd ensured Arthur would stand up for James. Considering their deep friendship, even the shy Arthur had been happy to agree. He pulled at his collar, but other than that, he did an admirable job.

To my relief, the service was over almost as soon as it had begun. I was expecting something like the church back home which went on for hours and hours. I'd worried about Thomas staying still for that long.

Colin pledged himself to James as tears rolled down

the men's cheeks. They'd been though so much together. Not just Colin's illness, although that was significant, but just all life had thrown at them. They'd survived. They'd made it through. They were clearly going to have a strong marriage.

I'd believed, all those years ago, that would happen for me. And maybe if I'd really loved Gerard instead of hero-worshiped him…

No. Don't go there. You did everything you could to make that marriage work. That it ended so disastrously is on him. Not you. I drew in a deep breath, holding Thomas steady. What would it be like? To marry someone I really loved. To be unified with someone who saw me for who I am and not who they thought I should be. Would I be as happy as these two men? As they exchanged rings, I blinked several times.

I wasn't going to give up on love. What I'd experienced with Gerard had never been love. Maybe in the future…? I spotted Danny wiping away a tear as well.

Our gazes met.

My breath held at the swell of emotion he conveyed. He loved his brother so much, but had been happy to stand up for Colin. A man who had no family here. Not that he would've wanted them. No, Colin was now officially a Reynolds.

I envied him that.

Barely ten minutes after Colin and James walked up the aisle, they kissed, cupping each other's faces, Colin on his toes, mouths fused like they were each other's oxygen. Then they walked back down. Only this time, they grabbed any niece and nephew interested in joining them and they had a weird conga line.

To my delight, Hallie wanted to join, and I let her go, even though I lost sight of her in the crowd of children. I didn't plunge after her. Possibly one of the hardest things I'd ever done. Because I'd spent four years being her shadow any time we left the house. My vigilance knew no bounds as I was aware of her every movement.

Her every breath.

And I knew that wasn't healthy. She needed to find her own oxygen. To find her own spirit.

To have a life beyond me.

Well, a few feet, anyway.

Gracie nudged me, and I let Thomas slither to the floor.

I snagged his hand. "You ready to go?"

He nodded with a toothy, gummy, drooly grin.

Teething.

I wiped his chin before we headed down the aisle with everyone else.

The grand ballroom of the venue was, in fact, grand. Danny joked they had three hundred and ten relatives who could be directly linked within one step or two. Most had been invited. Many had declined, saying they didn't get enough notice.

James didn't seem too upset about that. I had the impression he was of the *smaller is better* camp while Colin was the one who wanted James's family—and the entire world—to see how happy he was. How much he appreciated his second chance at life.

Danny scooped Hallie up and twirled her as several of his nieces clamored for the same thing. He was proving to be the most popular adult in the room for the under-tens.

A photographer snapped a few candid shots, then tried to gather the family members. Danny had said the photos would be on the beach while the venue staff set up for dinner.

My stomach rumbled. I'd remembered to feed the kids,

but had grabbed just a slice of toast as Gracie had piled us all into her car. That she'd come down to get us warmed my heart. Danny had wanted to drive us, but was needed way earlier, and Thomas, Hallie, and I would've wound up waiting around. So Gracie had stepped in.

You're starting driving lessons next week. Soon you'll be independent. Suddenly, that day couldn't come soon enough.

"Hey, let's go." Danny appeared before me. He had Hallie by the hand and, somehow, managed to scoop Thomas into his arms.

My boy poked Danny's clean-shaven jaw. For a guy who often went a few days between shaving, he'd cleaned up nicely today.

"Go where?" I asked.

"Pictures on the beach."

I squinted. "Uh, Danny, that's for family. Gracie's waving…you better go." I tried to take Thomas from his arms, but my boy squawked his protest.

"I want my picture, Papa." Hallie fingered her beautiful pink dress that Mama had so lovingly—and perfectly—selected. And she'd matched Thomas's tie the same pink and, my God, my kids looked adorable. Gracie had snapped a couple of pictures of the three of us, but they wouldn't be as good as the professional's.

Danny leaned close to my ear. "Just roll with it."

I had to chuckle. Of everyone here, I was probably the least capable of just *rolling with it*. But I owed him everything, and so I followed him into the bright sunlight. April's weather could prove unpredictable, but it was like Mama had waved her magic wand and everything was perfect.

The photographer, being a smart woman, had all the children pose first. She spotted Hallie and Thomas and insisted they be part of the shot.

"The more the merrier," Daddy said.

"They're like family," Mama added.

Like I'd argue with the couple I'd have done anything to have as my parents growing up. In the end, though, Danny's *please* won me over.

Hallie held Thomas who actually stayed still. Probably in awe of so many children at once. Mama and Daddy's entire pile of grandkids. Thomas looked like he belonged while Hallie obviously was the odd one out. Clearly, though, she didn't care. Maybe didn't even notice. She'd just met a great group of kids who wanted to play.

When the kids decided they'd had enough, several second cousins stepped in to corral them. I made a beeline for Thomas, who'd decided the water looked pretty. I had him scooped in my arms when Danny grabbed me by the waist.

"A quick shot." He had Hallie with him. In a moment, he had her in his arms. I had Thomas in mine.

The photographer took several photos.

My eyes burned.

Because of the sun, naturally. Obviously. Not because Danny wanted a memento of what he'd casually referred to as our first *official* date. Or of the fact he'd said he was so glad the kids were with us. I'd wanted to argue.

He'd kissed me into submission.

Now I'd have a photograph to hold close.

Gracie had her phone out as well and as Danny put Hallie back on the ground, my phone buzzed in my back pocket.

My gaze shot to Gracie, who had my number in case of emergencies.

She grinned and gave me a thumbs-up.

My heart soared. This family always thought of the

little things. They always had a camera at the ready. Or an adult there to help.

Leticia plopped one of the twins into my arms and headed back for a sibling photo.

I stared down at a wide-eyed infant who stared back up at me. "Are you Keyla or Malaya?"

She wiggled her butt, and I realized a diaper change was in order. Spotting Leticia's bag, I snagged a clean one and took Thomas in search of our abandoned knapsack. Timing was perfect as my son had just done his business too.

The baby wriggled a lot, but I eventually managed to get a clean diaper on her.

One of the aunts I'd been introduced to held her while I quickly changed Thomas.

I washed my hands and disposed of the diapers, then I took the baby back into my arms, grabbed Thomas by the hand, and we headed out together. I marveled at the infant being so placid. Hallie had wailed anytime anyone touched her other than me. Especially when Gerard had tried. I supposed this baby got passed around a lot—what with so many people willing to love her.

Gracie greeted me as I stepped outside. "Groom photos."

Hallie held her hand.

"We might want to get some liquid into the kids." I eyed the sun. "And move to the shade?"

"Sure." As we moved, Gracie cocked her head. "Where are Widget and Trouble?"

I coughed out a laugh. "Uh, Drizella and Widget are hanging out at Oscar and Hugh's house. They're big fans of Hemingway the Newfoundland. The three dogs love to play together. Well, Widget has a definite size deficiency, but she sure makes up for it in bossiness."

"Right…" Gracie nodded. "There are a lot of gay men in Gaynor beach with kids and dogs."

I chuckled. "And plenty of lesbian couples. And a few nonbinary and trans folk as well. Yeah, it's a welcoming place. I'm so lucky Anthony took me there." I winced.

"You don't have to tell me." Gracie offered a gentle smile. "You're safe now. That's all that matters."

"Right." I glanced down at the infant in my arms who'd fallen asleep and then over to my children who had found a patch of sand and were building a sandcastle. Without water, though, they were doomed to fail.

But they didn't care.

And for that, I was eternally grateful.

"Oh, there you are." Bryan, Leticia's husband headed my way. "How is she?" He held out his arms.

Mine ached, but I would've kept going. "An angel." I passed her over. "She's newly changed."

"Oh, bless you." He leaned in toward me. "I'd have done it, but…"

"Sometimes it's nice to have a break?"

"Yes. That." He cooed. "Malaya is much calmer. I think Leticia did you a kindness by handing her to you. And you did a kindness to us by watching her." He gave me a nod and headed off to where I spotted Leticia with a squawking Keyla and a heavily pregnant Felicia. Who'd complained to me about why James couldn't have waited until she'd given birth. And Martin's wife Shondra was also pretty close to due.

I was damn proud for remembering all that.

Later, as I danced in the curve of Danny's arm as he held Hallie and I held Thomas, I acknowledged in my mind what my heart already knew…I loved this man. Although it'd happened gradually, the realization had hit hard and fast.

I just didn't know what I was going to do about it.

CHAPTER 23

DANNY

"How'd it go?" I gazed into Rob's eyes as I waved goodbye over my shoulder to Anthony who drove away.

Rob just kind of stared.

I put my arm around him and guided him into the house.

Today had been a court proceeding. He wouldn't talk to me about it ahead of time—had just said Anthony was driving him up to LA, and he'd be home as soon as they could. A bad accident had snarled traffic on the 5, and he was now coming home in near-darkness.

The kids were already in bed. And, given how shell-shocked he looked, I wasn't certain that was a bad thing. "Come into the kitchen. Have you eaten? There's leftover stew." Mama had sent another massive care package.

Like I wasn't perfectly capable of cooking meals. Like Rob wasn't.

Still, I wasn't going to deprive her of her joys. I'd known today would be a rough day, so I'd thawed the stew.

I guided Rob to the chair, and he slumped as I headed

to the fridge. I poured him a glass of cold water, for once wishing I had something stronger to give him. I didn't drink, obviously, and neither did he. He said he didn't like to lose control. I had a liver to protect. We made a good pair that way.

And in so many other ways.

I put a bowl of stew in the microwave and waited impatiently to it to heat. I'd eaten already. Early on, I'd discovered Hallie didn't want to eat if I didn't join her.

Thomas totally didn't care.

Putting a finger on Hallie's thinking had eluded me, but she ate when I ate and therefore, we ate together. Secretly, I wondered if it was a Gerard thing. Or just a wanting to feel seen thing. Or…I hadn't brought it up with Rob. I should have, given Hallie was still in counseling. I'd seen huge improvements with her. With reading, certainly, but also confidence in asking for what she wanted. For asserting herself. Almost never in a rude way—her manners were well ingrained. It'd taken the dog of a lifetime to shake them. Trouble—excuse me, Drizella—was Hallie's shadow, and the gentle love of the little girl for that bouncy dog was sweet to see.

Unlike Thomas, who was a typical one-year-old, and had neither manners nor ingrained gentleness yet. Growing by leaps and bounds every day. I loved snapping a picture of him and sending it to Rob while he worked. Something to keep us all connected. I sent plenty of pictures of Hallie as well, but she wasn't as enamored with having her photo taken. Except if I said, "Help Drizella pose for a photo for Papa." That she would do. I had a feeling most of Rob's photos of Hallie for the next decade would have dog fur in her face.

Tonight, the dog was in Hallie's bed, warding off

nightmares. Rob said they'd vastly decreased with her at Hallie's side. Which left me to take care of the man himself.

The microwave beeped. Gingerly, I carried the bowl to Rob. Then I added a spoon and, finally, sat down next to him.

"I…" He gazed at me through glassy eyes.

"Eat first."

He looked down at his bowl, scrunched his nose, and sighed. But then, to my relief, he picked up his spoon and started to slowly eat the stew.

I sipped my water, patiently waiting. We had all night. "Hey, do you want a roll? I started to rise. "I baked a batch—"

"How do you do it?" He indicated I should sit back down.

I did. Then I cocked my head. "Do what?"

"Bake?" He rubbed his forehead. "I can barely take care of the kids, and…" He winced.

I placed my hand over his. "Where is this coming from? I bake after the kids have gone to bed and while I'm studying. I can multitask, much to Whitney's annoyance. She just forgets what she's baking and it burns. It's all about the alarms." I tried for a smile.

He didn't return it.

"Rob."

Finally, he met my gaze.

"You're exhausted when you get home. You barely get enough sleep to survive, and then you've got kids to deal with all day. You do the shopping, the cleaning, much of the cooking—"

"Some."

I glared.

He glared back.

"Right. And then you go back to work."

"Danny, you've got school and homework and you do all the stuff around here. Plus I'm sure you do stuff at James's…"

I twitched my nose.

He frowned.

"Well, his argument is that they're paying a cleaner anyway, so the guy might as well do my apartment and get paid more."

"Oh."

"Right. And then James says he's cooking for two, so why not for three?"

"Oh."

"And they both know how much time I'm spending here, so they want to make life easier for me." I scratched my belly under my T-shirt. "Look, I don't want to be beholden to them for the rest of my life. But right now…" I sort of nodded. "This is what Colin needs. He's buying me a new car, electric, and he's thrilled I'm giving you mine—"

"Danny, you're nuts." He might've whisper-hissed that.

"Oh." I grinned. "I forgot to tell you, right? It's not the greatest of cars. Leticia's when she first got married. A million years ago—"

"Don't let her hear you say that."

"Truth." I waved him off. My sister had a sense of humor about the differences in our ages—she being the eldest and me being the youngest. "So, like I didn't even pay for it. But I've treated it well, and she's got a few good years left. You're doing me a favor. Now I don't have to find someone to buy it. That would've just been a hassle."

"No one in the three hundred and ten relatives?"

I guffawed. Quietly. "Uh, no. By the time Mel's old enough, it'll be too late. You need one. No one else does."

"You can't keep doing things for me."

"Sure I can. That's what friends are for."

"Friends don't give friends cars."

"Who says?" I gave him faux indignation. "Friendship means whatever we want it to mean." Slowly, I eased my hand so I wrapped it around his.

He shivered.

"You going to tell me what happened in LA?"

Those luminous gray eyes shimmered. "Not yet."

"Well, I want to kiss you and make it better."

He managed a watery laugh.

"And maybe you'll let me do something else?"

"Do I want to know?"

"I can be very creative."

Hours later, after an epic kissing make-out session on the couch, he allowed me to gather him in my lap.

"This can't possibly be comfortable." He rested his head against my shoulder.

I'd learned, from more than a month being with him, that he tended to open up more when we weren't looking each other in the eye. One of his quirks. Whether because of his experience with his family, Gerard, or both, I couldn't be sure.

Mama was more *you look at me when we're working through shit*, so this felt like evasiveness to me. But it worked for him, and I was willing to do it tonight if I might get some answers. While Daddy would take us out in the car to talk, Mama wanted you at the table and looking her in the eye. That hadn't always been comfortable, and had been really hard for James, but we loved Mama and did what she wanted. I wouldn't let her push Rob and the kids around, though. "I'm comfortable." I wrapped my arms around him and tucked his mussed hair against my cheek. "Share what you can."

"I went before a Family Court judge." His voice wobbled.

"What happened?" I didn't want to assume it was bad, even as he shook in my arms.

"She asked me a lot of questions. About my life with Gerard, about my life before…Wynn said she was trying to get a sense of whether I was a fit parent."

"Did someone say you weren't?"

"Gerard."

"Son of a bitch."

"Yeah. But Wynn argued that the word of a man accused of two assault charges shouldn't carry much weight."

I'd yet to meet Wynn, but he sounded like a great lawyer. And he was handling Rob's case pro bono. "And?"

"And she asked me a lot of questions. Like how I was raising the kids. And did I have help…?"

I waited.

"I told her I did. I said my best friend was helping me raise them. Would watch over them when I was at work. Was helping Hallie with her reading lessons. I said Hallie was reading at a grade three level and she was in counselling. I told her Thomas was running around and smiling all the time. I told her we had a dog named Drizella—"

"Oh, I bet that went over well—"

"—who Hallie had named. And how the kids loved the dog and the dog clearly loved them." He rubbed his face. "Wynn showed her all the pictures you'd taken. And of our house. Of the life we've built here. I said I didn't need a mansion. Didn't want a mansion. Just wanted my kids to be happy." His voice broke on that.

I was afraid to ask, but I did anyway. "What did the judge say?"

"That she could see how happy we were. How she'd make sure the divorce went through in six months. And how she'd make sure I got everything I was due." He sniffed. "Wynn says he'd like to be there when you and James get the kids' stuff. The judge said she was fine with that." He hiccupped. "And Wynn said Gerard's pleading guilty to the assaults and is looking at jail time. The judge today issued a restraining order. She said I can ask to have it rescinded if I want to, in the future, and I promised her I never would. She also said I should petition to have him stripped of his parental rights because he'll be convicted of a felony."

"Oh, thank God. I hoped you would."

Finally, Rob tilted his head up to look at me.

"I'd been doing research into what was involved. But I didn't want to say anything because it's got to be your decision."

"Well, once his conviction is confirmed, Wynn said he'll start the paperwork. So it'll be a done deal. He'll never have rights to the kids again. They'll never be forced to see him. We can just move on." Again, he shuddered.

So I pulled him even closer. "Talk to me."

"I just…how can it be over? How can it be that simple?"

"Because sometimes the good guys win. And gals. Folks. Sometimes the good folks win. Sometimes it's okay for things to go your way. Sometimes it's okay to be—gasp—happy."

Another sniff. "That's not me, Danny. That's not my life."

"But do you want it to be for Hallie and Thomas?"

He reared back to face me. "Of course."

"Then it's okay for it to be that way for you as well. You can protect them from all the shit out there and still be happy. And happiness is all relative. If you're living your best life, and showing them that, then you've done your job as a parent. Mama and Daddy fought over the years, Rob. Believe it or not, our lives weren't always sunshine and roses."

"I have trouble believing that."

I chuckled. "Yeah...I admit those times were few and far between, but we did have rough patches. But we came together as a family to push through. We believed in each other...supported each other. Held things together. Like when Felicia had a miscarriage. When Martin didn't make the NBA, despite being a fucking awesome college player. When Gracie had her heart broken by the first girl she ever brought home..."

"And you?" He gazed up at me.

"Well..." I looked upward, searching my memories. "I came out about the same time as my brother who was seven years older. And by then Gracie was out. Life was interesting with three queer kids in the house. Mama and Daddy didn't give a shit, but some of our extended family members got all uppity." I smiled. "Which is why we had fewer people at the wedding than might've otherwise been. And they're not missed."

"My parents—"

"I know."

He swallowed. "I had an aunt. Have," he corrected. "I want to write to her. To send her pictures of the kids. But I'm scared..."

"I'm certain my cybersecurity brother could probably track down a way for you to safely contact her. I assume you're worried about her safety?"

"Yeah."

"Let's see what James can do. Mama could always write—a grandmother to an aunt."

"She'd do that?"

Clearly the wheels were turning. "Sure, if you asked her. If you want to just send pictures of the kids without too much detail, Mama could do that. We have a PO Box in Huntington Beach."

"I'd really like that. I miss her. Even just knowing she's okay—"

"Let me see what I can do." I rubbed my hand up and down his arm, trying to create some friction. "You're tired."

As if on cue, he yawned. "Yeah, I kind of am." He fidgeted.

Pressing his ass against my groin. How many nights had I left here verging on blue balls? We only ever just kissed. His hand never strayed below the waist and so mine didn't either. He had to be the one to make the first move.

Although, if he kept rubbing against me, my cock was going to become interested. It had been earlier, like always, but when Rob ended the kisses, it'd become clear to me he was ready to talk. So I'd ignored my hard-on and had instead focused on what I could do for him. Whatever he needed from me. Which was, apparently, talking.

"Why don't I get you into bed?" I hugged him tight. "You need a good night's sleep."

"Will you stay?" He didn't meet my gaze.

Gently, I tipped his chin up so our eyes locked. "What are you asking?"

His eyes widened. "Oh no. Not that. Like…"

Since I was afraid he might say *not ever*, I offered a smile. "Whatever works, Rob."

"Maybe…cuddle?"

We cuddled frequently, so I assumed I knew what he wanted. I loved when I embraced him tightly. "In your bed?"

"Yeah."

"That I can do."

I hadn't envisioned sleeping in my jeans that night, but, as I held Rob tight—and he drifted off to sleep—I had zero regrets.

CHAPTER 24
ROB

"Rob!"

Danny's cry of alarm rocketed through me and I was sitting up in just a fraction of a second. My addled, sleep-filled brain said I should worry about Danny being in the bed, but I was alone. *He probably snuck out before the kids woke up.* I rubbed my face, cut a quick glance to the clock radio, and nearly had a heart attack.

Ten o'clock.

How was that even possible? Thomas was up at six-thirty every morning. Train conductors could set their rides to his schedule. Panic seized me. I bolted from the room and stumbled down the hallway. Danny stood at the door as soon as he saw me, he ran out, slamming it behind him. Something he never did.

I located Hallie standing, clearly bewildered, in the middle of the room. "Where's Thomas?" My brain just really wouldn't kick into gear.

"Drizella's lost."

I blinked, then shook my head, trying to dislodge the cobwebs. "Thomas?"

She pointed to the playpen.

Where Thomas sat, playing with his train. Apparently oblivious to everything around him.

Lucky him.

Despite needing to take a piss super badly, I blinked at Hallie. "How did you get Thomas out of bed?"

"Danny."

"Right." That made sense. Then Hallie's words sank in. "Where is Drizella?"

"Gone."

"Gone? You mean like Danny took her for a walk?" I hadn't seen the dog, but maybe she was outside already and that was his hurry. Except we had a fenced-in backyard. If her need to go had been urgent, she could've gone back there.

Hallie shook her head. "No. Drizella gone."

"Okay."

Thomas, without warning, started fussing.

I knew that fuss. I darted into the kitchen, grabbed a frozen rubber teething ring, and brought it back to him.

He gave me *that* look. But he took it.

That felt like a monumental victory.

Still fuzzy, I yanked out my phone and texted Danny, asking him where he was. I tried for casual, but was wasting my time as his phone, on the coffee table, buzzed.

Well, shit.

My bladder was about to explode. All that water he'd convinced me to drink. He was always taking care of me and now…I didn't even know where he was.

"Hallie?"

"Yes, Papa?"

"Can you watch Thomas? Just for a moment?" He was in his playpen, and I wasn't putting Hallie in charge, but I needed to pee.

She rolled her eyes.

I was so stunned that I just stood there for a moment. My daughter had never rolled her eyes at me before. Which had sort of worried me…but I couldn't take a moment to savor this moment. "Be right back." I ran to the bathroom, emptied my bladder, splashed cold water on my face, washed then went into my room. I'd worn sweatpants and a T-shirt to bed last night, but those felt… too casual?

Right, because that's what really matters right now.

This time, I was the one rolling my eyes. I yanked down my sweats, then pulled on my jeans. After I'd done them up, I swapped for a fresh T-shirt. As I sprinted back to the living room, I lamented not having time to put on deodorant, but…priorities.

I returned to the living room where Thomas had pulled himself up and clearly wanted out. I hefted him out and put him on a blanket on the floor with his action-hero toy made for kids his age.

"Papa?"

"Yes, sweetheart?"

She just stared at me.

"Have you eaten?" Now I was getting my bearings, I needed to figure out what had and had not been done. I rubbed my face. "What happened exactly?"

"Danny said someone's coming and he'd get the door quick quick so the doorbell wouldn't wake you." Hallie frowned. Grammatical mistakes were rarer these days— except when she was upset. "He opened the door and Drizella ran away."

Slowly, the pieces were coming together. I noticed the abandoned package on the ground. I couldn't even remember what I might've ordered. Even as I had the thought, a burst of lightning rent the sky. I hadn't noticed the day getting darker. Or maybe it had always been darker. "Okay, so Danny ran after Drizella?"

"After you came out."

Ah. That makes more sense. He'd woken me, of course. And as soon as he'd been certain I was up, he'd bolted.

"And he said he'd be back?" I hadn't heard anything in my befuddled state, but maybe Hallie had.

She nodded emphatically. "Right back." She said the words with certainty. Then met my gaze. "But he's not."

I thought of the times Gerard promised to be home and then just never made it. I'd always covered, and told myself Hallie was too young to understand. Now I wondered if I'd been wrong. I crouched before her. "If he said he'd be *right back*, then he meant it. And if he's not here, that means he's looking for Drizella. That means we have faith in him." I doubted she knew what faith meant… but I did. And I knew, without a shadow of a doubt, he'd be back.

Well, even if just to get his phone.

Shut up.

I silenced my inner voice. Or tried to. Danny wasn't Gerard. Danny was the opposite of Gerard. If he wasn't here, then there was a damn good—

Scratching at the door pulled my attention. I gave a fraction of a second's thought to the paint as I flew over and opened the door.

A very soaked Drizella launched herself at me.

I'd never been so happy to see a wet dog.

"Drizella!" Hallie barreled over.

I put out a hand to stop her. "Close the front door and grab a towel."

Thomas, who'd been abnormally silent, playing with his toy, had spotted the open door and was heading straight for it.

Hallie, wonderful child she was, got to the door first and closed it.

My darling son wailed.

After retrieving the old towel we always used for Drizella, Hallie came over and wrapped the dog in it.

Drizella gave Hallie plenty of licks.

So where's Danny?

Even as I had the thought, rain lashed the window.

Then I did something I'd never done before I'd met Danny and his family—I called and asked for help.

And within twelve minutes, help arrived.

James stepped inside, deftly avoiding the wet dog determined to greet him. He offered a sheepish smile. "Sorry, just me. Colin's dead asleep. He had a rough night, and—"

I held up my hand. "You don't have to apologize. I'm glad he's sleeping. If you want to tell me later about his bad night—or not—that works."

"Sometimes he has dreams of waking up from the anesthetic and being on the operating table. It's...weird."

"Yeah." I winced. "Danny's never said he has that. Anyway." I swallowed. "I have to go find your stubborn brother."

James eyed the rain. "I'm assuming you called him..."

I pointed to his phone. "He went chasing after Trouble—"

"Drizella," Hallie insisted.

"Uh, right." I thought of all the mischief the husky had managed to get into in the past few weeks. *Trouble* suited her. "Drizella." I said the name with extra emphasis.

Hallie beamed.

"So I'll get in my car and go find him." James cocked his head. "You still don't have a license, right?"

"No. Even if I did, I couldn't drive on my own."

James nodded in acknowledgement. "So I go and—"

"I need to be the one to do it, James."

"Okay…"

"He needs to know everything's okay."

"I can—"

"He needs to hear it from me. I have an idea where he's gone, so I'll try there. If I can't find him, I promise I'll come back. He won't…" I swallowed. "He'd never abandon his phone."

James advanced on me—clearly mindful of his height. He didn't have Danny's bulk, but he topped six feet by a bit. "He'd never abandon you or the children." He glanced down to find Hallie watching use intently. "Just—" He met my gaze. "—he feels…forever about you."

I wanted to argue. Danny was just twenty-one. And I was an immature twenty-four. Neither of us should be making decisions like that. But I couldn't. Because I'd been married at eighteen—and that might've been a mistake, but I'd had Hallie by the time I was twenty and had exactly zero regrets. Danny had already donated part of his liver and found a serious course of study that would take him years to complete—but he was determined.

So…was it possible we did know? That what I felt might be more than infatuation and gratitude?

I couldn't tell right now.

"Let me take my phone." I tucked it in the back of my jeans and frantically tried to think of anything else I might need.

James now had Thomas in his arms.

Thomas was yanking my friend's beard.

Said friend was laughing.

Friend.

Suddenly I had people I could call. If Scott or Oscar hadn't been working, they would've taken the kids. If

Anthony wasn't working a critical case, he might've come over. And I'd met other people. That nice couple…Joe and Alec. With their son Kevin. I'd seen them a few times. A lovely older woman lived across the street. If Nai wasn't in school, she would've come.

A warm glow settled inside me, even as I donned my raincoat. That would do nothing to keep out the driving rain.

But I had to pretend.

I gave Hallie a kiss. "You be good."

"I'm always good."

"Yes, sweetheart, you are. You can show Thomas how to be good."

"It's handled." James managed to rescue his glasses before Thomas nabbed them as well. "I've done this a hundred times before." He considered. "Probably more. Just go."

And so I did.

CHAPTER 25

DANNY

"Drizella!" I wiped my forehead so the drips didn't go into my eyes.

"Gracie!" Still felt weird, but whatever.

"Trouble!" For good measure.

And still the rain came down.

You should go home. Call…animal control? Law enforcement? Arthur? Arthur felt vaguely logical. If any animal was found, they'd usually be taken to his home. Oh, or the Pam woman he'd complained about. Well, complain was a strong word. Had he said…indecisive. *What the fuck, dude? This is what you're focused on?* Well, anything was better than admitting I lost the dog. Hallie's dog, really. Thomas and Rob might love Trouble, but she really belonged to Hallie.

And the name *Drizella* just had to go. Of all the options I'd been shouting—that was the most painful. Hallie loving it swayed me ever so close to acceptance. Maybe I could call the mutt *Trouble* while everyone else—

"Danny!"

Even over the howl of the wind, there was no mistaking my name. I spun from the beach where I stood uselessly and gazed up toward the boardwalk. I'd first tried Druscilla's house. Then the three parks Trouble loved. Finally, I'd come to where I'd always had the sense she was happiest—the beach. I'd checked all along the boardwalk from almost the lighthouse to Riverside with no luck. I'd stupidly left my phone at home—

No, I'd left my phone at Rob's, and—

"Danny!"

Yeah, that was Rob's voice.

I waved and started to jog. The sand was heavy under my sneakers, but I finally managed to get some traction. Rain continued to lash my face. It hadn't been so bad when I'd first headed out. I didn't have a coat at Rob's and I'd been in a hurry, so I'd just headed out as was—sweatshirt and jeans. Both were, of course, completely soaked through.

Rob left the boardwalk and met me halfway. He gazed up at me, shielding his eyes from the pounding rain. "We need to get you inside."

"I have to find Trouble."

He managed a grin, although the strain on his face was clear. Only Rob could smile and still furrow his brow. "Drizella came home."

I crossed my arms.

"Trouble came home." Rob grinned. "Okay, but you have to convince Hallie. It's really her dog."

Lightning streaked the sky, followed by a crash of thunder.

I wrapped my arm around Rob's shoulder—as if I could somehow protect him from the storm. "Let's get you home. I don't suppose you brought a car."

"Uh, no." His teeth chattered.

Damn. "Should we call a cab?"

"Quicker just to run. And we'd soak the upholstery of a cab."

I loved how, even in the middle of a massive storm, he was worried about someone else. "Hey, who's watching the kids?"

"James."

I nearly tripped. "Great." Because I wasn't going to make a big deal of the fact Rob called my brother. I should've told him more before I bolted, but I figured I'd nab the dog and we'd be back home before Rob had time to panic. "How are the kids?"

He stopped and looked up at me. "They're fine, Danny. Hallie did great explaining."

"But she shouldn't have had to." I wiped my face. "I can't even look after a dog and two kids. I…" Worry poured out of me. "I keep waiting to make a mistake. I say it's easy, but it's not. I was constantly worried with my nieces and nephews. But I never…" I swallowed. "I lost the damn dog, Rob. If I can't even watch over a dog, how can I keep your kids safe?"

He blinked. "I have no idea what you're talking about. Of course you can take care of my kids. There's no one I trust them with more. I mean, James is great…but he's not you. And yeah, Trouble got out. So you know she's a little escape artist. She's almost made it past me a few times. We'll have to train the kids to be super careful and not to let her out. But…" He pressed a hand to my chest. "None of that detracts from your ability to care for my kids. They love you. Clearly you love them. I…" He wiped his eyes. "I can't do this without you, Danny. I thought I could…but I can't. And it's not the babysitting thing. That's great…but it's so much more. I can count on you. You get it. And you don't judge. You just help me be a better person. I…"

Say it. Please say it. Because I don't want to go first.

Yet he continued to flounder.

Okay, here goes nothing. Please don't let me be wrong. "I love you, Rob. I love everything about you."

A gust of wind nearly knocked me sideways, but I braced myself. At least I'd positioned myself so I took the brunt of that vicious wind. "And we should probably go inside. But not before I tell you how much I love you. Because when we go back inside, then it's about the kids. In your world, they come first. That's the way it should be. And I don't have a problem with that. If I've fucked up here—and you don't love me—then we'll forget we ever had this conversation. But...I hope we won't lose what we had. And I don't mean the epic kissing sessions...although those were pretty sweet." I managed another smile. "I mean the times when we just sit and talk. Or when we hang out with the kids and Trouble."

Another flash of lightning and another crash of thunder that reverberated through my chest. I knew we needed to get out of the storm—but he also needed to know just how damn important he was to me.

Then, to my absolute surprise, he threw his arms around me and pressed himself to me. He fit perfectly, of course. I wound my arms around him and pulled him close.

"I love you too." He whispered the words just before he crashed his lips to mine.

And then another lightning strike followed by a burst of thunder.

He laughed as he pulled back. "I think Mother Nature approves."

"Well, sure..." I pulled him close for one more hug, then shielded him with my body as we headed home. For once, I didn't mind my bulk. I could keep him protected. Several times, in fact, he'd said he liked me the way I was.

He used the word *sturdy*—but not in a bad way. Apparently his soon-to-be ex-husband had been a runner. All slender and obsessed with weight. That had driven Rob nuts. He just wanted people around him to eat food and not be constantly complaining.

I never complained. And as long as I stayed healthy, I was good. Maybe a few pounds might come off. Because if I was living with Rob, then I could walk—and train—Trouble more. I tripped on a board on the boardwalk.

"Hey, are you okay?" Rob met my gaze with concern. "You're probably freezing. Maybe we should call—"

"I want us to be together. Like, all the time. And that's crazy, right? Because we barely know each other, and—"

"Danny."

"Yes."

"You know me better than anyone in the world ever has. Even my aunt Lizzie, who loves me dearly, doesn't know all my dark secrets. The stuff I keep buried. The stuff I shared with you, night after night, while I mopped and cleaned and you listened so wonderfully."

I blinked. *Because of the rain. Just because of the rain.* "I can't ask you to move in with me. But I hate going home every night."

"So don't." He smiled. "Come home with me now and just…stay."

"That simple?"

"Yeah…pretty much…" He blinked rain out of those fathomless gray eyes that haunted my dreams.

I had to try. "I'm twenty-one. That's…"

Rob laughed. "I was twenty when I got Hallie. You think I haven't been fucking terrified every day since? But…" He sighed. "We're a package deal. I told the judge I had help with the kids. And even if you walk away, you'll have helped me through what I hope will be the worst—"

"Shush." I hissed the word. "That was the worst. It only gets better from here." I shook my head—as if I could somehow dislodge the falling water from my hair. "I love you. Nothing else matters. Well, that you love me too is sort of important. Now, let's go."

And we did, darting up to the road and practically running to our home. Not actually running...because neither of us was in that good of shape. We needed do better, though. We needed to be around and healthy so we could take care of the kids, grandkids and, God willing, great-grandkids. We were certainly young enough. The rest was up to Hallie, Thomas, and any children they might have.

Plus any more children Rob and I might have. Two was great, and if they were all we were blessed with, that was just fine. But if another child in need came along...we'd find room in our hearts and in our home.

We burst through the front door and I slammed it shut, wincing at how loud the sound was. I didn't think Thomas would be down for a nap...then realized if he was sleeping through the insane storm, then a little slamming of a door wouldn't be an issue.

He wasn't sleeping, though. He was sitting on James's lap and they were playing patty-cake.

I grinned. Then toed off my shoes.

Hallie handed me the towel I was pretty sure we used for Trouble. And as I wiped myself down, the pungent wet-dog smell confirmed my suspicion. Still, her kindness touched me. "Thank you for this."

"I noticed there's a lot of stew." James glanced over at me for just a moment before resuming his game.

"Yeah." I peeled off my socks.

"Way more than Mama ever gives me." A smile curled his lips.

"I have a family."

Rob stilled.

James's grin grew. "Yeah, that's what I chalked it up to. I'm going to heat up some lunch while you two warm up in the shower. You could always share the shower in the main bathroom. To conserve hot water, of course." In one smooth move, he was off the couch with Thomas securely in his arms. "You hungry, little man?"

Thomas gurgled.

James bent to my favorite small girl. "Are you hungry, my little friend?"

Hallie beamed. "Yes, please. Stew."

"Yeah, Mama makes the best stew." He held out his hand and, to my infinite joy, Hallie took it.

Rob and I exchanged a look as James took the two kids into the kitchen. He swallowed. "She just—"

"Yeah."

"You know what that means."

"That she sees my brother as trustworthy?" I wanted to make a joke about how she'd soon learn the truth, but I couldn't. Not only because Rob might not see it as a joke but also because of the solemnity of the moment. Hallie trusted someone other than us. Someone who would take care of her. Who would love her.

That meant everything.

Still… "We don't have to share a shower. If we each shower quickly, there'll still be lots in the hot water tank."

"And if…" He met my gaze. "I want to?"

My heart sped up. "Conservation is critically important."

"Yeah." He grinned wickedly. "You tell yourself that… if it makes you happy."

"You make me happy." I crashed our lips together as he grabbed the back of my head and held on tight. I could've told him how he only needed to say *stop* and I would. But he knew that. I could've told him we could slow down. But he knew how to speak up. A few weeks ago, I would've worried. Since the wedding, though, things had been different. Not just physically. He was more open. More honest. More trusting.

"Last one there…" He flushed.

"Yeah, that…"

And we were off.

CHAPTER 26

ROB

Nerves set in as I eyed the massive walk-in shower in the bathroom off my bedroom.

Even when I lived on the streets, I'd managed to not have sex with anyone. That meant often starving, but I hadn't cared. I'd sort of assumed I was going to die anyway, so that hadn't mattered. But not giving up my virginity to some rando felt...important. And so when Gerard pulled me out of the hellhole of homelessness and offered me...everything...I was able to offer him something that I considered sacred in return.

I'd never truly gotten a sense of how Gerard felt about that. Sometimes he'd been hard to read. Other times—mainly when he was angry—he'd been an open book.

"Hey." Danny made plenty of noise as he approached me.

I turned to face him.

"James doesn't know everything. He was, in his own awkward way, trying to say he approves of us. Not that we need his approval," he was quick to add.

"But it's nice to have it." I slotted in the words and he

smiled the luminescent grin I had fallen in love with. I bit my lower lip. "I've never been with anyone except my ex—"

Danny winced.

"Yeah, I know. Pretty pathetic—"

"Hey." He said the word quite forcefully. "That's not at all what I meant. Just...I don't want to think about your ex. But if he's on your mind, then that's okay. But if you're comparing your experience to mine, then just don't. I was out early and, with Mama and Daddy's permission, dating. I had to bring the person home—which could be awkward when I was dating someone in the closet. But I had fun. And was young when I lost my virginity. Maybe too young. I have no regrets. I've been careful. Never had sex without a condom. Tested regularly. Last month, in fact. I'm negative, and I haven't been with anyone since the day we met in December."

I blinked. "That was four months ago."

He grinned. "Yeah, but I was...what did Mama call it...? Oh, *smitten*. She knew I'd found my person, and she teased me. So did Gracie."

"And James?"

He shivered. "Not so much. We really need to get out of these wet clothes. I know colds are caused by viruses and not from *being* cold, but I still think getting out of these would be better."

"Agreed." I tried to unbutton my jeans. "I was tested at the hospital."

"Hmm?" Danny looked up from where he was unbuttoning as well.

"They tested me for, like, all the stuff. I think the doctor was being careful. I guess abusive spouses are often cheating spouses. Anyway, I went to a local clinic near here as well. They were…very kind. Otherwise, I would've had to go down to San Diego."

"Okay." Danny yanked his T-shirt over his head.

The expanse of glorious mahogany muscle lay before me—with just the right amount of chest hair. Gerard had manscaped to within an inch of his life. I really preferred the natural look.

Danny met my gaze. "You said you went for testing?"

"Yeah. All clear again. Which was not surprising because Gerard was meticulous. If he fucked around behind my back…" I swallowed. "*When* he fucked around behind my back…"

Sharp dark-brown eyes lasered in on me.

I persisted. "I would be almost positive he used a condom. He was very health conscious. A negative status wouldn't be enough for him, I'm sure. I was the exception, as his husband, but I was also pretty much forbidden to interact with any other men. Or women, for that matter."

"Jesus." Danny muttered the word under his breath.

Whether I was meant to hear it or not, was another question. "Don't feel sorry for me. I made the choice to stay over and over, even after I saw how things were going to be."

"Right." His jaw tightened. "You had the choice between going back to the streets or staying in a luxurious mansion."

"We all have choices." I blinked. "He actually wanted children, and that was my dream too. We'd planned to have our own by surrogacy, but then Hallie arrived, and he said yes. I thought we were working toward the family I always wanted, until I finally realized how little these kids meant to him. I will never regret my children."

Danny moved swiftly to my side. "Of course not. I get it." He grasped my upper arms. "I just have trouble dealing with what you went through. But that's on me. You need to be able to discuss whatever you need to. The abuse, the trauma, the manipulations—all of it."

"I'm afraid you'll judge me—"

"Damn right I will."

I took a step back.

He gripped me tighter. "I'll judge that you're the strongest person I know. That you survived all that and you've made a life for yourself. I'll judge that you had terrible decisions to make, and the ones you made brought you here. To Gaynor Beach." He offered a shy smile. "And to me." He shivered. "And if we're not out of here sooner rather than later, James will call the Coast Guard to come find us."

I laughed. "Yeah, okay." Then, to my surprise, Danny yanked my T-shirt over my head. I'd removed my coat in the front hall and it hung to dry. "We'll need to put everything in the dryer."

"Sure." Gently, he snagged my cell phone from my back pocket and put it by the sink. "For safekeeping."

"And you'll never leave home without yours again, right?"

He chuckled. "Yes, I promise."

"Good." I didn't stop him when he unzipped my jeans and slowly tugged them down. They clung to me, of course, and by the time they were off, we were both laughing.

He straightened. "Are you okay with this? We've only ever kissed."

"I wanted more." Heat rose up my chest to my cheeks, and I imagined I was blushing. "I didn't know how to ask."

"Which is why we never went further. You have to tell me what you want, Rob. What you need. I'll give it to you —all of it. But only if I know it's really what you want."

Craving clawed at my belly. "I *need* you, Danny. Want you. Desire you. I just…I wasn't good at that stuff."

"Says who?"

I was quite certain my cheeks turned scarlet.

Danny stepped up to me. "Here's the thing…I want to say I don't ever want to talk about your ex again. But he looms like a specter because you're still working through everything he did to you. I can rail against him—and I will—but he also facilitated your adoption of your beautiful children. You had six years together. Six pivotal years in your life."

I frowned.

He managed a laugh. "Okay, every year is pivotal when you're our age. But I want to believe, when we're in our thirties, that we'll have a few boring years. Or, hell, in our eighties would be okay too."

My breath caught. "That long?"

"Uh…" He blew out a breath. "I didn't want to say this—"

"Then don't." I couldn't imagine he was about to say something bad, especially after the *eighties* comment…but I couldn't be certain.

His eyes widened.

I gulped. "Sorry. I'm so sorry. I just…I panicked. Am still panicking. Because if it's bad news—"

"Rob."

"Yeah."

"We're standing here half naked, and I just said I want to be with you into our eighties."

"Yeah."

He grasped my hand. "What I was going to say… again…is that I love you. And yeah, I get that it's too soon. We haven't even…" He gestured between our crotches. "But I don't care about that. If we only ever kissed for the rest of our lives, I wouldn't be disappointed. I'd be grateful. And happy. You knowing that is important to me."

"You love me?" The rest of what he said, although clearly important, blurred. He loved me. *Loved* me. He'd said it outside. In the storm. But that had felt like an *in the moment* kind of thing. Something I'd never hold him to. Because, aside from my children, I couldn't remember anyone ever having loved me. Certainly not for who I was rather than who they thought I should be. The obedient son. The docile husband.

The doormat.

I had been none of those things the past few months. I'd tried to step out of other people's expectations and just be a good person. A good father. A good friend. I didn't always feel like I succeeded, but I certainly tried.

Danny repeated, "Yes, I love you. Like more than just friends…although I'd pretty much call you my best friend. When something good or bad happens, I pick up my phone to text you. Or make sure it's the first thing I tell you when we're together again. I hated leaving every night, but I also knew you needed space. Hell, you still might—"

Moving swiftly, I used where we held hands to propel myself into his space. "I don't. Need space. Or time. I got my resolution, Danny, when I went to court. As far as I'm concerned, my marriage is over. Now it's just a matter of waiting the appropriate time, and then—" Crap. He hadn't talked marriage or—

He grinned. "We can, you know, make it official?"

"We don't have to rush."

"If we're married, though, then it's easier for me to adopt the kids, right?"

My heart seized. One night, during an epic kissing session, I'd shared my greatest fear—that if something happened to me, there'd be no one to take care of the kids, or worse, that they'd go to Gerard or his family. Danny had said he would and wanted to run to the lawyer the next day. We hadn't done it together, but I'd gone to Wynn the lawyer and had him draw the papers up. I had them in my sock drawer—waiting for me to find the courage to ask Danny if he'd been serious. That he was willing to take care of my kids if something happened. I could tell myself a million times that nothing would, but my mind wouldn't settle. Gerard being in jail helped…but only so much. "Uh, yeah." I blinked. "I have papers for you to sign that would make you guardian if—" My voice caught.

He pulled me into a hug. "I'll sign them as soon as we're out of the shower. If we need a witness, James will do it. If that's not good enough, and we need a notary, we'll work it out. Okay?"

I nodded as I clung to him. We'd come in here for some *fun* and instead we were making lifelong commitments to each other that, thank God, included my children. I was totally overwhelmed.

"Rob?"

"Mmm?"

"We need to strip and get into the shower. I'm happy to use the guest bathroom—"

"No, here's fine." I pulled back. "Together."

CHAPTER 27

DANNY

REMOVING MY JEANS PROVED AN EVEN BIGGER CHALLENGE than Rob's, but Rob getting the water a perfect temperature spurred me into serious action. That and the sight of his pert ass. Seeing him naked, I saw fewer sharp angles…more muscle. He was spending more time walking with the kids. Carrying them. Connecting with them. And he was less concerned about being slim. He hadn't come out and said his ex demanded that…but he'd implied it.

Once my jeans were off and I was completely naked, I checked to ensure the bathroom door was locked. Probably should've done that first, but better late than never.

Rob held back the curtain. "The water's warm. But I'm still cold."

I grinned at his obvious coyness. I liked the fun side of Rob. I didn't see it nearly enough, but I sure hoped to more in the future. After piling our clothes on the closed toilet lid —because making him wait just a minute or two was a good thing—I stepped into the massive shower to join him.

He was soaping his hair, with his back to me.

"Got started without me?"

He laughed. "Oh, not so much."

"Let me do that." I moved to him and as the warm spray hit me, I replaced his hands with mine and worked the shampoo up to a lather. "Is this…?" I sniffed.

"Passion fruit."

"Okay." I held in the grin—but barely.

"The kids have lavender."

"Which is for calm. I get it." Had given the baths a couple of nights when they'd gotten too messy to just wipe down. Chocolate fondue with pudding on nights when they wouldn't settle could be fun. But the mess was… interesting. I continued to smile. "Passion fruit?"

"Invigorating?"

"Okay, that's reasonable." He fought fatigue pretty much all the time. He'd had yesterday off work—after I'd suggested he tell Dr. Louisa he had a personal thing to take care of in LA and he'd be too tired to work. Wonderful woman had given him the time. Me moving in wouldn't solve all our problems. I was years away from finishing my degree, and although Colin was footing my schooling expenses, I couldn't expect him to support my new family as well. His gratitude would extend that far…but my pride didn't. I'd need to find some kind of job as well. On top of full-time school and watching the kids would be a challenge, but we'd manage. Plenty of couples with kids did.

"Danny?"

"Sorry." I kept massaging his scalp.

He moaned.

My cock perked up. Although I found him attractive, that was about a tenth of the list of reasons to be with him. I didn't care if we ever had sex.

No, that was wrong. I cared. But the intimacy we'd shared last night was almost as good. "Okay, rinse."

He turned, closed his eyes, and angled his head into the spray so the water removed the last of the suds.

I might've stolen a glance.

To ensure he was okay.

Yeah, right.

His semi had definite possibilities. It matched my own chubby. But I wasn't going to push. No matter how much James teased, I'd never—

"Danny?"

I gazed down into amused gray eyes. "Mmm?"

"We're going to, you know, do *something*…right?"

"Well, you have to wash my hair first."

He chuckled and made a show of looking me up and down. "You'll have to duck."

"I can wash my hair after…"

"After…"

"What do you want?"

"This." He stepped into my space, grasped the base of my skull, and yanked my lips toward his.

As always, his eyes drifted shut. So did mine, at the last moment.

He opened his mouth immediately, so I snagged the implicit invitation and slid my tongue into his mouth. We tangled and fought for supremacy as he thrust his tongue into my mouth.

I dragged my hands from his shoulders, down his arms, and lower. I shifted to his back, scraped my nails along his flanks, and finally grasped his ass and pressed him against me.

His erect cock brushed my own very interested shaft.

Can I? Is he ready? If I stop and ask, will that slow forward momentum? But is being naked enough of consent?

Rob pulled back. "Danny?"

"Yeah?"

"Just do it. I appreciate you thinking…" He blinked up as the water continued to cascade down his back. "But we have limited hot water."

Not *that* limited, but clearly his patience was running out. "You're sure?"

He pressed our groins together. "I trust you. I wouldn't be here if I didn't." He blinked. "I wouldn't leave you alone with my children every night if I didn't."

I swallowed. Part of this I'd known—the bit about the kids—but to have his trust explicitly given in such an intimate way spoke volumes about the relationship we'd built. "Okay." I grinned. "I hope you're ready."

He bit his lower lip. "I think I've been ready for a long time."

Not asking how long took patience. I wanted to know the moment I'd earned his trust, but this wasn't the time for *that* conversation. Instead, I grabbed the bottle of shower gel.

"Oh, this is going to be fun." He gave me an impish grin.

Casually, I shrugged. "I might just be planning to soap your back."

He pretended to pout as he pressed against me. "You're not that cruel."

His words were meant in a casual and teasing way, but I took them seriously. No, I wasn't cruel. I was as gentle as someone might be. Mama always joked James was the one who would shoo flies out the door rather than swat them. But I was always a close second, often bringing home strays —human and beasts. The humans would become friends…the beasts made their way to other homes or the animal shelter. Mama's allergies were something fierce. But

I was also a nurturer. I hadn't been certain, until mere moments ago, if my future might include kids.

It apparently did.

And I couldn't have been happier.

I put a small amount of gel in my hand, put the bottle back on the ledge, then snagged Rob's cock.

He grinned as he thrust into my fist. "Yes," he hissed. "That."

Chuckling, I managed to add mine alongside his.

If possible, he grinned wider. Skin on skin always had a greater element of intimacy. And I considered dropping to my knees and giving him a blow job, but I liked the idea we might come at about the same time. Together.

He grasped my shoulder as I pumped faster and faster. I watched his face, trying to judge how close to the edge he was. He tipped his head back, his corded neck showing as he swallowed. "Yes, Danny. Please…"

Please what? Faster? Harder? I wouldn't ask, of course. I just needed to push him to the edge and beyond.

Then, suddenly he dug his fingernails into my flesh and convulsed as he came. He let out a choking sob that might've scared me if he hadn't been spilling all over my hand.

Moments later, I jacked myself to a stunning climax. I fought for breath even as I pulsed against him. My knees threatened to give way, but—with Rob clinging to me—I was pretty much holding up both of us.

Finally, he tipped his head so he could gaze up into my eyes. "That was…"

"Yeah."

"And you…?"

"Oh yeah. For sure."

"We'd better…"

"Yeah." I angled us so the water could wash away the

cum. Then I used more shower gel to wash him off as best I could. I worried about the hot water and, since I didn't want to run out in the middle of shampooing my hair, I gave him a kiss and hustled him out of the shower. In the end, I was just shutting off the water as it was turning cold. *I should probably note how long that was.* Because I definitely intended to repeat that experience.

Rob wore a towel knotted around his waist and held out a huge bath sheet for me. I stepped into it and he wrapped the terrycloth around me, trapping my arms.

I bent to kiss him.

He grinned just before our lips touched.

Everything would be okay.

CHAPTER 28

ROB

JAMES, SITTING COMFORTABLY ON HIS OLD COUCH AND holding a sleeping Thomas, listened attentively as Hallie read another advanced story.

At first, she didn't spot me. I stood in the doorway, wet hair dripping down my neck, with Danny at my back, just watching my daughter with awe. How she'd advanced so quickly blew my mind. Every day she seemed to be learning new words. I had a dictionary app on my phone. She had my password so she could access the app when she wanted. I probably should've just bought her a dictionary, but I trusted her with my phone. She knew she didn't have permission to answer it or anything like that. Plus, she knew how to search for Danny and James's names and how to call them in an emergency.

Danny pressed a kiss to that sweet spot just behind my earlobe, his lips as warm as they'd been in the shower. "You did that, Rob. You've helped her grow into this amazing child."

He didn't just mean the reading. She was growing in her confidence. Starting to ask for things she wanted. Not cowering in fear. The change had been gradual, but as I stood, watching her read with confidence, the transformation nearly stole my breath. Gerard had nearly taken something precious—her ability to grow into the person she was meant to be. I'd tried to shield her from the fear. She was far too empathetic, though. Now, I hoped my happiness would give her more assurance to be herself.

I reached behind me to snag Danny's thigh, still buzzing a little from what we'd done, still shaken that I had the right to touch him that way. "Thank you." I whispered the words with what I hoped was just the right amount of both fierceness and gratitude.

"It's going to be okay."

Trouble raised her head from where she sat on the couch by Hallie. I was pretty sure she shouldn't be on the couch, but Widget was allowed, so that was hard to police, when they often played together. "I need to call Jordan."

"Jordan?"

"The trainer Arthur recommended. I kept meaning to…"

"I'll get that organized. Figure out a time he can come when we're all around." He chuckled. "Least I can do."

I needed to sort out our financial situation, but now wasn't the moment. Neither of us had much. If he moved in, he would likely insist on contributing. At a time when he didn't have many resources.

"James wants to train me to do some data entry for him. Basic stuff but he can pay me a decent salary for the contract work."

I glanced behind me, my eyebrow raised.

Danny shrugged. "A couple hours a day, but the money'll help."

"A lot."

"We'll make this work, Rob."

When I finished my probation at the clinic, I'd be eligible for health insurance for myself and the kids. I planned to get everyone in for full physical exams. Hallie's counselling would be covered as well. "I'm still scared."

"Because shit happens. I get it." His gaze softened. "Together, Rob. And you're supposed to get some of your ex's money, right?"

My breath caught. "Yeah, but—"

"You can put it in a college account for the kids. Maybe some for an emergency funds thingy. You won't have to feel guilty, because it's for the kids."

He was right, of course. The kids deserved whatever money I got out of my ill-advised marriage. I got them—that was enough.

"Papa!" Hallie held up her book.

"That's great, sweetheart." I advanced into the room.

Trouble leapt off the couch and made her way over to Danny. She ducked her head, then butted against his hand.

"In no way is that dog trying to apologize." I eyed her. "She's not that smart."

James chuckled. "Maybe she realizes who she has to suck up to."

"Well, that's true." Danny ruffled her fur. "You're forgiven…but don't do it again."

Trouble woofed.

Danny cocked his eyebrow. "You realize we're going to call you *Trouble* from now on." He met Hallie's gaze. "Sorry."

She shrugged. "Drizella's a mean sister." She pursed her lips. "Trouble." She said the name, as if testing it out.

Damn dog leapt on the couch, went over to Hallie, licked her cheek, then dropped to the cushion and laid her head on Hallie's thigh.

Hallie petted her.

Danny laughed. "Oh yeah." He cocked his head at James. "Can I feed you?"

He arched an eyebrow. "Who said we haven't already eaten? There were only about two bowls of stew, so we left those for you."

"Uncle James made grilled cheese." Hallie beamed.

"Your favorite." And now I looked closer, she and Thomas both had ketchup on their shirts.

James grinned. "We enjoyed ourselves." He indicated I should take Thomas. "I'll be back around six. You have the night off, right?"

Dr. Louisa insisted I take both Friday and Saturday nights off. With pay. Something about having access to personal days.

"Uh, yeah. Back on Monday." I scooped Thomas from James's arms.

My boy woke, farted, then closed his eyes and went right back to sleep

Everyone except Hallie laughed. She was too busy talking to Trouble.

Danny cocked his head. "Why are you coming by around six?"

James's grin widened. "Colin and I are babysitting tonight."

As if that was the most logical answer in the world. I stared. "Uh…why…?"

"Well, Colin needs practice around kids."

"Your ten nieces and nephews aren't enough?" That sort of blew my mind. Even my family had only six kids. Well, the extended was pretty big. *Be fruitful and multiply* was a thing in my family's church. But we didn't treat all the kids as our own, the way the Reynolds seemed to.

James shook his hand in a *so-so* motion. "We rarely get one-to-one time. He hasn't had the strength to go up to

Huntington Beach and, as of now, with Colin's health, no one's come down with kids."

Danny chuckled. "You know Felicia's itching to drop the boys off for a weekend sometime before the babies are born."

"Or after," James added. "We've offered. But...we need practice." He gazed between Hallie and Thomas. "They felt like a safe way to start. I mean, if Danny can handle them..." He waggled his eyebrows.

Danny groaned.

James stilled. "But only if you're comfortable with us. I mean, you barely—"

"It's fine." I managed a laugh. "You really want the chaos?"

"Uh, they're two extremely well-behaved children."

I flashed back to the time Thomas managed to not just get spaghetti in his hair but also all over the floor, the table, and even the wall. I remembered all the nights Hallie had nightmares. "It's a lot."

"Colin and James are considering fostering." Danny nodded toward his brother. "When Colin's feeling better."

"Yeah." James glanced down at his socked feet before meeting my gaze. "We're both privileged. Me in coming from a big, supportive family and having a good-paying job."

"A company he built himself," Danny added proudly.

James rubbed the back of his neck. "Yeah, that." If he'd had lighter skin, I wouldn't have been surprised to see a blush. "And although Colin's family are assh...asshats... he put aside enough money, along with his inheritance, to live a comfortable life. We're in a position to help." James glanced at Hallie and Thomas. "Not all kids are so lucky."

I was grateful he saw the good—that I could care for

them. That they had a good life. Not the bad—that we skirted poverty, that I'd brought them into a marriage on the rocks, even if I hadn't realized how rocky. I reminded myself I'd get a raise and insurance shortly. Whatever I got from my marriage to Gerard would be our cushion. Maybe one day I'd find the time to get my GED. Maybe train for something. Although, frankly, I liked my job. Honest work for honest money. Helping people. Keeping pets safe from germs and disease. That made a difference in my self-worth. Yes, I was a dad…but I was also providing for my family.

We'd survive.

With or without Danny.

But hopefully with. *Be optimistic. He said he'll move in…*

"Okay. So maybe fostering." Danny met his brother's gaze.

James nodded. "I wouldn't mind adopting. I think I might eventually be able to convince Colin. Just…with the transplant…" He glanced over to ensure Hallie was still busy. She'd grabbed her book and was reading to Trouble, who appeared absolutely enraptured.

The dog would get an extra treat later…despite the running-away shenanigans. Thank God she hadn't been hit by a car during her escapade.

"The transplant," Danny prompted.

"You know he's facing a diminished lifespan. I mean, longer than if he hadn't had the transplant, but not as long as the average person." James winced. "Average is such a common word. I could be hit on the freeway tomorrow and he could live to eighty."

"Neither are likely," Danny reminded him gently.

James scratched his beard. "I know. So he thinks we should only do temporary fosters so that he doesn't leave me with the responsibility of a child when he dies."

Danny glared into space as if he could control fate. "He's not likely to die tomorrow."

"No, he's not. The infection cleared up and the anti-rejection meds are working perfectly. Everything is looking great. Dr. Milson is thrilled."

"Okay…" Danny arched an eyebrow. "I assume there's more."

"Yeah." James scrunched his nose. "And then Colin wavers over to adopting older kids so I'll have them to take care of—and to take care of me—when he passes."

"This is…" I rubbed my face.

"Morbid?" Danny snickered. "That's Colin."

James shot him a look.

Danny held up his hands. "I don't mean anything by it. I don't know what it's like to be on death's doorstep. That would change a guy. But he can't live the next however many years just expecting to die."

"You tell him that." James grinned. "Not like he'll listen to his husband."

"Have Mama set him straight."

Both James and I stared at Danny.

He shrugged. "You know Mama will have the perfect thing to say."

"I was hoping Dr. Milson might the next time we see her. How're you doing?"

Danny grinned. "Fit as a fiddle." He didn't look at me.

But I glared at him.

James glanced between the two of us. "What's going on?"

"Nothing." Danny cut me a glare. Then he smiled back at his brother. "So you want to babysit tonight."

"Colin's made reservations for you at Fiery's Italian. His treat."

"That's generous—"

James cut Danny off. "And a night at the hotel down the street from there."

"Uh…" I frowned.

"So we can practice overnight babysitting," James offered.

Danny snickered. "You just think I want to get lucky." He looked over at me. "Sorry."

I gazed down at Thomas. "I've never spent a night away from my children."

James's gaze softened. "I thought that. If we're pushing too hard, let me know. I just…" He pointed between Danny and me. "It seems like some time alone might be a good thing. We'll take good care of the kids, Rob—hourly updates. But if I'm pushing too hard, then I apologize."

"Reynolds men can be steam engines," I commented drily.

Both men burst out laughing.

James smacked Danny's arm. "He's got your number."

"Hey." Danny made a show of grabbing his arm. "What's with the violence?"

We all knew James hadn't hit hard, but I appreciated the reminder. That being said, Danny made it clear his nieces and nephews all understood the *smacks* to the upper arm were signs of affection and were never meant to be done with force. I could teach that to Hallie, but I couldn't envision Thomas understanding. Speaking of grabby hands… "I see you kept your glasses." I indicated to James.

"Nearly lost them a couple of times." He grinned ruefully. "That little guy moves fast."

"Yeah, he does."

"I do need to be heading home. Unless you tell us not to, we'll be here at six. We'll presumptuously bring overnight bags, but you can send us home at any time."

Danny snickered. "Steamroller."

James bumped him. "When are you moving in?"

"Uh…" Danny cleared his throat. "We haven't… that is…"

"As soon as he wants." Just so he was in no doubt of where I stood on the matter.

"Danny's moving in?"

Hallie suddenly stood between the three of us looking up.

James winced, but Danny crouched before her. "Your papa and I are discussing it. How would you feel?"

I held my breath, worrying this might be too much pressure for Hallie.

She pulled her lower lip through her teeth, then leaned over and whispered, "Will you be mean?"

Solemnly, Danny shook his head. "I won't be mean. I will love you and Thomas and Papa with my whole heart."

Again, her uncertainty ate away at me. *If she says no then what do I do?*

In the blink of an eye, she launched herself into Danny's arms, throwing her arms around his neck. "I want you to stay. I want you to keep us safe."

My heart broke, and I blinked back tears. She was four —she never should have known fear. Or felt unsafe. Gerard had done that to her. And I hadn't protected her.

But I would from now on.

CHAPTER 29

DANNY

COLIN ONCE COMPLAINED TO ME EARLY IN THEIR relationship that James had a tendency to run roughshod over people.

I couldn't see it. My brother was as mild-mannered as people came. Affable. Easy to get along with. Quick with a smile and an agreement. Gentle and considerate. No anger and no raised voice.

Still, I'd wanted to give Colin's observations some consideration. So I sat back and watched. In fact, James did have a tendency to just take over—at least when it came to people he loved.

Intrigued, I'd decided further study was required.

So I spent the next few months watching those around me...and discovered that tendency was a Reynolds family trait. We assumed we knew what was best and, because we loved someone, we would just step in and take over.

Like tonight. Not that I was complaining about a night out with Rob, but James sure had steamrolled it into being.

As I sat across from my guy at Fiery Italian's, I flashed

to a moment when Colin had made a casual comment that Rob probably hadn't been given much chance for agency in his life. And that possibly being assertive would be a challenge for him. He'd said the words at the end of a conversation we'd had about something completely different. I couldn't even remember what the topic had been. But James had left the room, and Colin had given me his simple observations. Then had deftly moved on.

I hadn't given the words the due consideration and weight they'd deserved.

To my shame.

I apologized mentally to Colin for not heeding his words. And I needed to find a way to apologize to Rob for being as bad as James—and just running roughshod over him. Or, at the very least, not protecting him from James's meddling.

"Danny?"

As I glanced up, I swallowed my discomfort. "Yeah?"

Rob offered a shy smile. "We're at this great restaurant." He scanned the room. "It's not fancy, but I'm glad I had this." He indicated his shirt. The shirt Mama had bought him for the wedding.

"You look good." I reached over to snag his hand. "I'm just thinking."

He tilted his head. "What?"

"Are you happy to be here?"

"Of course." His eyes widened. In the candlelight, the gray was barely visible. "Do you not want to be here? Because—"

I squeezed his hand. "I'm thinking about the fact you've never left the kids alone. I feel like James pushed you out, and I dragged you here."

He frowned. "I do realize I had a choice, Danny. If I didn't want to be here, then I wouldn't. And as much as

James had suggested we do—" He glanced around furtively. "—you know…I wouldn't have done it if I wasn't okay with it."

Relief flooded me. Along with a curl of desire at the memory of this morning.

Rob's phone vibrated. He held up a finger as if to ask permission.

I nodded.

He checked it, then held it for me to see.

Colin sat on the couch. Trouble, damn dog, was on his lap. Hallie sat next to him, with her arms around Thomas, and the four of them were hamming it up for the camera. Even the dog seemed to get she was on display.

I smiled. "That's pretty special."

"Hallie's too dependent on me." He typed a quick response, forwarded the picture to me—my phone buzzed —and then he put it back on the table, screen down. "I knew it back in LA. We were never apart. And…I needed her as much as she needed me. My ex…" He winced. "Yeah. He wouldn't let me go out and do things and he wouldn't pay for a sitter, so I was always taking care of Hallie. I never got any time off. And I didn't resent it—far from it—but I could see the relationship wasn't healthy. She could barely play with other children if I wasn't hovering five feet away. One of the mothers confronted me. What could I say? She was right—Hallie was too attached to me. I knew school was coming, and that just caused more dread. I'd have Thomas to keep me company, but she'd have to figure out how to cope.

"Then we're here and I'm working and suddenly she's alone with Nai. And…after a few meltdowns, she learned to cope. I panicked when Nai got sick, but you stepped up. And…she knew you. Was comfortable with you. Slowly, that comfort has extended to Colin and James because they've been so patient. I know it helps that Thomas is just rambunctious and fearless. Hallie sees people reacting positively to his energy, and she's starting to want some of that attention for herself. And yeah, I hadn't figured on adding Trouble to the family…" He snickered. "I tell myself that I did it for you and Arthur, while I know the truth is I did it for myself and the kids. She's the piece we didn't know we were missing. I wish all kids could have a dog growing up. My parents are shitty people—" He glanced around, but not one was paying any attention. "But we had dogs we loved. Sometimes I felt they were treated better than I was. My family knew I was different. They made sure to highlight that all the time. Kicking me out was an inevitability."

My heart broke for the sixteen-year-old who suffered such rejection from the people tasked with loving him. What kind of a God allowed that to happen? Or a society? Why was his family celebrated in their community for their tossing him out, rather than reviled? I knew these things happened. Had even happened to a lesbian classmate of mine. Before I could bring her home with me, though, a cousin took her in, up in Burbank. She'd done okay after that.

Mama had never spoken to the young woman's parents again. Her opinion carried weight in our community. People respected how she felt—and seeing how accepting she was of her queer kids, I believed, changed some people's minds. Or so I told myself to comfort me in those dark moments when I thought of the kids who weren't so lucky.

"Sorry." Rob flipped his knife over several times. "We should be celebrating, right?"

I reached out to grip his right hand. "Yes, celebrating." I tried to shake off my melancholy. "You were telling me how happy you are that Trouble's part of the family."

He grinned. "Jordan's coming for our first obedience lesson tomorrow. He said the first one was free." He pursed his lips. "I'm not certain that's true."

Jordan had trained Widget. Might James have made a call? Well, I wouldn't put it past my interfering shit of a brother.

I also couldn't be resentful. "We'll find a way to pay for the lessons ourselves without telling Colin and James."

"He said he leads group lessons, and they're less expensive. I think it would be good to socialize her as well."

The server, a lovely woman in her forties with jet-black hair appeared with our food. Lasagna for Rob and shrimp linguini for me. I was going all out and encouraged Rob to do the same. A splurge, but there was nothing I'd rather spend my money on than Rob, and I wanted this to be a special memory. I would've gone for the wine sauce, but wasn't going to take the risk with any alcohol.

After the server left, Rob held up his water glass. "To us."

"Yeah." I grinned. "To us."

We clinked glasses, sipped, then both started sorting out our very hot pasta dishes.

Suddenly, Rob put down his fork.

"What…?"

"I want to ask you to marry me, but I'm currently married, and my divorce won't be final for months, so I can't ask you because, you know, you might meet someone else and decide I'm not worth the hassle, and—"

Abruptly, I stood. I rounded the table and dropped to one knee.

Silence enveloped the room as all eyes turned to us.

"Rob."

"Yes?" That might've come out as a squeak.

"I love you."

He blinked. "And I love you."

"You've asked me to move in."

"Uh…yes?"

A few people tittered.

"I want to move in. And not just because it'll make our lives easier. But because I love you. And the kids. And even Trouble."

"Did he just say trouble?" A beautiful woman at the next table leaned over. "You need to speak up," she hissed.

"Trouble's the dog." I grinned.

"Of course he is," the woman agreed.

I didn't correct the misgendering. Then I blinked and looked a little more closely at our neighbor. Okay, so a drag queen. In a shimmering green hi-cut dress, skyscraper heels, and fabulous makeup.

"So I think we're comfortably headed toward marriage." I refocused on Rob.

"Uh…" He frowned.

"Did you not just say you wanted to marry me?"

"Well…yeah…"

"I'm going to pull a Reynolds and get there first."

Slowly, he smiled. "Bossy?"

"You bet. So…will you marry me?"

He blinked several times.

"Answer him, sonny." The queen next to us gently nudged Rob. "Unless you're not sure. If so, I can let him down easy for you."

Rob let out a watery laugh and turned to our neighbor. "Thank you for that kind offer. I think I'll accept his proposal."

"About time." The woman grinned. "You've been making shmoopy faces at each other all night."

I had no idea what *shmoopy* was, but I'd take the encouragement. "Oh crap."

Rob dropped his gaze to me. "Change your mind?" He laughed, but the worry was clear.

"No. No changing of minds. Just…I would've preferred to do it with the kids."

He closed his eyes for a long moment before opening them. "We can sit down and you can propose to Hallie. She'd…" He sniffed. "I think she'd like that."

"Who's Hallie?" Our neighbor leaned over. "Are you in one of those triad things?" She tried to whisper triad, but the entire restaurant heard her.

"Envie Allotta." Her companion hissed. "Leave the boys alone." He offered us a sympathetic smile. "Apologies."

"Hallie is Rob's daughter. And Thomas is his son." I turned back to Rob. "I hope one day to call them my kids as well."

About ten people in our immediate vicinity sighed and said *aw*.

I shot a quick glance at the couple next to us.

Envie pressed a hand to her chest. "You boys…what a lovely couple." She started waving frantically. "They need champagne."

"Oh my God." Rob whispered the words under his breath. "Danny…"

"Got it." I let go of his hand and quickly pivoted to the couple. "I donated part of my liver and can't drink."

"Good man." Envie grinned, then winked. "But you can have chocolate cake, right?"

"Yes."

"Lovely."

As I rose, she started waving frantically again.

I leaned over and pressed a kiss to Rob's cheek. "Just roll with it."

He tilted his head so he could catch my gaze. "Best proposal ever."

"Even with Envie?"

"Especially with Envie."

His grin didn't dissipate for the rest of the night.

CHAPTER 30

ROB

I'D BEEN NAKED WITH DANNY MERE HOURS AGO, BUT THAT felt different. Now, as I stood in a hotel with him, all my fears reappeared.

Fear of inadequacy.

Fear of failing.

Fear of feeling too much.

Fear of not feeling enough.

As I took him in, though, that particular fear slipped away. I felt…everything. Nervous. Anxious. Treasured. When he advanced, I held my ground. The hotel had a fantastic ocean view—and of course Colin had chosen that for us. I didn't care about the vast expanse of water outside. All that mattered was in this room. What we could do for each other. To each other.

Even Hallie and Thomas slipped into the back of my mind. There, to be sure, in a treasured place. The last picture James had sent was of everyone eating vanilla ice cream before bed. Definitely not something we did every day. Danny loved treating the kids, but he understood if you gave something every day then it wasn't a treat.

Had I thought I could push my kids to the back of my mind?

Not a chance.

"Hey." Danny, having removed his dinner jacket, moved into my space. He'd dressed up even more than I had, but that hadn't mattered. Nothing mattered except what happened to me every time he was in my space.

"Hey back." I tried to quell my anxiety.

Telegraphing his movements, he reached out to feather my hair, then to run his hand down my face to cup my cheek.

I leaned into his touch. Craved more. Didn't know how to express my needs.

"I could ask you if you're sure." His dark-brown eyes sparkled. "But you checked us in."

A laugh burst from my chest. That was true.

"But that doesn't mean you can't call a halt to this at any point. You say *no* and everything stops. No recriminations. No disappointments. Either we talk about it at the moment, or we discuss it later. But everything ceases."

I tilted my head. "You realize that goes for you as well, right?"

He grinned. "Yeah. And I could confidently point out I've never had to call things off, but that would not only be arrogant, but would give you the wrong idea. I get that things don't always go the way you want. Sometimes body parts do things unexpected."

"Like farting in bed?"

"Especially farting in bed." He winked, then the smile slipped a little. "I'm glad you get it. And you can fart in my bed anytime."

"Okay, this is like, the unsexiest talk ever." I couldn't help grinning.

"Sure." He raised his other hand and suddenly cupped both my cheeks. "But you're smiling, and we've come to an understanding."

"*Body parts do things unexpected*," I repeated.

"Yep." Our gazes held. "And I'd like to kiss you now."

I hesitated.

He cocked his head.

"I'm issuing blanket permission. Like you said, I can withdraw my consent at any time. I trust you not to push too far, but if you do, I'll speak up."

"So I can kiss you."

"I wish you would."

And so he did. A gentle pressing of lips. This was how we usually did things—he'd ease me into it. Rare were the times we clawed at each other. I appreciated the languidness of our affection. We had all the time in the world. Well, part of me knew that wasn't true, but the rest of me decided we were in our early twenties and we could pretend immortality. He'd signed the papers so if something happened to me, he'd take the kids. James had popped the documents over to Wynn Cavanah on his way home after lunch. One more safety measure Danny had given me.

Danny ran his hand down my back, then squeezed my ass through the khaki pants. "Want you," he murmured.

"And you'll have me."

He pulled away, with his glazed and unfocused eyes. "I want you to fuck me. If you're comfortable with that. I mean, blow jobs first, but—"

"I've never done that. I've always…"

"But you hinted you wanted to try being on top."

Heat crawled up my chest and into my cheeks all the way up to my hairline. "You remember that?"

"Babe, I remember everything you've ever said to me.

We were a little kiss-drunk, and you admitted you'd always wanted to try it."

I blinked. "I do. And you…?'"

"I'm as vers as they come. Trust me, I've done it just about every way possible."

I laughed. "You know, I believe you."

"As you should." He tried for faux officiousness, but broke into giggles. "I'm glad you're not holding my extensive experience against me."

"Well, as long as you don't hold my lack of experience against me."

"Never." He said the word as a solemn vow.

"Then we're good." I reached for the buttons on his pale-blue shirt and slowly undid them one at a time.

"You're going to kill me."

I chuckled. "What a way to go." When I finished with the buttons, I pulled the shirt from his pants, then slid my hands against his skin—from his belly, along his hipbone, to his back. I pulled him against me, laid my head against his heart, and inhaled his scent. A scent I'd become accustomed to. He didn't add anything, so the aroma was just deodorant and something that was just…him. So comforting.

He wrapped his arms around me and rested his chin on the top of my head. "You fit me perfectly."

"I'm short." I tried for a pout. The truth was that I'd ducked my head. When we both stood tall, the difference wasn't too noticeable.

Or so you tell yourself.

Danny's solidity drew me to him like a moth to a flame. I sought his warmth. His comfort. His strength.

"We don't have to…" He let his words trail off.

I pulled back while still in his embrace. "Oh yes, we fucking do. You think I'll be able to look James in the eye if

I go back and haven't fucked you?" I said the words with absolute solemnity.

The shock on Danny's face as they sank in was priceless. Then he laughed. A guffaw that resonated through his chest to me. He wiped at his eyes. "You're going to tell my brother that you fucked me?"

"Yep." I might've been putting more bravado into the word than I felt, but something about this felt important to me. I'd very much sensed there were few secrets in the Reynolds family. And yeah, if I asked Danny to respect my privacy, he would. But James's…discernment of my feelings for Danny had brought us to this moment. Somehow, I felt candor was important. And I'd find some way to make the gentle giant blush. For all his apparent audacity, he still had a strong sense of propriety. I very much got the sense the changes I saw in him from the time I'd met him were because of Colin. I'd never seen two people better matched. Except, perhaps, Mama and Daddy.

And, I hope, Danny and myself.

"I have to piss. When I come back, I want you naked in bed." I gave him a stern look.

Danny had, quite boldly, put a bottle of lube and condoms on the nightstand when we'd arrived. *In case*, he'd said.

As if I'd consider not getting into bed with him. We'd discussed condoms, having both been tested, and both found negative. I just…wasn't ready yet. Perhaps after tonight I'd have the courage.

He pressed a kiss to my lips, spun me toward the bathroom, then smacked my ass.

I mocked howled as I made my way out of the room. I only sort of needed to piss. More, though, I needed a moment to center myself. And the privacy to get undressed. Gerard would just order me to bed naked. I'd never undressed someone and somehow that felt even more intimate than the idea of penetrating him.

That's nuts.

Probably. But, I could admit this was easier. I pissed, washed my hands, then removed all my clothes. I gently laid the shirt over the folded pants and was planning to hang it up when I got back into the bedroom. Instead, when I spotted a naked Danny on the bed, palming his erect cock, all thoughts of creased linen fled. I dropped my clothes right on the floor and hustled over to the bed. I knelt and crawled over to him. The beautiful expanse of brown skin—that I'd seen just this morning—held even more magnetism. "I'm going to touch."

"I wish you would." Amusement laced his voice. "I'm all yours."

Mine. To have. To possess. To cherish. Vague notions of wedding vows flitted through my head as I crawled between his spread thighs. I touched his knees, then slowly drew my hands up to his hips, applying increasing pressure.

He moaned as his cock bobbed, a little drop of precum leaking on his belly where he had hair. The hair was sparse around his pecs, but arrowed downward all the way to his shaft, which stuck out from a nice bush. God, I loved the natural look.

I met his gaze. "May I…?" I indicated his cock.

"Oh, yeah." His grin was positively infectious. To my relief, he didn't show a slightest doubt. No moment of hesitation. No…nothing but clear eagerness. And although I expected nothing less, I appreciated having an enthusiastic *hell fucking yes.*

Slowly, I licked his tip. The salty precum tasted better than anything I could ever remember having savored.

He feathered his hand through my hair.

Emboldened, I licked around his tip.

His pelvis flexed, but he didn't press farther into my mouth. Instead, he moaned.

With more confidence, I sucked him deeper.

"Yeah, babe, that's perfect."

I smiled as I hollowed my cheeks and raked my teeth along his length.

"Fucking hell."

Again, he ran his hand through my hair. In such a gentle way, that I only gave a passing thought to how rough Gerard had been in comparison. Here, Danny was letting me set the pace. That gave me confidence to swallow him down.

"I'm coming, Rob. Pull off if—"

I sucked harder.

He came.

Even though he'd warned me, I was surprised and nearly choked as I struggled to swallow it down. He continued to pulse in me as I kept sucking. That had been the fastest anyone had ever come. Well, there'd only been one other guy, and I was so sick of comparing the two men that I swore I'd never do it again. I knew that *born-again virgins* weren't actually a thing, but I could pretend with Danny. That he was my first. That he was my only.

That he was my forever.

After he'd finished emptying in me, I laid my head against his pelvis and gently played with his fuzzy balls.

"Oh God, you're going to be the death of me." He muttered the words.

I glanced up to meet his gaze. "How?"

"I want to haul you up here so I can kiss you senseless, but I'm boneless after the best blow job ever."

My first reaction, of course, was to deny it. He'd had so

many partners—and not in a bad way. Surely I couldn't have been the best.

Except, maybe I had. Or, more importantly, maybe I was the most memorable.

Deciding to cut him a break, I crawled up his body, lay flush against him, pressed our lips together, then thrust my tongue into his mouth. I'd never done this before. The carnality stirred something primal within me. That possessiveness was back. But not in an *I need to control every aspect of your life* way. No, more like an *I want to be your everything because you're that for me*. I didn't ever want to be without him. He was like oxygen, and although that scared me, it also gave me hope that I could be whole again. After what happened on that horrible December night, I'd wondered if I could ever be a fully functioning adult. Not just a father…but a companion. A partner to someone who would love me as much as I loved them.

I had my answer.

CHAPTER 31

DANNY

I HADN'T BEEN LYING WHEN I'D TOLD ROB THAT'D BEEN the best blow job ever. Although I didn't want to think about who had come before me in his life, the real reason had been the emotional connection. I'd cared for most of my previous partners. But I'd never loved them. Never wanted to spend the rest of my life with them. Had never thought of them in *until death do we part* terms.

With Rob, I had those thoughts all the time. If not pushed by James today, though, I wasn't certain when I would've acted on that attraction. I'd treated Rob like he was made of glass. That the slightest movement might knock him over and he might shatter into a million pieces. In the past twelve hours, since Trouble had gone missing, he'd proved he was anything but fragile. He'd shown strength and resiliency. He'd also made it clear he was ready for intimacy again. Beyond the hot, but also weirdly chaste kisses I'd been living for. I could tell myself he hadn't been sexually assaulted, but his trust had been abused and devastated—so pushing him if he wasn't ready would've been a recipe for disaster. But not believing him when he said he was would be just as bad.

Apparently he was now *really* ready. I didn't know if he'd actually admit what we were doing—whatever that wound up being—to James and Colin. Judging by the light in his eyes, I wouldn't put it past him. Which told me he was healing. And accepting my insane family as his own.

He nuzzled my neck as I held him to me.

"That was…" I tried to find words.

"Best BJ ever?" He pushed up to meet my gaze and grinned.

That impish grin I was starting to recognize. And to see more and more.

"Well, frankly, yeah." I almost made a joke about technique, but I didn't want Rob's ex in this room. At least no more than absolutely necessary.

"So…" He moved sinuously against me, rubbing his very interested cock against my very flaccid one.

I tried valiantly to stiffen. Alas, the thing was just a little too spent. "You going to fuck me?" I flexed my pelvis.

His gray eyes lit with excitement. "Really?"

I chuckled. "Well, I might just lie here, completely exhausted, but I'm always happy to—"

He cut me off with a deep kiss. His taste always intoxicated me, even though I couldn't quite identify what it reminded me of. Just like he always smelled great—even after he'd just come home from work and still smelled like cleanser.

Huh.

Maybe that was why I now got turned on by cleaning supplies.

I was kidding.

Sort of.

Not really the time.

I laughed.

Rob cocked his head.

"I'm just thinking that I…" I closed my eyes. "Like when you come home smelling like cleaning supplies."

He poked me in the ribs.

My eyes shot open.

He laughed heartily. "And here I was thinking your deodorant was sexy."

I quirked an eyebrow.

"Yeah, exactly." He gave me another kiss. "Glad you don't mind the smell because that'll be my scent for a long time to come."

Before I could dissect that thought—beyond the obvious that he planned to keep working at his job, which I'd already known—he gave me another soul-searing kiss. When he pulled back, he reached for the lube. He held it between the two of us, clearly asking my preference.

I spread my thighs. "Do you want to?" Any chance to have his hands all over me was a bonus, as far as I was concerned. He'd probably never prepped someone else, if his ex always topped. Some guys got squeamish—which was a legit response—and I never judged. Still, as Rob nodded, he coated his fingers and positioned himself between my legs, and I couldn't help but grin. *This is going to be fun.*

As he moved my junk out of his way, my cock twitched. *Maybe?* Alas, the damn thing was truly requiring the entire refractory period. Which was just more proof of how good an orgasm Rob had wrung from me.

He ran his finger around my rim and then, slowly, pushed one finger inside.

"Oh, yeah, like that."

He grinned. "Ready for more?"

"With you? Always, babe." I'd worried he might not

like the endearment, or that it might be too close to something his douchebag ex used to call him, but his megawatt smile when I used it assured me that I hadn't misjudged.

After a moment, he worked a second finger in.

I sighed. I fucking loved this. And as he worked his way deeper, scissoring and opening me, my arousal only increased. I found the way his brow furrowed in concentration absolutely adorable. I suppressed the desire to smooth it, and instead of focused on the intimacy of his fingers in— "Holy hell."

He grinned as he continued to massage my prostate. "See? I know what I'm doing." For a moment, his face fell and a bleak look came into his eyes.

Concern rising, I smiled. "My cock agrees. He's very interested."

Rob glanced down and yes, my trusty appendage was perking right back to life. A grin replaced his frown. "I'm going to make you come again."

"If anyone can, it'll be you." I touched his thigh with my toe. "Please fuck me."

He blinked those stunning eyes at me, offering a smile. "Yeah, I can do that. I can definitely do that." He withdrew his hand.

I missed the contact.

He fumbled with the condom wrapper.

Ah, lubed fingers. I held his hand steady as I removed it from him. I opened the packet and removed the rubber. I pointed to his cock.

He nodded.

Carefully, I rolled it on. Then I applied lube.

He sighed as I massaged his shaft. "Jesus, keep that up, Danny, and I'm going to come."

I made a big show of stopping.

His laughter rang through the room. "Okay?"

"Yeah, okay."

He positioned himself between my thighs and slowly—oh so slowly—started to push in.

The pain burned and elongated as he struggled to press his head in. *Oh.* "Just push in, Rob. You're not going to hurt me."

"But…" He bit his lip in concentration.

"Trust me, I can handle it." Had certainly done so many, many times before.

Still, he held back.

I flexed my hips and tried to pull him in farther.

His gaze shot to mine. In the recesses of my mind, I acknowledged he'd not only never fucked someone before—which I'd known—but that he'd likely never made love face-to-face. I couldn't give voice to my suspicion, but I felt it deep down in my bones. This was truly a first for him.

Slowly, though, he sank deeper into me. He'd pull back a fraction of an inch, then slowly sank farther.

"That's good, Rob. So fucking good."

He met my gaze and…something passed between us. And understanding? A feeling? Something truly elemental. He was inside me. Despite my cavalier attitude sometimes, I always took this part seriously. Partly because I could be hurt physically…but mostly because this time, I saw this joining as sacred.

But this wasn't transitional with Rob.

This was forever.

"Danny?" He said the word through clearly gritted teeth.

"Yeah?" I swiped the sweat from his brow.

"I…" He grunted.

"Oh." I tried not to laugh, but found it a challenge.

He actually growled.

"Just thrust, Rob. It's okay if you come and—"

He was already moving inside me. Pulling out and pushing back. Frantically picking up the pace as he chased what was apparently an imminent orgasm.

To help myself along, I snagged my very interested cock and set a rhythm of jerks to go along with his thrusts. Normally I might've considered snagging some lube, but he was so close—and I wanted to be there with him—that I disregarded the dryness and sank into the climax that was mere moments away.

I didn't have long to wait. Four more thrusts and he stuttered to a stop and held himself still. His eyes drifted shut and his face contorted—as if he couldn't decide whether he was enduring intense pain or intense pleasure.

And just like that, upon witnessing something so… intimate…my own balls drew up, and I came. Hard. Cum covered my hand as I milked myself through my climax.

Rob's eyes popped open, and he stared at me. "I can..." He stopped, eyes wide.

I tried to breathe. "Yeah…" I cleared my throat, even as he lowered his full weight to me. "You can…?"

"Feel you. Around me. And…" He swallowed and blinked. His eyes shone.

I pushed up to press our lips together. I remembered the first time I'd topped. Wally Frum. Junior year. Cute kid. Lots of acne. No interest in coming out of the closet. The relationship hadn't lasted. But I'd always feel a connection to him—he'd been my first.

Rob eased out of me. "That was…"

"Yeah." I smiled, brushing his damp hair from his face.

He snuggled closer, so I angled him to my side. He tucked in, under my arm, resting his head on my shoulder, leg over my thigh, and his hand resting on my chest.

"I like your chest hair."

Again, I chuckled. "Well, I don't have as much as Bryan. Leticia's always asking him to wax. He asks if he should work or wax? Given they have five children, that answer seems pretty obvious."

Rob's hand stilled. "Waxing takes that long?" He sounded incredulous.

"Of course not." I feathered his hair. I loved playing with the soft strands. "He's just making the point that he chooses not to spend his spare time doing something he doesn't want to. Anyway, you'll see him shirtless one day and you'll laugh. He's, well, caveman comes to mind."

He stilled his hand.

"What? What's going on in that head of yours?"

"My family were more on the hairy side. I'm not, obviously."

I didn't respond because he didn't seem to need one.

"So my father said I was gay because my hair was so sparse and that if I took testosterone pills, then I would grow chest hair and then I wouldn't be gay."

"Jesus. He said that?" I didn't try to hide my disgust.

"Yeah. And then…" He swallowed. "Then I met Gerard who would've had lots of hair if he hadn't waxed and…" He cuddled closer. "I don't know what to think."

"Well, you can think that the amount of chest hair a man has involves zero correlation with his sexual orientation." Part of me couldn't believe I had to say this…and the rest understood completely. "I'm sorry for what came before, Rob. And I'm glad you're talking to someone about it."

"I want that someone to be you." He flexed his fingers against my chest.

"I'll listen, Rob, anytime. But I'm not a professional therapist. Someday, sure." *Hopefully*. I had years of schooling left. "But you need support I can't give you. You can tell me anything…but I might not always say the right thing in response."

"You're perfect." Rob said the words with a pout in his voice.

I chuckled. "Oh my God, you're going to see how not perfect I am. But I can hold you and help you fight your monsters. Your demons. I can't do it for you, though, and you know it."

"Yeah." He drew the word out. "I guess I do." He sniffed. "Can we…?"

"Shower?" Amusement laced my tone. "Because I'm sure we stink and—"

"No." He pushed up and met my gaze. "You never stink. You get this manly scent and—"

I poked his ribs.

He dissolved in a fit of giggles. Childish giggles. Happy giggles.

They warmed my heart.

Finally, as he wiped his eyes, he managed to say, "I miss the kids, Danny. We can be quiet when we come home—so we don't wake Colin and James."

"They might wake up when we kick them out of bed."

"We can sleep on the couch."

Inwardly, I winced. That would be a tight fit. Outwardly, I smiled. "Absolutely, Rob. Whatever you want."

"What I want is a blow job first." He removed the condom and tied it off. Then he rose and sashayed to the bathroom, ensuring he jiggled his ass in *just* that way.

I was hot on his heels.

CHAPTER 32

ROB

WE PARKED ON THE STREET AND MADE AS LITTLE NOISE AS possible as we approached the house.

"Okay, we're just going to slip in, check on the kids, and crash on the couch." Danny whispered the instructions.

I gave a momentary thought to just how much damage could be done to a very expensive cotton shirt while sleeping on the couch before remembering how much I wanted to see my babies. "Perfect." I slid the key in the lock, turned it slowly and held my breath as the mechanism gave way. "Okay." Gently, I pushed the door open.

Only to be met by the most God-awful howl followed by full-throated barks that would, I'd swear, wake the neighborhood.

Oh, sure. You never bark like this when I come home alone. Except Trouble had her other *person* at those times. Danny. She hadn't had him tonight, and she was, clearly letting us know what she thought of the two of us abandoning her.

Danny brushed past me, hustled over to the dog, and tried to shush her.

She was having none of it.

I closed the door in some vain attempt to keep her from waking everyone in Gaynor Beach.

"Papa!" Hallie ran into the room and barreled straight for me.

I caught her up in a big hug.

Next, the sound of Thomas's wail hit me. Sure…the kid who could sleep through everything chose *this* moment to show some normal reaction.

"I've got him." James yelled the words from down the hall.

Apparently while he did that, Colin wandered down to us and entered the living room. He rubbed his eyes and blinked several times. He looked healthier each time I saw him. Even clearly tired, he glowed in comparison to the wan man I'd met before the surgery. Again driving home how much of the gift of life Danny had actually given him. "Problem?"

I tried to shush Trouble even as I met Colin's gaze. "I, uh, missed the kids."

He chuckled. "I win the bet."

James entered the room behind him with a wailing Thomas in his arms.

Danny was there to rescue his brother and scooped up my screeching child.

As soon as Thomas realized whose arms he was now in, he stopped.

"Oh, so that's how it is." James chuckled, clearly not upset. "That's okay, I'd be calmer in Danny's arms too."

Colin guffawed.

Hallie continued to cling to me. "Thought you'd stay away all night."

James crouched to meet the dog's gaze, which completely derailed her. "Thank you for being a superb guard dog. Would you like a treat?"

Trouble sat. She associated sitting with treats. Hopefully Jordan could help her obey the rest of the commands we needed her to. I wasn't certain *shut up* was a viable command or something I wanted to teach my children. *Quiet*, perhaps? Anyway, she followed James into the kitchen in search of treats.

"Papa, I'm hungry."

"Really?" I gazed into her bright-blue eyes, not a sign of sleep anywhere.

"I am too." Colin grinned. "Ice cream?"

I should've glared because sugar in the middle of the night really wasn't the best idea, and they'd had some earlier—but Hallie's grin had me smiling as well. "Just this once, sweetheart."

"Yep." She put her arms around me. "You're the best Papa."

"I try." I eyed Thomas who had his arms around Danny's neck. "He okay?" I whispered the question.

Danny nodded. "He's a little warm, but I think because he was worked up. If I keep holding him, he should be fine."

My chest tightened. In a good way. I had someone in my life who could calm my child as well as I could. That... was amazing. "You want ice cream as well?"

"Of course." He gave me a mock-indignant look. As if daring me to suggest otherwise.

"Okay."

Colin had headed into the kitchen, so Danny and I took the kids there as well.

Between Colin and James, they had five bowls organized and the ice cream was nearly entirely scooped.

"You work well together," I observed.

The men exchanged a look in question, as if they'd never really thought of it. Finally, James grinned. "Yeah, I guess we do."

"That helps a lot when you have kids." Danny maneuvered himself into a chair, still holding Thomas.

Does he realize how easily he says those things? How easy he makes this all look?

I managed to sit, still holding Hallie in my lap. I rotated her so she faced the table just as James set a bowl with a small scoop of strawberry ice cream before her.

"Thank you." She grinned.

"You're welcome."

She poked her spoon in, scooped out a strawberry, and showed me. "Real strawberries."

I caught Colin's eye. He shrugged. "Danny said she loves strawberry."

And so they'd picked up the more expensive brand with real fruit chunks.

My heart squeezed and then expanded.

"You're spoiling your future niece and nephew." Danny held out a small spoon of vanilla ice cream and Thomas accepted. Apparently his tears and upset were a distant memory.

James and Colin stilled, looking back and forth between Danny and myself. I held in the grin.

Barely.

Danny turned to Hallie. "I have something very important to ask you."

She nodded solemnly.

I held my breath.

"I love your papa."

Hallie nodded.

James grasped Colin's hand and squeezed.

"I would like to be here all the time. With you, Thomas, and your papa." He was always so careful with any derivative of the word *daddy*. "Might you want that?"

Hallie glanced back toward me. "Papa?"

"He's asking you, Hallie. It's okay for you to be honest." If she said *no*, we'd deal. We'd figure out a way to make things work and to gradually ease into things instead of the more abrupt—

"Are you happy?" She whispered the question to me.

A question she'd asked more than any four-year-old should. That she'd seen my unhappiness and was able to articulate the question terrified me. Still, at least here I could reassure her. "I'm happy, sweetheart. As much as I love you and Thomas, I think I have room to love Danny too."

"Okay." She stroked my cheek. "Okay." She turned back to Danny. "You move in?"

"That was my hope, yeah. So I can be here all the time. So I can take care of you and Thomas and your papa." He stretched his large hand across the table.

Hallie gently laid hers against his palm.

"I'll always be here for you."

She scrunched her nose. "Will you still be Danny who takes care of me? You won't be different?"

Danny blinked several times, tried to speak, cleared his throat, and then managed, "I would like to be the same Danny…if that's okay with you."

Thomas grabbed for the bowl of ice cream which James deftly managed to nab first. He snagged the spoon from Danny's loose grasp and put some ice cream on it. "Are we going to play choo-choo train, or are you just going to eat it?"

My darling son gave him a *you think I'm giving you a hard time about ice cream?* Then he obediently opened his mouth.

Colin laughed, drawing my attention to him. His eyes were suspiciously wet.

I smoothed Hallie's tangled hair. "I love you, sweetheart. Just like I love Thomas and now..." I swallowed hard. "I love Danny."

Hallie gazed back at me. "I love Danny too. He takes care of me."

"I love you too." Danny gently squeezed Hallie hand. "I'll take care of you. And protect you."

"From the bad people? People who make Papa cry?"

We all stilled.

Well, except Thomas who pounded his little fist on the table.

James gave him more ice cream.

"Bad people?" Danny kept his voice steady.

Hallie leaned over and beckoned him close.

I worried I might not be able to hear, but her whisper of, "Daddy," carried.

Danny held her gaze. "He's gone far away. He's never coming back. Your papa was brave, and you don't have to worry."

"So you'll protect Papa too?"

"Of course I will." Danny's gaze flicked to mine before returning to Hallie. "It will be my honor."

We'd need more counselling sessions in Hallie's future —as well as for me—but this felt like the optimistic, hopeful, new beginning we all deserved.

Colin yawned loudly. "As much as this deserves a celebration, this old man needs his rest."

James snickered. "Wait until we have kids and you're up all night."

I stilled, waiting for Colin's response.

He smiled softly. "Fair point well made. Guess I'll figure it all out when I have to. But right now..." He rose, then placed a hand on James's shoulder. "We'll organize a celebration for you. With Mama's help, of course. But for now, we'll leave you in peace."

Danny groaned. "I have to tell Mama."

A stab of pain went through me. *Danny doesn't want to tell his mother about me? About us?*

"Mama's going to go over the top." James's gaze met Danny's and then he flicked his head over to me.

Danny glanced my way and winced. "Sorry, right. I didn't mean that in a bad way. Mama's...going to be excited."

"I like Mama." Hallie grinned. "She gives me treats."

"Oh, really?" I'd suspected, and it didn't bother me, but it did amuse me. Then I turned to Colin and James. "You go back to bed. Danny and I can crash on the couch."

Colin snickered. "Uh, no. But thank you."

James grinned. "He has this super expensive orthopedic mattress set to his exact specifications. As nice as your mattress is, my husband likes his creature comforts. Old man."

Since I knew there to be less than ten years between the two of them, I chuckled. I wondered about James's assertion, but clearly they were keen to leave us alone. I appreciated that.

"You get the two munchkins into bed while Colin and I make up your bed with fresh sheets. Then we'll get out of your hair." James rubbed his nearly bald pate. "At least you have some."

Danny laughed. "You shave by choice. Nice try, though."

"Why does James have a bald head?" Hallie asked me the question in what she considered a whisper. We'd really have to work on her quiet voice.

"Uncle James was going bald prematurely," Danny quipped. "He didn't want to look funny, so he decided to look like that." He pointed.

Hallie smiled. "It's soft."

James did a little bow. "Thank you." He rose and snagged the empty bowls. Then he caught Colin's gaze.

"Yeah, I'll find the fresh sheets."

"In the linen closet." Danny and I spoke at the same time.

Colin rolled his eyes. "I did used to live here." With that, he left the room.

James wet a clean washcloth and brought it over to hand to me. "Ice-cream faces." Then he left.

I gazed between each of my children who did, in fact, have ice cream faces. As I wiped Thomas, I chanced a glance at Danny. "You okay with this…chaos?"

He cocked his head. "Of course." He grinned. "I just think we should tell Mama in person. Otherwise she might fry the wire in her excitement."

We had a cell phone, as did his mother, but I understood what he was trying to say. He wanted to be there in person. Perhaps to curtail her excitement. She had a heart condition after all. "You realize this leaves Whitney and Gracie as the two last Reynolds singles."

Danny grinned. "Oh yeah. I can't wait."

The next day, we drove to Huntington Beach to tell Mama and Daddy. Who promptly commanded all the Reynolds children, their spouses, and their offspring, to descend unto the house where we had a huge barbecue.

Mama sat at the head of the backyard table, beckoning me to her. Rashon and Bryan had been tasked with watching all the mobile children. Theirs and everyone else's. Danny and James held Leticia's twins while Daddy held Martin's newborn son. Leticia, Felicia, and Shondra were talking Whitney and Gracie's ears off about the joys of motherhood. To my best estimation, Gracie wasn't even trying to be interested while Whitney, to me, looked a little bewildered. Much how I must've looked when the nurse placed Hallie in my arms that first time.

"Now." Mama gestured to my hand.

I extended it and she grasped it. "What's this nonsense about you boys wanting a small wedding?"

"Mama." Danny's tone might be warning, but I doubted his mother would listen.

I was right.

"Hush, you. James and Colin had a big wedding. Would've been bigger if we'd had more notice."

Colin, whose lap had been co-opted by my son who apparently felt *right now* was the time to nap, grinned. "I couldn't wait any longer."

"Mama." This time James spoke. "We don't need all three hundred and ten relatives."

Daddy held Jeremiah up. "Thee hundred and eleven."

"Oh, three hundred and thirteen. Felicia's twins will be born by then." Colin grinned.

The father of Felicia's twins, who was chasing a wayward son, hesitated, looking a little peaked. "Yeah, don't remind me." Bryan put on a brave smile for Mama. "Can't wait."

She rolled her eyes. "You, my boys, are getting snipped."

Neither Rashon, nor Bryan were her actual boys. And I wasn't certain she meant Martin as well, who only had two. Two was plenty, as far as I was concerned. With our finances and Danny in school for the next however many years, we wouldn't be expanding our family. We were okay with that.

"Got the surgery booked." Bryan now looked a little queasy. "Gotta go. Rashon looks swamped."

"You'll be fine." Daddy grinned. "No complications."

Bryan nodded and headed off toward what looked like an impending fight.

I cocked my head. But held my peace. I supposed after seven children, Mama and Daddy had decided their family was complete. I didn't blame them.

"Be that as it may…" Mama turned her focus back to me. "I want you two to have a huge wedding."

"It's my second marriage," I mumbled. The first had been a lavish affair with all of Gerard's work colleagues and friends. He, like me, was estranged from his family. He'd put me on display that day. Behind my back, although within my hearing range, more than a few attendees had commented about my age and speculated on the true nature of my relationship with my new husband. If only I'd listened…but then I wouldn't have Hallie and Thomas. So…whatever.

"Pshaw." Mama scowled. "You think that matters to me?"

"Mama." Danny spoke up again. "We want small and intimate. Just the immediate family."

His mother turned to me. "My sons seem to be speaking for you. I warn you—if you don't speak up for yourself, a Reynolds will fill the space." She gave her sons a look. "I'm glad to see Hallie's learning to speak up for herself. I don't want her railroaded."

Martin nodded in agreement, apparently, that Hallie should not be run roughshod over by their very opinionated children. "I'll remind Rashon and Bryan."

"See that you do."

He rose and headed toward the pile of children.

Mama returned her attention to me. "Quiet?"

"Yes, Mama."

"Six months?"

"California law."

"You could do a commitment—"

"That's enough, Mama." Danny smiled at his mother. "Don't overwhelm him. We're having this…engagement party. That's enough for now.

She harumphed, clearly not pleased with this turn of events.

Hallie ran up to me. "I'm tired."

"You want to sit on my lap?" Mama held out her arms.

With only a fraction of hesitation, my daughter managed to settle herself on Mama's lap. I might've worried about Hallie's size, but Felicia's middle son—who was about the same age and bigger—had occupied that exact spot earlier.

Mama wrapped her arms around my daughter. "They're only this age once. You have to treasure every moment."

Then the five women joined us. Gracie handed me a gift bag. "Danny should be giving you this, but his arms are a little full."

I was pretty sure he was holding Keyla while James had Malaya. The few times they calmed, I stayed as quiet as possible. Especially since, as Danny suggested, they could sound like sirens when they wailed. Thank God Thomas never hit that decibel level.

"Open the gift." Whitney gestured, miming me opening the bag.

I did. And pulled out a small album of some kind.

"Oh, you did not." Danny glared at his sisters.

Felicia rubbed her belly. "Oh yes, we did. You're marrying him. So it's time."

I caught Colin's eye who grinned widely. "You're family now."

I opened the album and the first photo was the one of Danny, Hallie, Thomas, and me on the beach at James and Colin's wedding. My eyes watered.

"Keep going." Danny's glare softened a little. "Because I'm certain—"

I flipped the page and burst out laughing.

"Jeez Louise, you just had to put in a copy of *that* picture."

"Of you naked in the bathtub?" Gracie grinned what I was coming to know as her shit-eating grin. "You'd better believe it." She smiled. "Lots of family photos with captions so you'll know who's who."

Leticia nudged Felicia. "I'm the pretty one."

Felicia nudged back. "Yeah, you go on believing that."

Whitney cleared her throat. "There are some blank pages at the back. To start adding your own memories. But you'll need to do a separate album for your wedding photos or Mama will howl."

"You're asking for trouble, my girl." Mama glared.

A lot of glaring in this family. But all in fun. Or so I was discovering.

Still, I blinked a number of times, finally finding the courage to look each of the women in the eye. "Thank you." I held the album to my chest. "This is truly the best gift I've ever been given."

Mama smacked my arm. "You're one of us now. Don't forget that. Ever."

I gazed over at Danny who blinked several times. I'd found my family. My found family. They welcomed me and my children. They accepted me as a partner for their youngest child. They protected us. All of them.

My life felt rife with possibilities instead of narrow with fear.

I couldn't have been happier.

EPILOGUE
DANNY

TWO WEEKS LATER

"You're certain we should be bringing Trouble?" Rob eyed our pooch as she sat at the front door.

Clearly, she understood we were going out. Clearly, she believed it was her right to come with us. Clearly, she would not take well to being left behind. She wasn't destructive, per se, but she made it very clear she didn't enjoy being *abandoned*.

Serious drama queen.

Jordan, our trainer, assured us that she needed to learn to cope on her own. That as much as usually someone was home, there would come times when we went out as a family and she'd need to self-soothe.

Today was not that day.

I got her into her harness, hooked up her leash, and grinned at Rob. "All set."

"All set." Hallie repeated my words. She wore a little canvas knapsack she'd gotten for her fifth birthday last week. Because, dear Lord, she was starting school in

September. She'd also declared she wanted to wear it to the wedding. Engaged two weeks ago and getting married next Christmas. Mama'd taken Rob's request for a quiet ceremony, and we intended to have only immediate family. I wanted to get married the day Rob's divorce was finalized, but he wanted to wait a few months. Not because he didn't love me and didn't want to make it official. No, he just wanted there to be a decorous distance between the two events. He wasn't marrying me because he was no longer married to fuck-face. He was marrying me because he loved me and wanted to spend the rest of his life with me.

I was okay with that. Christmas in SoCal was a beautiful time to wed—not too hot and not too cold. And, if Mama's discussion with Mother Nature went as planned, not too rainy either.

Today, on a beautiful May afternoon, the sun shone and we were headed to the Safe Haven Animal Rescue opening. Hallie sat in her car seat behind the driver, Thomas was opposite, and Trouble sat harnessed in the middle. Although she enjoyed being between the kids, her true goal in life was to stick her nose out the window. The SUV Colin insisted on buying me fit our family perfectly. I'd transferred my old car into Rob's name. She ran well and had been cared for. Good safety features. The perfect vehicle for Rob to get around—once he got his full license. He was well on his way.

"Dad?"

I glanced in the rearview mirror as I pulled out of the driveway. "Yeah, Hallie?"

"Are we getting another dog?"

Rob sputtered in the front seat while Thomas clapped. Whether out of agreement with his sister or just because he was happy, I couldn't tell. I cleared my throat as I pointed our vehicle toward Marina Park. "We're going to support Uncle Arthur, Uncle Colin, and Uncle James." For a child who'd spent the first four years with just Rob, she was figuring out this extended family thing quickly. Like how to get special attention. Mama lavished the same love as if Hallie were a blood grandchild. And Hallie lapped up the love and attention.

"Is Widget going to be there?"

"I'm certain she will. Although your uncles aren't looking to adopt any more dogs either, so don't try to pressure them."

"Okay."

I glanced in the rearview mirror when I stopped at a red light. "You'll be good?"

She sighed. "I'm always good."

Rob chuckled. "You walked right into that one."

I laughed right back. "I did."

Within five minutes, we were at the shelter. Mylar balloons in animal shapes were probably the biggest indication something was going on. As well as people milling about. We had to park down the street because the lot was full, but that wasn't a bad thing, since we were able to organize the kids and Trouble before we pushed through the front doors and waded into the crowd.

James grinned, waved, and headed our way. As always, he crouched down to greet the kids first.

I didn't mind.

He and Hallie engaged in a very solemn conversation while Colin made his way over with Widget.

Her little tail wiggled with excitement when she spotted her favorite canine friend as well as her two little buddies.

Thomas, having no sense of propriety, threw his arms around the bulldog.

In return, she licked his face continuously.

We had some wipes in the car, and we'd clean everyone up before heading out to the boardwalk for lunch. Of course, Trouble might sneak a lick. We were constantly dealing with happy animals who loved showing affection.

"Oh hey," Colin turned toward two approaching men. One was slim and about Colin's height, with blond curls and clothes that fit so well they had to be expensive. The other was my height, lean and angular, with straight amber hair falling into his eyes. And, startlingly, an orange-and-white cat draped around his neck like a scarf. "These are Theo and Shane, who helped Arthur start the shelter."

The blond stuck out his hand. "Theo. You must be James's brother."

I grinned. "Yeah, and this is my fiancé, Rob."

Another shake of hands. Shane, meanwhile, was dealing with Thomas who tugged at his pants and was pointing at the cat. "Hey there." He glanced toward me. "Cute kid."

Probably thinks he's mine.

Wait…he is mine.

People would make assumptions about both Hallie's and Thomas's parentages. Rob and I had the discussion. The kids would always know they were adopted and loved —and that we were their fathers in every single way that mattered.

Before I could speak, though, Arthur hustled over. "Great to see you folks. I can't believe how busy it is. We've already had some possible adoptions."

Rob's gaze clearly took in the old wine tasting mansion Arthur had told us about converting. "This is quite a place."

I noted the marble floor and chandeliers, and big plate glass windows. "Pretty fancy."

"And no better use than to house all creatures looking

for a home." Something dark crossed Theo's face momentarily, then he gazed affectionately at Shane. "Or a better person to help run it."

Shane's running it? I'd sort of thought that was going to be Arthur's work, but maybe he wanted to keep his medical transcriptionist job to earn some bucks. Regardless, hopefully he wouldn't have so many strays at his small house anymore. I'd visited once with James, and the place had been pure chaos. No doubt Arthur was looking forward to moving his menagerie of foster dogs and cats here to the shelter once this opening party was done. Although, would he miss them? Sometimes two kids and one dog were pure chaos too, but I'd never give them up.

Rob surreptitiously took my hand.

Casually, I glanced over.

He gave me a look that let me know he was feeling a little overwhelmed. That happened sometimes when we were around a lot of people. He was learning to cope with the Reynolds crew, but he didn't have as much experience with strangers. Six years of being isolated left him unsure of how to cope with groups of people.

"Excuse me." Someone had come up behind us while we were talking. She held a cat cage in one hand.

Of course, I tried to see in, but all I could make out was a furry black shape.

"Oh, today's not an intake day." Shane grinned in what I'd term a disarming smile, a hand rubbing his cat's cheek. "This is the grand-opening party. If you could come back—"

"Mrs. Rousseau?" Arthur stepped forward. "Is that...?" He crouched to peer into the carrier. "Hey, Zeus."

James crouched as well. "You kept the name. At least I'm assuming this is the same kitten."

The nice lady with the bouffant blonde hair and rueful smile winced. "Yes, we kept the name. She's truly a lovely cat—"

"What's wrong?" Arthur rose and, after a moment, James did as well.

Mrs. Rousseau looked out toward a car pulled up to the curb by the front door with a couple of kids in the back seat. "My daughter is deathly allergic. Lovely cat, truly— but her doctor said yesterday that it has to go. My kids are devastated." She glanced around. "We might get a hypoallergenic dog when they're older, but..." She thrust the cage toward Arthur.

Reflexively, he took it.

"Sorry." She scurried out and, within moments, had driven away.

Theo cleared his throat. "That was...unexpected."

"Kitty." Hallie planted herself in front of the cage and stuck her fingers right in.

"Uh, we need to be careful, sweetheart." Rob gently extracted those fingers. "Remember how we don't approach dogs without permission? It's the same with cats."

"Zeus is pretty docile." Arthur blinked bleak blue eyes. "The timing—"

"We can take her." James started to take the cage. "I named her, after all."

I cleared my throat.

Everyone turned to me.

"Colin's immunocompromised. Even the cleanest cats—"

"You're right." Arthur met my gaze, nodding. "I

should've thought of that." He turned to James and Colin. "That was very generous of you to offer—"

"Kitty." Hallie gazed beseechingly between Rob and myself, throwing in looks at the rest of the men for good measure.

James laughed. "Seems to me, this is how you wound up with Trouble."

The dog, who'd been very well behaved to this point, started howling her agreement.

Not to be outdone, Widget added a few barks.

Shane winced. "Not certain the neighbors are going to love the cacophony."

Theo waved him off. "It's an animal shelter, and we're having an open house. Any uppity neighbors will survive."

"How did you get this place renovated so quickly? Wasn't there opposition at the city council meeting?"

This time, Theo winced. "Yeah, don't remind me. But we swayed the council—especially the mayor—and received expedited permits. The council recognized the need for a shelter. Once the decision was made, city hall worked some magic. Even the inspectors were here as soon as any work was done. A bit on the miraculous side." He eyed a tired-looking Arthur. "Not a moment too soon."

"Kitty."

At Hallie's insistent demand, Trouble stopped her caterwauling and dropped to lie down on the pavement.

Widget lay down next to her, chin on her stubby paws.

Colin whipped out his phone, snapped a picture, then quickly sent a copy to the Reynolds family group chat. Therefore, both my phone and Rob's buzzed.

Because he was part of the family now. He glanced over at me.

I read the question in his eyes. And sighed dramatically. "I suppose I'm going to be scooping the litter."

He winced. "No, I can—"

"You get to bathe the husky."

"Well…with your help."

"Yeah, but it's always your shirt that gets soaked."

"You know, he could just bathe the dog without a shirt
—" James suggested, winking.

"James." I glared at my brother.

Who grinned sheepishly.

"I don't mind scooping litter. I always wanted a pet growing up. Now we have…two." I feathered Rob's hair in a gesture that was perhaps too intimate, but had to convey so much. "And I always wanted kids growing up."

He blinked several times. "And now you have them too."

"Kitty." Hallie gazed between the two of us. "Please."

Shane said, "We might think twice, if you have that husky. A lot of them are not great with cats."

"Her foster home had a cat," I told him. "The woman said they were best buddies. And Trouble's super gentle, despite her name. When we meet smaller dogs on our walks, she tones right down and doesn't play too rough with them."

"Is the cat okay with dogs?" Rob asked.

"Should be. She was raised in my house, which is full of dogs. She's got a bad leg, though," Arthur began. "She copes just fine, but—"

"We'll take good care of her." I grinned. "Maybe that will keep her out of mischief."

James chuckled. "Uh…no. I helped with her when she was a kitten, and she was just as much trouble as her littermates."

I snorted. "Of course not." I turned to Arthur. "How much is the adoption fee?" I was already tallying all the stuff we'd need to buy just to bring her home. An envelope taped to the top of the cage read *vaccines*. Likely more of those. And if she wasn't spayed, we'd have to do that too.

"Oh, we'll waive that fee. We didn't actually take her in. And Dr. Louisa gives a special rate for spays under some circumstances." Arthur winced. "Sorry."

Theo and Shane, who'd been pretty quiet to this point —likely relieved the cat wouldn't actually be staying— exchanged a glance.

"Or, since Rob's an employee, she'd likely give a discount." James smiled.

Silently, I thanked him. I didn't mind people knowing we weren't well off…but I didn't like admitting it to virtual strangers. I worried about how they might perceive Rob and myself. If they might wonder if the kids were deprived.

"We can waive the adoption fee." Shane grinned, making a show of checking us over. "We're working on cutting weeds in the back next weekend…"

"We'll be here." I eyed the kids.

"Uncle Colin will be thrilled to babysit since he's not helping with the weeds." James eyed his husband.

Colin mock glared back, but I could see a smile touching his lips. He turned to Rob. "Happy to watch the kids, Trouble, Widget, and…Zeus. We can hang out at your place."

I appreciated he was willing to keep the kids in their environment. That being said, visiting Uncle Colin and Uncle James was always fun with all the kid-friendly stuff they had in their house.

Rob nudged me. "Is that…Gracie?"

As I turned, I narrowed my eyes and tried to make out the couple approaching from down the street.

"Dr. Milson?" Colin might've squeaked that.

Colin's hepatologist. Yes. Holding hands with my sister. Okay. Mind blown.

James laughed. "Oh yeah. Saw that coming a mile away."

"Auntie Gracie!" Hallie abandoned her admiration of her new cat and took off at a run to my sister.

With ease, Gracie scooped her up.

Jezebel Milson approached with a bit more caution, likely trying to suss out our reactions.

I was the first to offer my hand. "So great to see you." I spun to my sister. "You didn't say you were coming."

She offered what I termed her megawatt-actress smile. "Didn't think we had to." She turned to Colin. "Great shot of the dogs."

Said dogs were now up and examining the newcomers. Jezebel was clearly at ease as she cooed over both Trouble and Widget. Who, in turn, showed their appreciation at another human to do their bidding.

Arthur smiled. "It's great that you're here to support the shelter. Gracie and…"

"Don't mind the lack of Reynolds manners." I grinned. "Dr. Jezebel Milson, this is Arthur, the local animal rescuer; Shane, the manager of the shelter; and Theo…" I squinted.

"The money," he supplied.

He and Colin laughed.

I was well aware Colin had made a hefty contribution and would be donating a nice sum every year from now on. I couldn't help financially, but I would volunteer whenever I could.

"You're here to visit?" Arthur eyed my sister who had, not so subtly, thrown her arm around Jezebel in a very possessive manner. Given the doctor had almost twenty years of living compared to my sister, I was finding this an interesting twist. I was assuming this wasn't an ethical conflict as Colin appeared perfectly at ease with his doctor dating his sister-in-law. The doctor a fraction less so, but with all us standing around looming over the petite woman —including my very tall sister—I could understand.

Arthur indicated I should take the cat cage. I'd kept an eye on Thomas who had lain down on top of Trouble and appeared to be taking a nap. Man, that kid could go at one hundred miles and an hour and then come to a full stop, drop, and snooze anywhere.

Hallie watched me closely as I took the crate. I was completely healed from the surgery, and back in fighting form, so helping with the weeding next weekend wouldn't be an issue. Knowing Rob, though, he'd be keeping an eye on me.

Rob scooped Thomas into his arms.

Thomas's eyes popped open, and he squawked his indignation.

"I think he wants to walk by himself." I eyed my boy. His independent streak was going to be the bane of our existence…and I couldn't have been happier.

Hallie snagged Trouble's leash and handed it to me. "All good?" Her blue eyes settled on me.

"All is perfect." I nodded to the group. "Lovely to see everyone. Gracie, Jezebel, James, and Colin, feel free to drop by later to visit our growing menagerie."

"Oh, that would be great." Gracie grinned. "And the next time we come, we can bring our new dog."

Arthur cleared his throat. "I'm sorry…?"

"We're here to adopt." Gracie nudged Shane. "You got the paperwork we submitted, right?" She ducked aside as Shane's cat meowed loudly at her from his shoulder.

Shane grinned. "Cool it, Mimsy, that was a friendly bump. I got your paperwork, yes, although we're not sending any animals out today. If you'll head this way, you can meet Smokey and Tigger, the two dogs chill enough to bring to the grand opening, see if either of them is what you're looking for…" He led my sister and her new amour toward the back of the shelter.

Colin guffawed. "Oh my God, your house is going to be a zoo."

"Good thing Mama's got those new antihistamines." She'd admitted recently—when we'd said we'd board Trouble whenever we came to visit—that her allergies were mild. She just hadn't wanted to add animals to seven crazy kids.

I would legit respect that. I was wondering what we were thinking, bringing home a new cat to go with the rescue dog and two kids.

And I couldn't have been happier. "We'll take our leave."

"We'll be over later." James clapped his hands in glee. "I can't wait to see the puppy Gracie adopts."

Colin snickered. "Yes, this will be one for the ages. Do you think that means they're moving in together? Dr. Milson released me from her care, and I'm seeing an associate of your Dr. Patton."

Ah, that suggested Jezebel was serious about Gracie. I wished her all kinds of luck with my sister.

"We'll do a barbecue." I did an awkward wave. Colin had left behind a sweet grill for us when he'd moved. His new mansion had one of those built-in fancy things. Way more than I'd ever need. At some point, Rob and I would need to figure out how to pay for our house. For now, Colin charged us minimal rent and said it was going toward the eventual purchase of the house. I wasn't sure I liked that… but the kids loved our house and I was pretty sentimental.

The place where I'd fallen in love. With an entire family. Who were now mine.

Rob nodded to Colin and James, then we as a family headed back to my SUV. Only when we were settled, with Zeus in her crate secure in the back and the kids and Trouble locked in, did I chance a glance at Rob. "Oh my God, I love you."

He grinned. "And all the chaos?"

"Especially the chaos."

Despite our seatbelts, we managed to lean in for a kiss.

"Forever." I whispered the words as I gazed into his eyes.

"Yeah, forever."

And we headed into our new adventure.

NEXT IN THE GAYNOR BEACH SERIES

RUFF START BY ROAN ROSSER

SAWYER

I'm deathly afraid of dogs, so why am I signing up to volunteer at an animal shelter?

When my therapist sends me to the newly opened Safe Haven Animal Rescue to get up close to a dog in a safe environment, my nerves almost get the best of me in the lobby. But a run-in with a handsome employee makes putting up with the terror worth it. I'm so besotted, that before I know it, I'm signing up to be a volunteer at the shelter.

NEIL

Crushing hard on my first volunteer is not a good way to start my new job as a volunteer coordinator.

When he starts flirting with me, I shut him down despite his pushing all my buttons. Yet the more time we spend together, the more my crush deepens, and the more I regret staying so professional. But even if I do jump despite the consequences, will he still be interested when he finds out I'm trans?

Ruff Start *is a slow-burn gay romance novel between a work-a-holic corporate professional and a laid back artist who needs to learn when to ask for help.*

Grab it here: books2read.com/ruffstart

ALSO SET IN GAYNOR BEACH

Friends of Gaynor Beach Animal Rescue
Love Furever by Gabbi Grey
Impurrfections by Kaje Harper
Husky Love by Gabbi Grey
Iguana You to Want Me by Meredith Spies

———

Single Dads of Gaynor Beach Series
Jake by Charley Descoteaux
Finn by Jessie G
Wynn by Amelia Hayden
Hugh by Gabbi Grey
Anderson by Foxy Valentine
Alec by Kaje Harper
Demetrius by SA Sway & Amaya Knight
Leo by Meredith Spies
Anthony by Gabbi Grey
Hiroshi by Amaya Knight
Jaime by SA Sway
Nate by Amelia Hayden
Tress by Michele Shriver
Eden by Leona Windwalker
Xavier by Gabbi Grey

Mattie by Elouise East

Lucien by Alice La Roux

WANT MORE GABBI GREY?

Check out her *Love in Mission City* series, set in beautiful British Columbia.

The first book is Ginger Snapping All the Way (Love in Mission City Book 1)

Also available:

Ginger Snapping All the Way (Love in Mission City Book 1)

Stanley's Christmas Redemption (Love in Mission City Book 2)

Sleigh Bells and Second Chances (Love in Mission City Book 3)

The Beauty of the Beast

Love in Mission City: The Boyfriends Duet

Love in Mission City: The Shorts

Page Against the Machine

The Lightkeeper's Love Affair

Ace's Place

Marcus's Cadence

Not in it for the Money

Also:

Axe to Grind

Grindstone's Edge

Hugh (Single Dads of Gaynor Beach)

Anthony (Single Dads of Gaynor Beach)

Xavier (Single Dads of Gaynor Beach)

Love Furever (Friends of Gaynor Beach Animal Rescue)

Husky Love (Friends of Gaynor Beach Animal Rescue)

My Past, Your Future

If Only for Today

Catch a Tiger by the Tail

Solstice Surprise

Valentino in Vancouver

You See Me

Sun, Surf, and Surprises

Love Without Reservations

An Uncommon Gentleman

Caressa's Homecoming (Bound by Love Book 1)

Cole's Reckoning (Bound by Love Book 2)

Audiobooks

Ginger Snapping All the Way

Stanley's Christmas Redemption

Love in Mission City: The Shorts

Page Against the Machine

The Lightkeeper's Love Affair

Ace's Place

Marcus's Cadence

Not in it for the Money

My Past, Your Future

If Only for Today

Catch a Tiger by the Tail

Solstice Surprise

An Uncommon Gentleman

·

Want a free short story? The story is set in Gaynor Beach, California where there are plenty of single dads and puppy rescues! You can sign up for my newsletter so you can keep up with all the great stuff I'm doing as well as pictures of my own pooches, Ally and Finnegan.

<u>Hemingway's Happy Day</u>

·

INTERESTED IN KNOWING MORE ABOUT GABBI?

Sign up for her newsletter
Follow her on Bookbub
Follow her on Instagram

USA Today Bestselling author Gabbi Grey lives in beautiful British Columbia where her fur baby chin-poo keeps her safe from the nasty neighborhood squirrels. Working for the government by day, she spends her early mornings writing contemporary, gay, sweet, and dark erotic BDSM romances. While she firmly believes in happy endings, she also believes in making her characters suffer before finding their true love. She also writes m/f romances as Gabbi Black and Gabbi Powell.

www.ingramcontent.com/pod-product-compliance
Lightning Source LLC
Chambersburg PA
CBHW021442240626
47153CB00001B/252